I0525086

# Stripped by Passion

# Mahagony Redd

ChocolateRoze Publishing

*Stripped by Passion* Copyright © 2012 by Mahagony Redd

Cover Design by Donna Osborn Clark at: creationbydonna.com

Interior Design and Typesetting: interiorbookdesigns.com

ISBN 978-0-9884712-4-5

## ~Sending Love and Appreciation~

First and foremost, I want to thank God for giving me the gift of writing. I want to send my love and appreciation to my mother Bernice Forrest, my children Maliya and Derrick, and my Nana Audrey Grinnage; thank you for teaching me what forgiveness is all about.

I want to send my love to my sisters for life (Tawana, Mecca, Shamekia, Kim and Anneka). My siblings (Robert aka Boom..Sharima, Asalma, Munira, Shijuana, Munira, LaQuan and Hashim. I would also like to send my love and appreciation to the entire Forrest and Grinnage Family. A special thanks to Lisa Smith and Rosalind Kelly (I thank the both of you for the love and support you gave at a time when I really needed it.) Last, but not least, thanks to my dad Ron Grinnage. Thank you to all who have supported me throughout my journey....Smooches!

"Life isn't about finding yourself. Life is about creating yourself."

# It Ain't Over

## Taraine

As I lay in bed holding on to LaQuan with everything in me, I felt overwhelmed, but so grateful it was just a dream. A dream that felt so real. I was so anxious and ready to get out of New York and start over with my man, or should I say my husband and my baby girls.

"Are you okay, baby?" LaQuan asked as he looked at me with fear in his eyes.

"Yes. I'm okay, Daddy. Just hold me please."

"I had a dream Lance's bitch ass was released from jail early. He came straight here from jail to rob you but you weren't home, so he decided he was going to kill me instead. Damn, it felt so real, LaQuan. I hope that's not a sign. I'm just ready to get the girls and leave all this bullshit behind us."

"Daddy got you," he said, kissing me gently on my neck. "I love you," he said, looking into my eyes. "This is just the beginning. We have so much to look forward to, Moc."

My heart was pounding hard. I couldn't express exactly what I was feeling. I just wanted to be held. *Damn, I have been through so much,* I thought as I began to have flashbacks of all the mishaps in my past. Jay and all his bullshit, then there was Rell and all his bullshit, and all the other bullshit in between. I'm not going to allow anyone to nullify my happiness. *I'm in love. I'm happy and at peace with life and it feel so damn good,* I thought.

"Baby, I need to relax. I think I'm going to take a long bath, relax my body and my mind."

"I got you, baby," LaQuan said as he got up to run my bath water.

He knows just how I like it, that's what I loved so much about my man. He pays attention to the small stuff.

"Your bath is ready, Moc!" he yelled.

When I got into the tub, LaQuan grabbed my loofah and started massaging my back and shoulders in circular motions.

"Come join me," I said, looking at him.

He undressed and slid down into the water behind me. I leaned back on him and closed my eyes as he continued washing and caressing my body.

He began massaging my breast. He then glided his hands down to my precious jewels and caressed her gently. I moaned slightly, letting him know I was enjoying what he was doing to me.

"Do I make you feel good, Moc?"

"Yes, baby, all the time!"

He always made me feel sexy and desirable. *I love my baby so much,* I thought to myself as he suddenly glided two of his fingers inside of me. He was taking me to a place I was ready willing and able to go. He definitely knew my body and he knew just what it took to make me reach that higher plateau. I leaned my head back against him and we began kissing and tongue-locking passionately. He continued massaging me gently until I began to release all over his fingers. We got out of the tub, dried one another off, and proceeded to the bedroom to bless it one last time.

Our love-making was the greatest. You know you're in love when just a kiss to the neck sends your body into convulsions; when you wish that very moment could last forever. When every thrust feels so good it makes you shed tears—not tears from pain or sadness, but tears from joy and fulfillment in your heart. I love my husband. He was not just my husband; he was my soul mate. He loved to take his time and satisfy my every need. He loved trying to find pleasure spots I never knew I had. Then when he found one, he would look at me, wink, and tell me to close my eyes, relax, and enjoy the moment.

There's nothing better than an unselfish man; a man who finds pleasure in pleasing his woman. I did exactly as I was told – I relaxed my body, closed my eyes, and I enjoyed every pleasurable and passionate minute.

*****

I woke up, turned over, and noticed LaQuan was gone, but I could hear the shower running. I decided to go spend some time with Deb. I really wish she was moving to Georgia with us. She is such a big help with the girls; maybe after a while, I can convince her to move down there with us. *I am going to miss New York so much, but it's time to move on,* I thought as I lay in bed, smiling at the thought of our new journey.

I had mixed emotions. I never thought I would be leaving New York City, not ever. NYC is the place to be; the city that never sleeps. I can't be selfish; my girls deserve so much more and I'm going to do whatever it takes to make sure their upbringing is better than mine.

LaQuan walked into the bedroom glistening, looking as sexy as he did the very first time we got it on. He was so delicious; all I wanted to do was eat him up. I was ready to taste every part of him all over again. He looked at me and smiled.

"What's up? Why you looking at Daddy like that?"

"Because I adore you and I was just thinking about the first time you came walking into the bedroom wrapped in a towel. It feels like déjà vu. You sent electricity throughout my body then, and to this day, you have that same effect on me," I said with the 'I want you now' look on my face.

"I do?" he asked blushing.

"I love you so much, LaQuan, and I am very happy we're together. Bonnie and Clyde ain't got shit on us," I said laughing.

"Not a damn thing on us, baby. I'm going to the club to sign some documents. When I come back we can finish packing whatever is left. It's not much; whatever we don't need we'll leave behind," he said.

"Okay, well, I'm going to go over to Deb's for a while. I will meet you back here in a couple of hours. I'm going to leave Raine' and Nicera there. There's nowhere for them to sleep anyway," I said.

"You're right, Moc. I should be back no later than 8," he said.

"What time is it now?" I asked.

"It's about 3. When I get back we can continue where we left off. I want to try some new things tonight."

"I thought we tried everything possible."

"Not everything, Moc," he said winking.

"Come give me a taste of chocolate before you leave," I said.

He leaned in towards me and tongued me down.

"Damn, you taste good, baby. You better leave now, daddy, or else you might not make it out the door," I said.

"I love you, baby," he said as he walked out the bedroom.

Once LaQuan left, I decided to get up and take a shower before heading over to Deb's house.

As I turned the water on, I heard my doorbell ring. I threw my robe back on and headed to the door.

"Who is it?" I asked.

"Sidora!" the small voice on the other side of the door said.

"Yes, may I help you?" I asked.

"Is LaQuan home?" she asked.

I was startled by who she was asking for. I immediately opened the door. Standing in front of me was a light-skinned, slim woman with long, reddish hair and a big mole on the right side of her nose.

"Who are you looking for?" I asked again, just to make sure I heard her right. Knowing I just heard this bitch ask for my husband.

"LaQuan," she said once again.

"No, LaQuan is not home, but I'm his wife, Taraine. Can I help you?"

I waited anxiously to hear her response.

"Oh, I'm LaQuan's cousin, Sidora," she said with a slick cackle.

I just got into town today and his mother gave me this address. Do you know where I can find him? I really need to talk to him about some family issues."

*Family issues,* I thought to myself. *What family issues? And most importantly, who the fuck are you? I never heard of no-damn Sidora. Maybe she's a lost cousin he never spoke of.*

"Well, LaQuan will be home in a couple of hours. I will call him and let him know you're here. Come in."

"Oh, you guys look like ya'll are all packed up and ready to move," Sidora said.

"Yes. Tomorrow we will be leaving the city that never sleeps and moving to Georgia. His mother didn't mention that to you?" I asked.

"No, she didn't, but that's great. I guess I made it just in time."

"We're all packed, but I do have some glasses out and a bottle of Rose' in the fridge. Would you care for a glass?" I asked.

"Sure, I would love a glass," she said.

I poured us both a glass.

"Oh, let me call LaQuan," I said searching for my cell phone.

"Damn, voicemail," I said before leaving a message. "Hey, baby, call me when you get a chance. Love you."

"Okay, Sidora. My baby didn't answer, but I left a message for him to call me back. So how are you and LaQuan related?" I asked.

"His mother and my father are brother and sister," she said, as she sipped her Rose'.

"So you guys are moving to Georgia, huh? I guess my cousin is doing very well for himself," she said.

"Your cousin is the shit, girl. He knows how to handle his business quite well, and he definitely knows how to support his family. I couldn't have asked for a better husband. So, I guess you know what took place between Lance and LaQuan?" I asked.

"No, girl! What happened?" she said.

"Oh, that motherfucker put my husband through some bullshit. He robbed a jewelry store in Manhattan, then jumped into LaQuan's car without letting him know anything. To make a long story short, they both were locked up. I'm surprised you don't know about any of this."

"Girl, this is all news to me," Sidora said, as she sat anxiously waiting to hear more.

"My daddy had to do time over this bullshit; all because of that selfish bastard, Lance. I know Lance is family, but I always felt a bad vibe coming from him. He always seemed shady to me. Fortunately, my man is home and that psychopath is still in prison where he belongs," I said happily.

"Wow, that's fucked up!" Sidora said. "Can I use your bathroom? This drink is running right through me, girl," she said.

"Sure, straight down the hall and make a left."

Sidora came back into the living room looking through her Louie Vuitton bag as if she'd lost something.

"Is everything okay?" I asked.

"Yeah, I'm good. So, has LaQuan heard from Lance since he's been home?" she asked.

"No, but I had the craziest dream about him. It felt so real. I really don't want any connections with him, and I'm quite sure LaQuan feels the same way," I said.

"That's real fucked up, but do you know the sad part about the situation?" Sidora asked.

"Yeah, I know the sad part. The sad part about the entire situation is that I lost a lot of time without my man — all for nothing. Because at the end of the day, LaQuan was innocent," I said.

Sidora sat there shaking her head. "Yeah, that's fucked up, Taraine. But the sad part would be losing your man forever," she said angrily.

I looked at her in confusion.

"I know how it feels to lose someone," Sidora said. "I lost my man; he was killed a month ago over some dumb shit. I wouldn't wish this pain I'm feeling on no one. Well, maybe the person who caused his death. We had a great future together. We were looking forward to getting married and having children and now that's all gone," she said as the tears filled her eyes.

"Damn, I'm sorry to hear that. And you're right, I don't ever want to experience that," I said, shaking my head. "Did they catch the person who killed him?"

Sidora looked up at me. "Yes, they caught one of them, but its two left, and eventually, they will get what's coming to them."

She searched through her bag, as if she was looking for some tissue to wipe away her tears.

"Trust me, Taraine. They will get what's coming to them, and I will be the one to take them down," she said.

Before I knew it she pulled out a .38.

"Bitch, did you hear what the fuck I just said? I will be the one to take you and your motherfucking man down. Now, get the fuck up, bitch," Sidora yelled.

I just sat there in shock.

"Bitch, I said get the fuck up," she yelled again, walking towards me pointing the gun in my face.

"What's going on?" I asked sarcastically.

"What's going on, bitch, is what I'd like to call Sidora's revenge. That's what the fuck is going on," she said.

"I don't understand, Sidora. What do I have to do with your man being killed?" I asked.

"Are you serious, or are you just dumb as hell? You and your man, or should I say husband, have everything to do with my man's death. Since you can't figure it out, I guess I have to explain it to your dumb ass," she said, pushing me down the hall toward the bedroom.

When we got to the bedroom, she closed the door behind us.

"I was waiting for my man to come home and surprise me with a little gift, but he never showed up. Days turned into weeks and weeks turned into months and I heard nothing from my man, which was odd because he never let a day go by without talking to me," she said angrily.

As she rambled on, things became clear to me who this chick was.

"You know why he didn't call me, bitch? Do you have any idea why? I'll tell you why. It's because he was locked up. Then, he was placed in the box. When he was released from the box, they put him in the psyche ward. I finally received a letter from my man, and do you know what it said?" she asked.

As she fussed and cried I knew I needed to find my way out of this situation and I needed to figure it out fast. This bitch was just as crazy as her man.

"The letter said he was locked up because your motherfucking husband set him up in a botched robbery," Sidora said.

"Who – my husband?"

"Shut the fuck up. Yes, your motherfucking husband, but I'm here to get revenge. Either I can take you out and let LaQuan suffer the way I'm suffering, or I can just take the both of you out. Okay, it didn't take long for me to figure this shit out. BITCH, you're a dead woman," Sidora said.

"Sidora! Why do you want to kill me?" I asked.

"You love your husband, right?" Sidora asked.

"Yes," I replied.

"I loved my man, too, and guess what? He's gone. Lance is gone, bitch, and our dreams are over. Your man hated on his own fucking cousin."

"I'm sorry, Sidora. I don't know what Lance told you, and no disrespect to you, but your man lied to you. He was the one who robbed that jewelry store, then he got into the car and didn't tell LaQuan what he had done. Lance was the one with the diamonds on him. LaQuan was the one who did time for nothing," I said.

"Shut the fuck up, bitch, before I blow your fucking head off. I don't give a shit about you or LaQuan. And why would Lance lie to me?" she yelled.

"I really don't know, but like I said, I lost my man, too!" I said.

"Well, bitch, you're about to lose so much more because I'm about to take your life," she said, as she swung and hit me across the face with the gun.

As I fell to the floor, things began to feel like déjà vu. I felt like the dream I'd had this morning was turning into reality, but just from a different perspective.

Lance didn't win in the dream and I refuse to let this bitch take me out. *Hold on,* I thought to myself. *I'm too strong for this, I've been through too much and I'm definitely a survivor.* As I lay on the floor in excruciating pain, she began kicking me in my stomach and yelling at the same time.

"I hate you, bitch. I hate you and your motherfucking man. This is the day your life will come to a motherfucking end," she yelled.

Suddenly, everything went black.

*****

When I woke up, Sidora was sitting on the floor directly in front of me talking to herself. I know she was in mourning, but this bitch was crazy as hell. I continued to lie still and just listen to what she had to say.

"My man may be dead, but he made me promise to take you and LaQuan's punk ass down if anything was to happen to him. Then I get a phone call telling me he was dead, and how he was killed by another inmate. I know LaQuan's low-down dirty ass set him up. He took my king away from me, and now I'm going to take his queen away from him," Sidora mumbled to herself.

As I lay there, she must have thought I was still unconscious from the blow I took to my face. She got up and looked through my belongings. She couldn't find anything because everything was packed away. She didn't find anything in the bedroom, so she walked out of the bedroom and back down the hall into the living room. This was my chance to get up and find a way to take this bitch down before she killed me.

The only thing I could find in my room was the ice pick LaQuan had used on the ice last night. I got up holding my head, and walked quietly out the bedroom, trying to listen to her footsteps to at least figure out where she was exactly. As I approached the living room, I heard her opening up some of the boxes. I looked over towards the couch and saw my phone. It was lit up, which let me know I had a missed call. It was probably from LaQuan. As she continued to rip open the boxes, she cried hysterically.

"Lance, please help me, baby. I don't know what to do. I don't want to kill this bitch but that was your wish. You told me to take her and LaQuan's ass out. But, baby, she said you lied. She said you twisted the story and that you were the reason shit went wrong. We were supposed to be happy right now. I know you wouldn't just leave me out here like this. The money you said would be here, I don't see. I don't see no damn safe and I don't see no jewelry. Fuck, fuck! Where is the safe? Where are the jewels? Damn, I got to wake this bitch up and question her ass. She is going to tell me where the safe is and then I will kill the bitch," Sidora, said continuing to sort through the boxes.

At that moment, my phone rang. She went and looked at the caller ID.

"Daddy," she said, looking down at the display screen. "Well, daddy, your little queen is about to meet her maker," she said and dropped the cell phone back onto the couch.

Once she dropped the phone, I quietly walked back into the bedroom. I lay back on the floor with the ice pick in my hand. She walked into the room, reached down, and pulled me up by my hair.

"Um, excuse me," she said, slapping my face. "Wake the fuck up. You slept long enough. Where is the motherfucking safe that has the money and jewelry in it?"

"I don't know what money and jewelry you're talking about," I slurred.

"Stand up, bitch. Don't play with my fucking intelligence. Take me to the safe now, or else I'm going to blow your fucking head off," she said, pointing the gun to my head.

"The safe is in the kid's room," I said, holding the ice pick tightly in my hand.

She put the gun to my side. "Then let's go to the kid's room. Take me to my shit."

When we reached the girl's room, I went to their closet knowing there wasn't a safe in there. I had to think fast. I needed to take her out before she tried to blow my damn head off. I opened the closet door, and at the same time, turned around and jugged her with the ice pick twice in her chest. When I tried to stab her a third time, I heard a loud pop and immediately felt a burning sensation in my chest. Then I heard another pop and felt pain in my head worse than any migraine I'd ever had. I fell back into the girl's closet. I could see her pulling the ice pick out of her chest. I watched her as she stumbled out of the room.

My heart raced as I thought to myself, *No, bitch. You can't die. My girl's would never forgive me for this.*

My body felt numb. I felt like I was in a deep sleep and I was trying to force myself to wake up.

*Help me!* I tried to yell, but nothing came out.

My chest was hurting and so was my head. I tried once again to scream for help, but still, nothing came out. *Damn, I let this bitch take me down. She shot me!!! LaQuan, baby, please come home and find me before it's too late,* I thought to myself.

As I lay there in pain, I felt my eyes getting heavy. I just wanted to go to sleep. I could still hear movement going on in the other room. Suddenly, it stopped and everything went dark.

I was awakened by the sound of LaQuan's voice calling out to me. His voice appeared to be getting closer. I tried my best to move, but nothing was happening. I tried to call his name, but still nothing. I couldn't even open my eyes. All I saw was darkness. Suddenly, I felt his lips on mine as he cried for me to wake up.

"Open your eyes, baby," he said.

*I'm trying to, LaQuan, but I can't,* I thought.

I heard him on his cell phone.

"Hello, I need an ambulance at 527 Bainbridge Street. Please hurry, my wife has been shot. Yes, it looks like one shot to the chest and one to the right side of her head. Please hurry," he said before hanging up. He continued talking to me.

"Moc, baby, who did this to you?" he asked. "What happened here, baby? Please open your eyes for me. Open your eyes for daddy. Squeeze my hand, Moc. Do something…just don't leave me," he said, crying hysterically. "Moc, I love you so much. I need you and the girls need you. Don't do this to us, baby."

He picked up his cell phone to call for help again, but the paramedics were ringing the doorbell. LaQuan opened the door and guided them to the bedroom.

"She's been shot twice," he said.

They laid me on the floor and went to work. I heard more voices; it sounded like the police. I heard their conversation and their movements, but I couldn't see a thing. I was extremely scared and confused.

They placed me on a stretcher and put me into the ambulance as they continued working on me.

You're a fighter, Moc," LaQuan said over and over. "You can beat this; it's not your time. We need you here, baby. I forbid you to leave us."

I could hear in his voice just how afraid he was.

"Who did this to you, baby?" he asked. "Who?"

*Baby, I'm so tired and my head hurts. You got to get that bitch. Lance's so-called fiancé did this to me. You have to find her trifling ass and make her pay. Do you hear me, LaQuan? It was Lance's fiancé, her name is Sidora.*

I managed to open my eyes and looked directly at him, but his head was down as if he was praying.

*Look at me. Pick your head up!* I said, but it seems as if he didn't hear a word I said, or at least I thought I said it.

My eyes began to feel heavy again as the tears began to fall down the side of my face. Then, once again, there was only darkness.

I felt LaQuan wiped the tears from my face as he whispered in my ear. "I'm here for you and I will always be here for you. I love you." Those were the last words I heard him speak.

*****

The doctor worked for hours trying to remove the bullets without causing more damage to my brain and my chest. There were a couple of close calls, but I made it out of surgery without any problems… or so I thought.

"Doc, why hasn't my wife shown any signs yet? She has opened her eyes from time to time, but that's about it," LaQuan said with concern in his voice.

"Well, Mr. Cummings, as I told you before, your wife has gone through a couple major surgeries. Looking back at what has happened to her, it's a miracle she's still alive. We had to put her in an induced coma to try to keep her under control throughout the surgery, and to keep the stress on her heart to a minimum. I cannot tell you that she's going to wake up at this very moment and be back to normal. I'm sorry, I just can't promise you that. Talk to her; let her feel your presence. Pray and thank God for bringing her this far," Doctor Graham said.

*What? I thought. What the hell does he mean I'm in an induced coma? I'm lost. What just happened here? Why am I still unable to open my eyes? Why am I still struggling to move my hands and toes? Am I paralyzed? What's wrong with me? Did you catch that bitch, Sidora? That motherfucker Lance did it again, baby. He set us up again.*

The more I thought about it, the more aggravated I became, thus setting off my machine.

"What's wrong with her, Doc?" LaQuan yelled. "Why? Why is this happening?" LaQuan asked as he kissed my lips. "I love you, Taraine. Please come back to me."

*I love you, too, LaQuan.*

I knew he was afraid because it's been a very long time since he called me Taraine, so this had to be more serious than I realized. I felt his head on my chest, but I was unable to rub his head, reassure him and tell him how much I loved him.

"Baby, I need you to wake up. I need you to tell me who did this to you. I've already been questioned by the cops twice. My story checked out, so they're moving on with the investigation. I understand why they questioned me, but I only wish they knew how much I love you and I would never in a million years hurt you, baby. I called all your girls and they all were here while you were in surgery. They have been spending time with Nicera and Raine, giving Deb a piece of mind. She is hurting and wants to know who did this to her daughter. You know Fatima has been up here causing a ruckus. She is not having it. She is making sure these nurses are doing their jobs," LaQuan said.

*Oh yeah, that's my girl, Fatima. I know when she catches that bitch Sidora she is going to rag-tag her ass. Baby, I wish you could hear me. Laying here unable to speak or move is killing me. Damn it. I don't deserve this. Why are you punishing me, God? I ask you this over and over again. My family, my children, my husband, and my friends don't deserve this heartache. They can't handle it,* I thought as I lay there, crying on the inside. All of a sudden, I heard the bitch of all bitches, as her voice got closer to me.

\*\*\*\*\*

"LaQuan, we have to find out who did this to my girl. We're going to find this bastard," Fatima yelled as she leaned over and kissed me on my cheek.

"Oh, hell no! I hate this wrap around your head, chica. But you still look good. I'm thankful you're still here, but you have to wake up. I can't live this life without you. Who's going to keep my ass in check when I need it? I know you think I can hold shit down, but I can't, Tee. I need you. I need you to open your eyes and give me that look you give whenever I pissed you off. I need you to spread those lips and say 'what did you get yourself into now Fatima?' I really need that from you, Taraine. I know I may sound a little selfish, and I know it's all up to God, but I have to say what's on my mind. Am I being selfish for that? You damn right I am, because I need you," Fatima said as she wiped the tears from her face.

"I'm going to step out for a minute to see if Deb wants to come inside. I'm also going to see if they will allow Raine' and Nicera to come in as well," LaQuan said, rubbing Fatima gently on her back.

"Okay, Q. I am going to stay here and talk to my bitch…I mean, my girl. She'll get tired of my ass and will come out of this damn coma just to tell me to shut the hell up," Fatima said with a slight chuckle.

"Well, chica it's just you and me. But on the real, Tee, I need you to get stronger and come up out of this, especially for that fine ass husband of yours. You don't want these starving ass bitches out here trying to take what's yours, do you? He's looking so worried and stressed out. He's been up here every day, all day. We are all showing love and support, waiting for you to open up them pretty brown eyes. Plus, there's really no one I can talk to but you. You're the only one who will give me the real feedback no matter what, and right about now, I need someone to talk to. I got some serious issues and I can use some good advice on what I should do next. I decided I can no longer stay in this relationship with Karl's ass. I know what you're thinking; he's a good man, but, Taraine, he is a drag. He's slowing me down. I know I said I was ready to settle down, but I didn't say I was ready to retire from living an active life. He got us ready to start looking for senior citizens homes. He has the maturity, he has the money and he knows how to make love, but I like to fuck every now and then. I like to go in, you feel me? Be spontaneous; have sex whenever and wherever. Not him. Not Mr. 'It's Not the Appropriate Place'. It *is* appropriate if your ass is horny. So, guess what, boo boo? You got to go. Yes, I did, Tee. I kicked his ass to the curb. I will love his ass from a distance—a far, far distance. Maybe ten or fifteen years from now we can get back together, but as of today, he's a done deal. And this bitch right here is back in the game," Fatima said, clapping with joy.

"Now, let me tell you what happened to me last week. I know you were packing to move, so I dragged Slim's ass with me to test drive this X5 out in L.I.C. But it all went down like this...

# Test Drive

## Fatima

When we got there, this fine-ass chocolate brother came walking up to us. I smiled and checked him out from head to toe. He smiled and sized up my breast.

*Size 'em up, boo. I know you like what you see, because I'm loving what I see. Yum, yum!* I thought to myself.

"Hello, ladies. I will start off by introducing myself. My name is Chris. Is there anything I can show you?" he asked as he smiled at us showing off his one deep dimple on the left side.

"Yes. I'm interested in purchasing an X5, but I would like to test drive it first. I would like to test drive something else, too," I mumbled.

"Excuse me?" he said.

"Oh, I was just saying I love that dimple of yours."

"Thank you. By the way, did you know BMW has the X6 out now?" he asked.

"Yeah, but I'm really feeling the X5. The X6 looks like a damn spaceship. Nah, boo, that's not for me," I said.

"Okay," he said, "follow me and I will get you set up to test drive the X5."

We walked into the office to signs some papers. As we walked, he asked my name. I gave him my driver's license and smiled.

"My name is Fatima, but you can call me extraordinary if you like," I said sitting down to fill out the forms.

He looked at me and smiled. Right then and there I knew he wanted me. He was thinking about how good of a fuck I would be, and I was thinking the same damn thing.

I turned back and looked at Slim. "Damn, he's fine," I mumbled to her.

She started smiling shaking her head. In other words, she agreed.

We all jumped inside the all black X5.

"Oh yeah, this right here is all me. I'm claiming this – black leather interior fully loaded, sexy and hot, and it has Fatima written all over it," I said. I turned the music up loud and was ready to cruise.

"I look good in this don't I?" I asked.

He looked at me and said, "You look extraordinary in it; this is all you, sweetheart."

I put on my Gucci shades and rolled out. After a couple of blocks I had made my decision.

*I'm taking the X5 and Chris, too,* I thought as we pulled back into the lot.

If Slim wasn't in the car with us I would have shown him what I was working with. I was definitely in need, especially after being in a committed relationship with Karl. Karl's ass had me damn near ready to commit myself into an asylum. I was ready to release all this backed up stress and I know I would have done some damage to his ass in that X5.

"You know I can't keep no secrets from you, Taraine. We eventually met up later that night and we fucked like crazy. It was so good. He definitely laid the pipe down. Tee, he is into that freaky shit like me—whips, cuffs, blindfold – you name it, he had it. I put it on his ass for real. Then he turned around and put it right back on me. Slap it up flip it rub it down, oh no. We were out of control and I loved every minute of it. He tried to get next to winky (my ass), but I had to let him know there would be no ass action that night. I told him he could kiss it, blow on it, he could even lick it, but he wasn't sticking a damn thing in that area. That's exit only and he was fine with that. The only thing I didn't like was when he wanted to snuggle after. He was fine as hell, but oh no, no, no, there would be no snuggling going on between us. I did enough of that with Karl. I kind of brushed him off of me, then got up to get dressed. He lay there watching with the biggest smile on his face."

"So, Chris, when can I see you again? When are you going to take me out and show me off?" I asked him.

He laughed at me, but bet that ass he was down. "We can hang tomorrow. I would love to show your sexy ass off," he said.

"Sounds like a plan," I said. I kissed him gently on the lips and made my way towards his door.

"See you tomorrow. By the way, the sex was great. Can't wait to do it again," I said as I closed the door behind me."

*****

He picked me up near the house. I couldn't let him know exactly where I lived – not until I get Karl officially out of my life.

"Where do you want to go?" he asked.

"Let's just drive. Let's get on the I-95 and go. Are you down for that?" I asked smiling.

"Sexy, I'm down to do anything with you."

Before I knew it, we were on the strip of Virginia Beach, a nice simple state, but I knew we were going to turn this motherfucker out. We laid up in a resort with the balcony facing the beach and it was on. We were getting it on right on the balcony. He picked me up against the gate and banged me out. I just went with it. I wrapped my legs around him and went to work.

After our little private performance, we headed out to the beach and got it on some more, but this time we had an audience. We definitely put on a performance and they enjoyed it to the very end."

"Taraine, I think I found my match, girl. Your ass got to wake up and let me know what's good. I'm back to the stage of just wanting to have fun, and you know what that means, right? Karl and I had to come to an end. I didn't want to hurt him and that's what would have happened if I didn't let him go. Do you think I'm wrong?" I asked as I rubbed her soft hands.

*"Nah, you're not wrong, that's just you, boo,"* I said, even though she couldn't hear a word I was saying.

"I don't know who did this to you, baby girl, but you best believe he's a dead man. You have been through so much, but it's not your time. I'm praying to God that he gives you the strength to come out of this coma. We all love you and need you here with us. You know I'm not a crier, but I'm angry, sad, and scared, and all I want is for you to come back to us. The other bitches are on their way. I guess we are going to have our sessions here in this room until you decide to wake up. We will continue to help Q and Deb out with Raine' and Nicera. This is not over; trust me, a motherfucker is going down for this one. This shit ain't over until that motherfucker is caught," Fatima said, her voice filled with anger.

*I know you got my back, Fatima. And when I get out of this hospital, that bitch Sidora's ass is mine!*

# Never Give Up

## Taraine

The more I lay here stuck inside my own mind, the more frustrating things became. I was frustrated at the simple fact that I had this amazing husband of mine singing in my ear and letting me know just how much he loved me and I was unable to respond to him. He was asking me to show a sign letting him know that I could hear him, and as much as I tried, I was stuck. I was paralyzed, physically and somewhat mentally.

*LaQuan, baby, I'm here and I'm fighting to come back to you and my girls. I refuse to give up, baby,* I thought as I listen to him read my favorite poem to me.

Pretty women wonder where my secret lies
I'm not cute or built to suit a fashion model's size
But when I start to tell them
They think I'm telling lies
I say
It's the reach of my arms
The stride of my step
The curl of my lips

I'm a woman
Phenomenally
Phenomenal woman
That's me.

He continued reciting the poem and it was killing me – literally killing me. I heard my heart beating stronger and faster. I felt trapped and the darkness seemed darker. I just can't accept this; I refuse to give up on life or my family. LaQuan sounded lost and hopeless and I knew my baby's heart was broken.

*Yes, daddy. I am a phenomenal woman and I will fight to the very end.*

After he finished the poem, he grasped my hand.

"Baby, the detectives have no leads as of yet. I'm so fucking angry; it seems as if the motherfucker who did this to you just vanished into thin air. This is killing me. I hate to see you lying here like this. I miss hearing your sexy voice. You are still so beautiful, lying here peacefully. Are you dreaming about me, baby? My Mocha Chocolate…my angel. I just want to assure you of one thing—I am not going anywhere. I'm going to stay here and talk to you, sing to you and read your favorite poem to you. It's always about us and we still got a lot of living to do," LaQuan said.

"I hate to tell you this, Moc, but me and Boom went and dragged Rell's ass out of his mother's apartment. He was crying like the little punk bitch he is. Boom put the glock to his head and he swore up and down he had nothing to do with shooting you. You know I've wanted to get at his ass since I came home, and this was my chance. He has been fucking with you for far too long. I took everything out on his ass. As soon as I looked at him, I started having flashbacks. That was my time to get his ass for every 'bitch', 'hoe', 'slut', and any other name he called you and for every punch, kick, slap and anything else he ever gave you. He always wants to play the victim. I told him to forget he ever had a daughter and that Nicera was officially mine. Moc, what did you see in his bitch ass? I promise you one thing – he won't be trouble for you any longer. I'm quite sure he got the message," LaQuan said.

"Your mom is going to bring the girls to see you today. The doctor gave us permission he said it might do you some good to communicate with the girls. They miss you so much. Nicera cries herself to sleep and Raine' holds her tight until eventually they both fall asleep," he said sadly. "Baby, your hands are so cold." LaQuan rubbed them gently trying to warm them up.

*Damn, I wish I could just gently rub his cheek. I love you so much, daddy and I need you as much as you need me. But I don't have enough strength to move or to open my eyes. I wish I had just enough strength to part my lips and tell you just how much I love you. You are my everything, and as God is my witness, I'm going to find the strength to open my eyes and move my arm so that I can wrap them around you and whisper in your ear just how much I love you.*

"Moc, this is killing me. I can't lose you. I need to find out who did this to you. Who had the courage to try to turn our world upside-down? We can't let them win, baby, and the detectives need to step their game up."

All of a sudden, I heard voices yell "Daddy" in unison. It was the most beautiful sound a mother could ever want to hear.

"Hey!" LaQuan said with excitement.

"Mommy, wake up. Me and Raine' came to see you," Nicera said.

"Daddy, why don't mommy open her eyes?" Nicera asked.

"She's very tired; she's just getting a little bit of beauty rest. Come over here so you can give mommy a kiss," he said.

"Love you, mommy," Nicera said.

"Now, let your sister give mommy a kiss; you can't have all the kisses," LaQuan said.

"Yes, I can, Daddy," Nicera said giggling.

He picked Raine' up so she could give her mother a kiss, but Raine liked rubbing noses; that was her way of kissing.

"Can I lay next to mommy?" Nicera asked.

"Yes, I think mommy would love that," Laquan said as he laid both the girls beside Taraine.

*Hi, my Angels. Mommy loves you guys so much. I wish I can just hold you and kiss you all over. Oh God, please give me one more chance to hold my babies. They mean the world to me.*

*****

"What the hell are you doing in this bed?" I heard a voice ask. "You need to get your ass up out of that bed."

As the voice got closer to me, I realized it was Monica, aka 'Slim Boogie'.

"You know I am the cry baby out of all of us, but I kept telling myself not to cry the closer I got to the room. I was expecting you to be up by now, but I guess you're being stubborn, as usual. You still look beautiful, even in your head bandages. Damn, I should have brought my makeup kit with me. I would have fixed you up. You can still be a diva, girl. You can't let this tragedy stop you. I know you just needed some good rest, but I'm here to talk your head off anyway."

"My hubby and I are about to leave Brooklyn and start off brand new. We had a couple of therapy sessions and they went pretty well. I'm just trying to stay positive and get back on the right track. I really want our marriage to work. The sex is still boring, but I'll manage. Eventually, I'll get him to do things the way I like and to explore different things. I'm going to bring that shit up in our next counseling session. To be honest with you, Taraine, I really want to have a threesome with him, but I know he would not be down for that. He barely wants to do shit with me, and if I see him putting it on the next bitch, I might have a fucking fit. I know Fatima has been doing her thing as usual. She is too much. Ain't no stopping that chick," Monica laughed.

"Tee, I'm kind of lost. Why would somebody want to hurt you like this, girl? I know I am the quietest one out of all of us, but if I was to find the motherfucker that did this to you, I would probably kill him my damn self. I know one thing for sure, Tee – your man is not having it. He is on his job, hard. He is definitely holding it down while you take your personal vacation. I respect him for that! He is remarkable, Tee, and I can definitely see why you fell in love with him. He didn't get selfish and decide to leave the girls with your mother. That sound like some bullshit Rell would pull. I hope Rell didn't have anything to do with this happening to you. I know that God will see you through this. He has you hanging on for a reason," Monica said sympathetically.

I could feel Monica softly rubbing my hand, but I was still unable to move my fingers. It felt as if I had no circulation in my hand. Just knowing I could feel her a little gave me plenty to be happy for. There was hope that I could come out of this. If only I could just squeeze her hand or open my eyes.

*Slim Boogie, I hear you, girl. And believe me, I'm going to get up out of this comatose state I'm in. This is not how I plan to leave this world. I'm a fighter and I refuse to let some bitch named Sidora end my life. I wish you could hear me, Slim, because I would tell you to keep fighting for your marriage, but if you don't feel him fighting back, let his ass go. Someone out there would love every part of you. Damn, this hurts so bad. Why can't anyone hear me? This is so confusing to me, God.*

"This chick I went to college with said I should look into this gated community in Philly where she lived. When we saw the home we fell in love with it, and decided to take it. I will keep in contact with LaQuan while I'm gone to see if you decided to come back to us. I just hate seeing you lay here like this. I know you would have some good advice for me. I always loved you for that. You are the realest friend I could ever ask for. I don't know what I would do without you – none of you girls. I truly love you," Monica said.

*Aww! I truly love you, too, Monica. I don't want you to leave, but you have to do whatever it takes to make sure your family is okay.*

"By the way, Fatima is back at it again. I went with her to test drive an X5 and it looked like she was ready to test drive the salesman. What are we going to do with her, Tee? Poor Karl! I thought he had a hold on her, but I guess not. As for Shantae, she should be here soon. She told me to meet her here. She's still going through the motions of who she wants to be with," Monica said.

"Oh, I guess your ass talking about me," Shantae said as she walked into the room. "Taraine, what's up? Why are you being so stubborn? You wanted our attention, and now you got it, so you can stop all this playing around and wake your ass up. You're suppose to be in Georgia by now setting shit up so I can come down there and make some of them Southern bitches fall in love with me, but instead, you've decided to go on vacation in this bitch," Shatae said.

"Shut up!" Slim said.

"Seriously, Tee, you have to wake up. I need some counseling right about now. We need to have a session because I need to vent," Shantae said.

"Yeah! We do," Monica agreed.

*Damn, Shantae. What did you get yourself into now? What would you girls do if God decided it was my turn to leave this world? While I'm here trying to survive, you girls are out there doing all type of shit.*

"Okay Taraine, you pulled it out of me," Shantae said laughing. "I went back to the bar we all went to. You know, the one you decided to have a fit in because the bitches were getting too close to you? Yeah, the gay bar. So, I'm at the bar getting my drink on and who do I see? Angela. You heard me right . . . Angela. Fatima's friend. So, I get my drink and go sit next to her. 'Hey, Angela. What you doing up in here girl?' I asked her. She turned around and looked as if she didn't quite recognize me. After taking a second look, she realized who I was. 'Hey, Shantae! Long time, girl. I'm doing the same thing you're doing – trying to get my buzz on,' she said. Damn, Tee. I didn't realize how beautiful she was when we were younger. I never really paid her that much attention when Fatima would bring her around. Then again, I wasn't checking for bitches at that time. Or was I?" Shantae said.

"Yeah, that's true. You wasn't checking for girls back then, and if you was, I hope your ass wasn't looking at me," Monica said laughing.

"Bitch, I was not looking at you. You're too light and too damn skinny, to be honest with you," Shantae said.

"Kiss my ass," Monica said jokingly. "My man likes it!"

*I wish they could hear me tell both of them to shut the hell up. Shantae, are you going to tell your story or not? Damn, even while I'm in this coma, these bitches still manage to get on my nerves.*

"Anyway, as I was saying, Tee, she is beautiful and so soft-spoken. I wanted to throw her ass on that bar table and eat her ass up," Shantae said.

*There you go, Shantae! You are unbelievable.*

"We sat and talked for hours. Well, come to find out, she don't go by the name Angela anymore. Her name is Kandi, but that ain't even the big news. She is a call girl. This bitch was into the escorting world. She ran it all down to me – what she did and how much she charged. I asked her what made her get into that type of business – if it was to pay her bills? She said she had a job and that she did other business outside of her job. It wasn't for the money; that's what she claimed. I don't know, but I can only believe what she told me. She talked about the white lawyers, teachers, and hustlers that would make appointments. She said when she first started, she tried to walk the strip, but she didn't feel safe, so she started doing her own thing online. The more she told me, the more I wanted to fuck this chick. Her lip-gloss was nice and shiny and I wanted to taste her bad. I asked her if she had ever been with a woman, I mean, we were in a gay bar. She said no, but she had participated in a threesome with another woman and a guy, but the women did the guy, she and the chick didn't have any one-on-one action. I didn't believe her. I knew right then and there I was going to fuck this chick. She didn't know it, but I did!"

"So anyway, we ended up at my place," Shantae said.

"Stop lying," Monica said.

"Seriously . . . and I gave her the business," Shantae said.

"At first, she was going there with me, but something happened and she stopped. I don't know if she was embarrassed. How could that be; she was fucking and sucking on them white dicks, but then again, she was getting paid for it. I think when she tried to do me back, she was so good at it that it took her by surprise. Deep inside, I knew she wasn't new to this. She just lay there, so I asked her what was up, but she remained quiet. I gave up, turned around, and went to sleep. Two weeks later, I dumped the youngins and she has been with me since that night. She stopped her escorting job, even though she still gets calls every now and then. I hope she really stopped, but if she hasn't by the time I'm done with her, she will," Shantae said.

"Girl, you are too much for me," Monica said. "So, what did you tell your young tenders?" Monica asked.

"I told both of them I needed time to get my mind right and they needed to go out there and enjoy life. To be honest, they were just a project to me. I explored it and loved it, but I found something more entertaining for me. I'll keep ya'll updated on my new quest for love," Shantae said laughing.

"You are crazy, Tae. You know you are going to meet your match one day," Monica said.

*I agree with you, Slim Boogie. This girl is out of control and she will meet her match one day. The sad part is, she won't even see it coming. She has to stop taking people for granted. How I wish I was able to speak my mind right about now. I would let her ass have it.*

"Yeah, I may just meet the one who's going to hurt me bad, and Kandi may be that one. I can't predict shit, but what I do know for sure is that I really like her. She is easy on the eyes, easy to talk to, and now she gives head like a motherfucker without feeling embarrassed," Shantae said smiling.

*Oh, damn! I know you think I can't hear you, Tae, but I can and I don't want to hear that. I don't even want to visualize it.*

"I'm glad to know you're still getting good head. My husband is still acting like it's the nastiest thing to do on this planet. Don't get me wrong. He will do it, but it's only because he did some foul shit and he's trying to get back on good terms with me," Monica said sadly.

*I wish I could hold my husband for one second. All I got now is great memories. LaQuan is, by far, the best husband ever, and that's why it's imperative that I find my way back to him and my girls.*

As Monica and Shantae continued with their conversation, I tried with everything I had in me to move my fingers or open my eyes, and nothing. I felt helpless and hopeless. *Why me?* I thought as I continued with everything I had. Finally, I moved my finger.

"Oh, shit! Did you see that?" Monica said.

"See what?" Shantae asked.

"She moved her finger!" Monica said excitedly. "Taraine, you moved your finger, girl. Can you move it again? Can you try to open your eyes? Where is LaQuan? We need to get the doctor. Call LaQuan's phone to see if he's still around."

"Hey, Tee, you just moved your finger – that's a good thing. Can you try to move it again?" Shantae asked.

*I'm trying, but it's so hard, Tae. I feel like I'm playing tug-of-war with myself. The only thing that's working perfectly is my hearing.*

"What happened?" LaQuan asked, rushing into the room.

"I was telling her about my new chick and Monica said she saw her move her finger. I keep talking to her to see if I can get her to move it again, or at least open her eyes, but I haven't gotten another response from her yet," Shantae said sadly.

"Well, I had the doctor paged, so maybe he can tell us something. Hey, baby!" LaQuan said, grabbing my hand. Moc, can you please squeeze my hand? Daddy is here, baby. I love you so much. I need you to come back to me," he said, shedding a few tears.

*LaQuan, I am trying so hard, but I don't know why I'm having such a hard time. I have tried everything, but nothing is working. I just ask you to not give up on me, baby. Promise you will never give up on me.*

The doctors came into the room and checked me thoroughly. I could hear Monica explain to the doctor what she saw.

"I don't see a change in your wife," Dr. Graham explained. "I'm quite sure it was just a reflex, but I advise you and your family to continue talking to her."

*No, it's not just my reflexes. I can hear every last one of you. Please don't give up on me. You guys know I'm a fighter. You're right, Slim. I did move my finger.*

"That damn doctor don't know what the fuck he's talking about, Moc. I'm going to be here with you every day. I know you will open your eyes and be able to talk. I will hear you loud and clear when you tell me just how much you love me," LaQuan said confidently.

Minutes turn into hours; hours turn into days. I didn't know what day or time it was, but I knew for sure I was still fighting. I was going to continue to fight because I have a purpose. One, my family. Two, my friends. And three, getting my sweet revenge on that bitch, Sidora. She fucked with the wrong one.

# The Move

## Monica

"Hey, Monica. Welcome to Philly," said a voice coming from behind the door.

"Thanks, Dee," I said as I walked into the home of my college friend.

"How was the ride here from NY?" Dee asked.

"It was pretty good, the traffic was flowing smoothly. I'm just glad to be here and ready to see if this is where I want to begin my new life," I said.

"Let's go, girl," I said. "Show me Philly. Take me to where it's live. I can't meet no men, unfortunately, since I'm already married, but ain't nothing wrong with looking."

"Well, I'm not married yet, so I can look and talk as I please. I've been on sabbatical for a minute but we'll talk about that later. I think I can let loose just a little bit," Dee said.

Dee was a beautiful woman. She dressed and carried herself well. I was curious as to why she was on sabbatical. The first day of class we hit it off but after two months she left school and moved to Philly. She said she was missing her man, so I wonder what happened. She would have graduated with me if she would have stayed at N.Y.U. *The things we would do for a man,* I thought.

"I want to get this famous Philly cheese steak everyone is always talking about," I said. "I don't want to stay out too late. I need to get back to my husband."

The tour around Philly was nice. It was definitely a place I could get used to, although I'd probably get homesick and miss my girls. Suddenly, I remembered that I needed to call and check on Taraine. *I pray she's still hanging in there. She is one of the strongest women I know and she's a fighter for sure,* I thought to myself as we headed back to Dee's house.

"Okay, Dee thanks for the tour. I'm going to get back to my new home and help my husband and the boys unpack," I said.

It took me a minute to find my way back home. I felt like I was going in circles for a while. *I need to install that damn GPS system in my car before I find myself in another state,* I thought to myself. We were renting a four-bedroom townhouse. We weren't financially ready to buy a home yet and the economy was still bad, but I'm satisfied, for now. All I wanted was to give my boys a better life. We were both able to transfer our jobs, which was a good thing. If our marriage was meant to be it will be. Making the decision to move was the best decision we've made overall.

"I'm home!" I yelled as I walked into our new home. The smell of fresh paint usually made me nauseous, but not today. I felt nothing but happiness as the sound of my boys yelling "mommy" echoed in my ears.

I walked into the living room and Ron was unpacking.

"Hey, what's up?" I said. He just gave me a look and nodded.

I knew I should have stayed home and helped him unpack, but he just gives off bad vibes at times and I refuse to bring the bullshit here. Dee gave me a bottle of wine, so I decided to pop the cork, get in my relax mode, and help him unpack.

The wine had me feeling good and horny. The boys ate their dinner and were ready for bed. I was due for some loving and was ready to bless our new home as soon as my boys were asleep. I decided to take a nice hot bath, put on one of my teddies, and make my way back into the living room for a little romance.

"Hey, Big Daddy!" I said seductively. He wasn't into role playing, but it was time for a change, some excitement.

Ron looked back at me and I watched his knees almost buckle at the sight of me. Not only was I gorgeous, I was looking sexy and seductive – a sight he hasn't seen in a while.

"Are you ready to explore the dark side?" I asked. I couldn't believe I was saying all this, but it felt good and I felt powerful. I felt like I was in control and shit was going to go my way for the very first time.

He sat on the couch with his mouth wide open. I just walked over to him and guided his head to my cherry pie. He pulled back, which meant he was not going there. So, I decided to put one foot on the chair and get aggressive with it. *Tonight, I'm in control and I had to let it be known,* I thought. I guided his head towards me, and gave him the 'try it or else' look. Now he had no choice but to taste me. It took a minute for him to give in, but eventually, he did. He licked my clit softly. It felt so good. I felt myself instantly start to flow. He sat me on the couch, got on his knees, spread my legs wide, and went to town.

I couldn't believe it. *Was this my husband? The one who acts as if eating pussy was a crime?* He was eating it as if he was at a seafood buffet and I was enjoying every bit of it. Soon, I began to release and I held on to him tightly. I didn't do much, but I was drained.

He looked up at me. "Did I do the damn thing or what?"

"Yes, you did, baby!" I said giving him a wink.

Now, it was time for me to go to the rodeo. I need this ride to relieve some of this stress, and I'm sure he will enjoy it as well. Being on top was the best. I knew I could control everything and please myself in every way possible.

As I rode him, I gently nibbled on his ear, and then I whispered, "Do you want to have a threesome?"

He acted as if he didn't hear me, so I decided to go over to the other ear and asked him again. This time I said it while moaning and grinding on him.

"Baby, do you want to have a threesome?" I asked again.

I knew he was loving every minute of it, as he moaned softly and said yes.

I was instantly turned on even more. I felt myself climax all down his long pipe. I couldn't believe this was happening. I was finally going there with my husband and it felt so good. I continued to ride him until he grabbed me tightly and let it all go. I looked down at him and noticed a slight sense of embarrassment on his face. I kissed him gently on his lips. "It's okay, baby. Enjoy yourself, let go, and just live in the moment."

I woke up feeling like a different woman. A new home in a new state, a new job, and an old – but new – husband, I hope. But only time will tell.

*****

My first day at the job was going well. I was learning the ropes and meeting my coworkers. Dee worked one floor above me, so she came down to see how things were going. We decided to meet up for lunch since I was still unfamiliar with the area. I enjoyed hanging with her, but it was nothing like being with my Divas. I needed to call and see how Taraine was coming along.

*God, I think you gave Taraine more than enough sleep. Her family needs her, but I know she will wake up when you decide it's time for her to resurface.*

"You ready, girl?" Dee asked walking towards me.

"Yes, I'm ready, and I'm starving," I said.

"Good. Let's go get our grub on," Dee said.

"I'm so happy you convinced me to move to Philly. I wish I could convince my girl, Fatima, to move out here. Maybe when she comes to visit me she might fall in love with this place like I have," I said.

"Tell her to come for a visit. I can show her a good time. If she decides this is not the state for her, no worries, boo. You got me," Dee said.

"You are absolutely right," I agreed.

# Caught Off Guard

## Fatima

"Baby girl, it's been two months and you still haven't budged yet. I'm not going to cry, I refuse to cry this time. I have to remain strong for you. I know you're probably tired of me coming up here talking my bullshit to you. You can't be tired of me yet, are you? If so, just open your eyes and tell me to shut the fuck up and trust me, I will. You know you're the Yen to my Yang and I will always be here by your side telling you the everyday drama of my life," I said, rubbing Tee's hands gently.

I can hear your big ass mouth, Tima. I'm still fighting, I'm still here and I will open my eyes. Believe me, I will. Just tell me, what you did now, girl.

"Baby girl, I know I've been talking about Chris and how nice he is to me and everything is still working out fine. He has definitely stolen my heart. But your girl has some news for you. I got caught up in some more shit, as usual," I said laughing.

"I don't know if you remember Khalief from Prospect Heights, but anyway, he found me on that social media bullshit. I know what you thinking, chica. What the hell was I doing on a social outlet, right? Well, a couple of months ago we were chatting and catching up a little, but I didn't think much of it. Then, a couple of weeks ago, he hit me up again. But this time he was coming on to me. He asked to take me out to dinner. I found it kind of weird. Why didn't he ask me out a couple of weeks ago? Well, Tee, you know how the story goes with my hot ass. And, shall I say, dinner was kind of nice. This is how it all went down…"

*****

"So do you want me to pick you up or would you like to meet me," said the mild but strong tone voice on the other end of the phone.

"I'll meet you there, sweetie. Just give me a time; better yet, would you like me to pick you up?" I asked.

"No, babe. My Benz gets me around just fine," he replied.

"Okay, boo. So I'll just see you there. By the way, where is *there*?" I asked.

"Suzie Wong's, it's on 7th Ave in lower Manhattan. Have you heard of that restaurant?" he asked.

"No, love, but there's a first time for everything. See you at 8, or maybe 9. I love making a grand entrance," I said seductively.

"That sounds good, baby. I would love to see what this grand entrance looks like. I look forward to watching you walk up to me as I picture in my mind the things I'm going to do to you," he said.

"Well, whatever you have in mind, make sure you come correct. If not, you will definitely see my grand exit," I said.

"Well, if I don't come correct, teach me. I don't mind taking directions," he teased.

"Sounds good. I'll see you at 8."

*****

As I walked into the restaurant I automatically felt this seductive vibe taking over. The restaurant was beautiful inside. Red walls, red velvet chairs, with red sheer covering over the tables.

"May I help you?" the host asked.

"Yes, I'm here to meet Mr. Banks."

"Oh yes! Please follow me, madam."

As I walked towards the table, there was this fine brother standing tall. He had to be maybe six feet tall – a little taller than I had remembered! He was dressed casually in a nice linen top, and slacks. Once I looked at the Gucci shoes, it all came back to me. Yes, this is Khalief, and he still loved his Gucci. *Oh, he is so fine,* I thought as I bit my lip the closer I got to him. By the look on his face, I could tell he liked what he saw as well. I was dressed in an off-white sleeveless, fitted dress with a red belt to show off my curves. I was also rocking my red Roberto Cavalli pumps. He reached out his hand to grab mine and kissed it gently. *Damn, his lips were soft.* It definitely sent chills all through my body.

"You look so beautiful, Fatima," he said as he stared directly into my eyes.

"You are looking very handsome as well." *Damn, I want to fuck you, Mr. Banks,* I thought, and I'm quite sure, he was thinking the same thing.

He pulled out my chair like a real gentleman would.

"Thanks, love," I said. "I guess chivalry isn't dead after all, huh?"

"Not in my eyes, baby. Trust me, I will always be the perfect gentleman, that's just who I am."

He ordered some red wine as we looked through the menu. I didn't see anything of my taste, so he decided to do the ordering. As we waited for our food, this gave us some time to catch up.

"So where have you been hiding all this time?" he asked.

"I've been around. But once I moved from around the way, there was really no reason to return. You know, I always had the biggest crush on you," I said smiling. "You always stood out amongst your friends, especially when it came to dressing, and hands down – the ride was always on point. There was just always something about you."

"Wow, it's funny that you said that. I always wanted to get with you, too, but there was never an appropriate time for me to approach you," he said.

"I don't believe that," I said as I gently bit on my bottom lip.

Damn, he looked so edible. I wanted him in the worst way. We got our food, it looked delicious. He even fed me some of his. *He's already trying to charm his way into my panties,* I thought. *And hell yeah, it's working. I feel like my heart has fallen between my thighs and she's ready to be pumped up some more. I can guarantee he's on the rise,* I thought as I sipped on my wine. *Should I tease him a little by licking my lips? Hmm…of course I will.*

He fed me once again and I noticed a little bit of sauce on his finger, so I decided to swirl my tongue around it and lick it off. Then I smiled, giving him that 'I want you bad' look.

"I see somebody's not playing fair," he said. "But I like it, so…your place or mine?" he asked.

"Sorry, love. Thanks for dinner, but not tonight. I have to go home and pack. I'm leaving for Philly first thing in the morning and I can't miss my flight," I said.

"Can I see you when you get back?"

"Maybe," I said as I winked at him. "I have to check my red book to see if I have any space available on my calendar."

He laughed.

"Okay, that's what's up, babe. I'll wait for you to get back to me, maybe," he said authoritatively.

"Oh, I'm quite sure you'll be waiting," I said.

"I'm quite sure I'll be waiting, too."

"What time is your flight in the morning?"

"My flight leaves at 5:45 a.m."

"I could drop you off, if you like."

"That's sweet, are you sure?" I asked. "I don't want to interfere with any other plans you may have."

"The only plans I have is getting better acquainted with you, babe. I can pick you up when you get back as well. Just let me know when and where and I will be there."

"I'm only going for the weekend. I'll be back Sunday. My flight gets in at 1 p.m."

"Sounds good, I will pick you up. I hope you have something special for me for all my generosity," he said.

"I sure will have something for you, a nice hug and a kiss. That's all the appreciation you need from me, love." I laughed.

He laughed with me. I loved the sound of his laughter. It was turning me on in the worst way.

When I got home, all I could do was think about Khalief, totally forgetting about Chris's sexy ass. And as far as Karl went, he was definitely a has-been. Karl who? Thinking about Khalief made my packing much easier. I poured a glass of Moscato Rosé just to relax a little and calm these chills that were circulating all throughout my body. Shit, I hadn't felt this since I was younger when I was with my teenage love.

*Oh, damn, bitch. You need to calm down,* I thought. I taught you better than this. I'm taking and breaking hearts not the opposite. I tried the falling in love thing with Karl and it is not happening. I'm back to dating and sleeping with whoever I want. "No, Khalief, you are not doing it to me!" I started yelling as I threw my panties in my traveling bag. So why am I thinking about what type of panties to put on to impress him and to get him open at the same time? Mmm…. I can still smell his Dolce and Gabbana. He didn't have to tell me what he was wearing. I knew that scent anywhere. Damn, I think I want him. Yeah, I want him. And I want him bad.

*****

I slept well, and the next morning I was up and ready to catch my flight. I called Khalief to give him my address. I made sure everything was secure, and I proceeded to Philly. *Philly, here I come. I hope you're ready for a bitch like me.*

I got into Khalief's Benz it had that brand new smell to it.

"Good morning," I said, reaching over and kissing him gently on the cheek.

*There's that scent again; he's trying to send me on the plane all out of control,* I thought.

"Good morning. You look nice," he said.

"Why thank you!"

He was playing Avant's CD, which I loved, especially that song '4 Minutes'. *Shit, in about four more minutes, he might be getting the goods,* I thought.

"Are you going to think about me while you're in Philly?"

"Of course not! When I'm in Philly, trust me, New York will not be on my mind," I said with a straight face.

"Yeah, okay," he said. "Well, have a safe trip, babe. Go out there and do it up. Is it alright if I call or text you while you're away?" he asked.

"Sure, Khalief, that won't be a problem. I look forward to it."

"Make sure you call me when your flight lands. I just want to make sure you made it there safely."

"Aww, that's so sweet. Yes I will make it my business to call you. Miss me while I'm gone," I said as I blew him a kiss then proceeded inside the airport.

I was looking forward to seeing my girl, Monica, but I wished it was Sunday already. I enjoyed being in the company of a sexy man. Throughout the entire flight, all I thought about was our dinner date and how wonderful it was. It had been a long time since I've been down that path.

It felt like more than just lust. I wanted to really get to know Khalief. I would usually meet men, fuck them, and forget all about them. What the hell is going on with me?

I walked out of the airport, and of course, I didn't see Monica. *Damn, this bitch is never on time,* I thought, but it's all good I had other things on my mind. I pulled out my cell to call her and that's when I heard her calling my name.

"Damn, Slim, you will be late for your own funeral," I said, walking towards her car.

"Oh, shut up, and show me some love, chick," Slim said.

"What's up? You up in Philly, huh?"

"Yes, boo, I'm out here to tear shit up," I said.

"Well, I haven't really been out to explore much since I moved here, but my girl, Dee, took me to a couple of places – but nothing spectacular."

"I don't know, Slim. There's something about that Dee chick. I wasn't feeling her the first time I met her. I'll see what she's about this time," I said.

"Tima, you don't like nobody. If they are not in our circle you don't rock with them! She's cool. Trust me, she helped me out a lot here in Philly. But since you don't like her I know you won't agree with what I'm about to tell you."

"What are you about to tell me? Let me put all my focus all on you because I'm dying to hear this one."

"I'm thinking about asking her to join me and Ron in a three-some," Monica said.

"Get the fuck out of here! I don't believe that."

"It's not for you to believe, Fatima. I'm dead serious. I want to try this, and I think she will be the perfect person for this. It's time for me and Ron to try something different. I know he's not with it, but he's going to get with it. I've been playing by his rules for too damn long. And now it's time for him to play mine," Monica said with attitude.

"I hear you talking, but are you sure you want this chick to be a part of this new venture of yours? I don't know, Slim. I'm telling you, I don't trust her ass. She couldn't get within two inches of my man."

"Which man you talking about?" Monica said laughing. "I just want to try it once, Tima. What's wrong with that? I won't plan it; I will just go with the flow, but trust me, I'm ready for this. I haven't talked to her about it yet, but I plan on doing it very soon. As far as Ron is concerned, I asked him once while I was on top of him doing my thing. He said yes, and I'm not asking him again. That's every man's fantasy, even if they don't admit it. So, I'm quite sure when it's about to go down he won't stop it," Monica said.

We finally reached her home.

"Damn, Monica, this is nice. This is definitely something I would love to have for myself in the near future. But you know I'm not ready to leave the city, ain't nothing like New York."

I took my things into the bedroom and then I proceeded to take a nice shower. After my hot shower, I laid down for just a moment to get my thoughts together. I decided to call Khalief to let him know I arrived safely. I sat up on the bed, got my cell, and dialed his number.

"Hey, love. I made it to Philly."

"That's good, I was waiting for you to call me. I'm glad you made it there safely."

"So how's work?" I asked.

"Work is good. My day is even better now that I hear your beautiful voice. So, what are you getting into tonight?" he asked.

"I don't know yet. I'm not sure if my girl and I are hanging tonight or tomorrow night."

"Go out, babe, and enjoy yourself. Have fun and turn Philly out."

I started laughing.

"Why you laughing?" he asked.

"It's unusual for a man to want a woman to go out and have fun, especially if he's trying to get close to her. He would rather she stay at home, especially if he's not going with you. Men don't want to take a chance on letting someone else scoop their women up," I said.

Then he started laughing.

"Now, why are you laughing?" I asked.

"Babe, I'm laughing because I'm secure. I know who I am, and if somebody really wants me the way I want her, there's no person out there that can change that. We only live once, babe. So, why not go out and live it up? You could have stayed home and laid in bed for the weekend," he said. "Put your fly shit on and live it up with your girl."

"We'll see. But you're definitely right. I could have stayed home if I was just going to come here and lay around."

"If you want, I can catch a flight and come out there with you."

"Stop it! Why are you trying to get me all hot and bothered now that I'm miles away?" I asked.

"Seriously, babe. I would catch a flight right out there with no problem. You're worth it."

"Aww, that's so sweet, love. But I'll be back in a couple of days and we'll hang out and enjoy each other's company."

"I'll be waiting," he said. "Damn, I don't want to end this call. I still question why I never approached you back then; you never know where we would be today. How about you give me her address so I can send you something special?"

"Khalief, why are you trying to get me open? Anything you want to give me, you can surprise me with it on Sunday. How does that sound?"

"Okay, babe. No problem. I'm not going to push it. I do look forward to getting to know you better."

"I look forward to getting to know you better as well, Khalief. We will continue where we left off when I get back," I said. "Will you be able to pick me up?" I asked.

"Yes, babe. I'll be there."

"Okay. I can't wait to see you again. Call me tomorrow, I'm going to go in here and see what we're getting into tonight. Enjoy the rest of your day. I hope you dream about me and all my sexiness tonight."

"I hope so, too," he said.

*****

"Bitch, what we getting into tonight? What type of outfit should I lay out?" I asked. "Should I wear the 'buy me a drink outfit' or should I wear the 'you think you're going to fuck me, but sorry, not tonight' outfit?"

We looked at each other and said in unison, "Sorry, not tonight," and started laughing.

"Dee is going to roll with us," Monica said.

"Oh damn. I don't think I'm going to like this," I said.

"Relax, Tima. Damn, get to know the girl before you start judging her."

"I'll try, chica, but something about that bitch rubs me the wrong way and I'm not going to pretend. If I'm not feeling her, hey, that's just me. But I know how to control myself, just as long as she don't come at me the wrong way. If she does, I'm going to let her have it – in a nice and respectable kind of way. You just better remember who your real friend is. If we get to rumbling, you better rumble with me."

"You know what's up. Don't doubt my loyalty to you, Fatima, but stop searching for shit. We're adults; let's go out and have fun, get right, mingle with others, and enjoy the night. Can you do that for me, chica? Monica said.

"I hear you," I said, rolling my eyes as I picked up my 'let it all hang out' dress. "This dress right here is fire, ain't it, bitch? Go hard or stay home. That's my motto and I'm going hard tonight, boo boo."

We rolled out at about a quarter to 12. I love to make my grand entrance. I just love the attention I get – even from the females who look at me from the corner of their eyes. I see you watching, boo. Like me, love me, or hate me, boo. But you're still watching. I had my armor on to shield me from any bullshit that might be thrown at me. Monica decided to drive, which was good for me. She didn't drink as much anyway, so I knew I could count on her to get me there and back to her house safely.

The Night Shift was suppose to be one of the hottest spots in Philly; at least that's what Dee said. When we walked inside, it was hot and they were definitely watching. It was a mature crowd, this spot reminded me a little of LQ's in Manhattan. Would this be my first choice for a night out on the town? Probably not, but hey, I'm not from Philly. I'm just a visitor, so I'm rolling with it. The music was flowing nicely. We walked across the floor and found a spot to lounge and take in the surroundings. It was a corner spot where we could sit and sip and enjoy the scene. We could see everything that was going on around us.

"I'm going to get me something nice and mellow. What you having, Monica?" I asked.

"Just get me a club soda."

"Did you say club soda?" I asked, looking at her like she was crazy. "Come on, now. One glass of wine won't kill you, but I'm not going to argue with you. Only because you are the designated driver, so club soda it is, boo."

I didn't even bother to ask Dee what she wanted. *That bitch could get her own damn drink,* I thought.

"I'll be right back," I said, not even giving Dee a second glance. *You're a shady bitch. I'm not blind. You may have my girl Slim under your wing, but not me, boo – not this bitch here,* I thought as I walked to the bar. I ordered my drink and got Slim her club soda, ewh. As I stood waiting for my drink, this seductive smell glided across my nose. *Damn, I know Khalief didn't come all the way out here just for me.* That Dolce and Gabbana had my Kat twirling. *Bitch, get it together. Don't forget you're bare under this dress; if you can't control yourself it will show.* I directed my eyes in the direction of the cologne. *Damn, baby. You smell good and you look good, too,* I thought. He looked at me and I turned my head quickly back towards the bartender.

"How you doing, sexy?" he asked.

"I'm fine as I look. Thanks for asking," I said smiling.

"I watched that dress escort you inside," he said with a slight smile.

"I'm quite sure you did!" I said.

"Once I saw you walking over to the bar, I knew it was my chance to see you up close and personal." He smiled, showing off his dimples.

*Damn, I love a man with dimples,* I thought, looking at his kissable lips.

"What's your name?" he asked over the loud music.

"Fatima," I replied, reaching my hand out to shake his. "And yours?" I asked.

"Ramell!"

The bartender returned with the drinks. I reached for money to pay for the drinks when Ramell gently pulled my hand back.

"I got this, sexy. There's only one thing I want in return and that's a dance. Can I get that, sexy?"

I looked at him, smiled, winked, and thanked him as I grabbed my glasses and turned to walk back to where we were sitting. I turned back toward him. "I'll think about it," I said before walking away.

I made sure that when I walked away, he noticed the sway! He needed to see what he would be working with *if* I decided to give him one dance.

"Okay, don't forget about me!" he yelled to my retreating backside.

As I got closer to our spot, I noticed that bitch, Dee, giving me the eye. *Yeah, watch me, bitch. I already got my eyes on your twisted ass,* I thought.

"Here's your Long Island Ice Tea," I said to Monica, laughing.

"Don't play with me! You know what I asked for," Monica said.

"I know. Calm down and take your club soda."

The DJ in here was all right, but out-of-town clubs never really did it for me. It ain't nothing like NY, but I was enjoying myself so far. The DJ started playing old school music.

"Aww, shit. Monica, they're playing our shit right here," I yelled, bobbing my head to the Jeff Redd song.

Me and Monica started dancing with each other, doing our thing. The DJ played "I Like" by Guy and we really got it in when the DJ played "Before I Let Go" by Frankie Beverly. We were jamming. Then the DJ slowed it down a little bit, and to my surprise, who was standing right behind me an inch from my ass? That's right, Mr. Ramell himself. R. Kelly song "Slow Dance" came on.

*Hey Mr. DJ, why don't you slow this party down...*

I decided to give Ramell his one dance. We started dancing and he smelled so damn good. But all I could think about was Khalief. Ramell was very attractive, but I wanted Khalief bad. *I guess I'll just give him the dance of his life and then leave him right here on the dance floor.* He probably felt like we were doing the damn thing right then and there. I was grinding all on him and felt his nature rise. I could tell he was definitely working with something. Suddenly, he whispered in my ear.

"You are so sexy! You make me want to lick you from head to toe."

I heard him, but it wasn't happening. I had other obstacles to tackle, so he'd better settle down and enjoy this one-time mind fuck he was getting on the dance floor.

Monica looked at me and shook her head. I winked at her. She knew how I got down. It was easy for me to blow a man's mind and then step.

I let him have his little fantasy about 'doing me' until the song ended. As soon as it was over, so was I. I looked at him and thanked him for the dance. He was sweating as if we were in a sauna. I'm quite sure he was drenched somewhere else as well.

"Enjoy the rest of your night," I said. *Sorry, I can't help you, boo boo. I got something in NY waiting on me,* I thought as I walked away. I walked back to our cozy hideout and sat next to Monica.

"You know you are crazy, right?" Monica said.

"We both know that, and we both know I turned his ass out right there on the dance floor. Monica, I'm not here to hook up with anybody. I got someone I'm trying to get with when I get back home, but we'll talk about that when we get back to the house. Wait until I tell you who it is," I said.

"It's kind of dull up in here tonight; it's usually packed," Dee said.

"Really? I kind of like it like this; sometimes, you just want to go out and feel comfortable, and not worry about a bunch of freaks all up in your face, thinking they got a chance," Monica said.

"I know that's right! But you know it don't matter to me. Empty or packed, Tima is going to turn it out, as I proved to you tonight. In state or out of state, I'm turning heads," I said, taking the last sip of my drink. "I need another drink. Do you want another club soda, Monica?" I asked.

"Nah, I'm good!"

When I got back to the bar, Ramell was standing there. Thank God, he was talking to some other chick. *That's right, boo. You better try your luck with somebody else because it's not going to happen with me,* I thought. *I don't care how good you smell or how fine you thought you were!* It wasn't happening.

I ordered my drink and turned around to check out the action. Ramell looked over at me, so I smiled and winked. *Do your thing, boo! That's what you're here for,* I thought as I got my drink and danced my ass back to our table.

"I'm about ready to blow this bitch," Dee snapped.

I ignored the bitch and continued to sip my drink.

"They need to play something good. I'm ready to dance some more before I decide to blow this bitch," I said sarcastically. "We need the *real* divas here," I said, looking in Monica's direction.

"We sure do! Let's not go there; you going to make me cry. I think I'm going to come up next weekend. I need to check on my girl Tee," Monica said sadly.

"I don't want to talk about it Monica. It's all good; we all got each other and God works miracles on the right people."

Dee just sat there looking stupid.

*Yeah, bitch. That's all you better do is look! You will never be down with us! I don't like you and you will never be a part of our sisterhood,* I thought.

"Alright, I'm done with my drink and the DJ seems like he's done as well. You ready, Monica? I did what I needed to do on the dance floor, I'm feeling good and I'm ready to take it down." We left because I was ready, not because Ms. Dee was ready to blow this joint.

Monica dropped Dee off at her house, and we reached Monica's house around 3 a.m. I took a shower, got into bed, and decided to text Khalief to see if he was up.

*Hey, love, are you up?*

*I'm up now!* he responded. *Did you decide to go out?*

*Yes, I did!*

*Did you enjoy yourself?*

*I would have had more fun if you were there.*

*Can I call?* he asked.

*Sure!*

When the phone rang, I answered seductively trying to turn him on.

"Hey, love!" I said.

"Damn, you sound good, baby! You got me ready to catch a flight right now!" he said.

I laughed.

"So, what's up? Did you do it up tonight?"

"It was okay. Ain't nothing like NYC! You know how that go!" I said.

"I can't wait to see you, babe. I'm missing you like crazy. It feels like we've been talking for a while," he said.

"I know, Khalief. I feel the same way, which is totally out of the ordinary for me. Maybe because we knew each other from way back! I just wonder why you never said anything to me back then."

"That's not how I am. I never had the appropriate time to talk to you. I always saw you in passing," he said.

"I guess your right, but if you wanted me bad enough, you would have tried. I'm not falling for the 'it's wasn't the appropriate time'. When a man likes something he sees, he usually goes after it. Maybe you were a little intimidated by me. Yeah… I think that's what it was. Intimidation," I said. "But it's all good. I'll give you a trial period, see what you're working with now."

"A trial period?" he asked.

"Yes, a trial period, and it starts now. So what you got in mind for us when I get back in town?"

"We can do whatever you want. I just like to have fun and stay drama-free. We can go out to dinner again, the museum, the aquarium… I don't care where we go. It's all good; just as long as we're together."

"So let me ask you this. Are you seeing anybody?" I asked.

"No, not seriously. I've just been dating, I haven't found that right one to commit myself to yet. I'm just living life to the fullest. My last relationship lasted for about a year before the both of us realized it wasn't going anywhere. Either she changed or I did, I'm not sure. But we are much better off as friends. I work six days a week, sometimes ten to twelve hours a day," he explained.

"Really? Where do you work?" I asked.

"I'm working down at the World Trade Center. I'm a part of history — something I will be able to talk to my children and grandchildren about."

"I hear that. Speaking of children, do you have any?" I asked.

"No, I don't. I was waiting for the right woman. Parenting is no joke and you have to make sure you're bringing children into the world with that right one," he said.

"I know what you mean. I don't have time to be getting knocked up by some deadbeat leaving me to take care of the baby on my own. I don't play that. Don't fuck with me, but most of all, don't fuck with my babies. I will take you down for that. I guess that's one of the reasons why I don't have any children yet."

"So what about you babe, are you seeing anybody?" he asked.

"I'm dating as well, but nothing too serious."

"I was checking out some pictures of you on the net. You are so beautiful!"

"Of course I am! You don't have to try so hard, Khalief. You already got me where you want me."

"Do I?"

"Yeah, you do. I know you want to get between my thighs, don't you?"

"Yes, I do!"

"Do you think I want you as well?"

"I don't know. Do you?" he asked.

"Yes, I do Khalief. You're like this new type of dessert that I'm anxious to taste. I hope you taste as good as you look. But let's be clear; just because I may decide to give you the goods don't mean you're in. The trial period still stands."

"I understand, babe."

"Can I take you there before you go to sleep?" he asked.

"How you know I didn't already go there?"

"If you did, that's good."

I laughed. "No, I didn't go there. But your voice is definitely doing something to me."

Next thing I knew, he started talking dirty to me. Damn, that shit was turning me on. I haven't felt like this in a while, at least not while talking on the phone. I was so busy trying to transform into a certain type of woman to please others. Being in a relationship with Karl had me lost in the moment and I stopped being me. *Damn, am I letting go too fast with Khalief?* I thought to myself as I listen to him talk that talk to me. *Relax and let go, bitch; it's okay.*

"You know what you want just as well as I do," he said.

"You're right. It's obvious we want each other."

"If you weren't going out of town, do you think I could have had you last night?" he asked.

"Maybe, I can't answer that because last night is a has-been. Just know this, I was attracted to you back then and I'm still attracted to you now."

"That's good to know. I guess we'll take it from where we left on Sunday."

"That sounds like a plan. I really look forward to seeing you, Khalief. Sunday can't get here soon enough," I said. "But I'm drained, love, and this diva right here needs her sleep. But I will call you tomorrow."

"I will be waiting," he said.

*****

I woke up to the smell of bacon.

"Damn, Slim! Philly has really changed you; your ass is up cooking, huh?"

"No, Philly hasn't changed me; I'm just being nice, bitch." Monica laughed.

"So, what we getting into today?" I asked.

"We'll get into something, but first things first. You said you had to talk to me about something, so let's talk."

"Oh yeah, guess who I reconnected with?"

"Who?"

"Khalief!"

"Khalief who?"

"Khalief from the Heights. Mr. Fly Guy himself."

"Get the fuck out of here! Where did you see him? What's he been up to?"

"Well, he still looks the same. Still loves the nice rides. He works at W.T.C, Ground Zero. You know they've been rebuilding it since forever. He appears to be a very intelligent man; one who has his priorities in order. At least, that's what I got from him on our date."

"What date? What happened to Chris? When did all this take place?"

"Thursday night, he took me to a nice restaurant. When I walked up in there and saw him, Monica, all I thought was damn! I'm glad I met him on my grown and sexy shit. I turned it out just as well and he was watching hard. He better be lucky I was in my 'act like a lady' mode and didn't fuck him right there on that table." I laughed.

"You crazy, Tee. But are you feeling him like that?"

"I don't know if it's the thrill of the chase, or if I really want to get to know him. I'm just being me, Fatima, the bitch who don't give a fuck anymore! I don't know, Slim, but we'll see. He's picking me up from the airport on Sunday."

"Well, what's up with Chris?"

"I'm still doing him, but going out with Khalief caught me totally off guard. I'm doing a test drive with Khalief on Sunday, and his ass better know how to handle me. I'm an expert when it comes to driving a stick."

"I know that's right!"

"Come on, chica. Let's get out of here. The City of Brotherly Love needs to feel my presence today." I smiled and winked at her.

*****

We headed out and, of course, you know who had to tag along.

"Damn, Monica. Don't this bitch have a life of her own?" Dee was starting to piss me off and my attitude was showing.

"Don't start!" Monica said.

"What's up, ladies? What we getting into today?" Dee asked.

I just looked at her. *Please, bitch! Why you even here?* I thought.

"I'm taking my girl to the mall; she wants to do a little shopping," Monica said.

"Yes, shopping is the second best thing I love to do, besides giving head. And I don't do any window shopping either. I purchase," I said arrogantly.

The ride to the mall was blah. I refused to be phony and act as if I was feeling that bitch when obviously, I wasn't. I could see right through her, but Slim would just have to figure it out on her own. I popped in one of Monica's CD's. She's back in love with her husband, so all she had in her collection was R&B. I didn't want to hear that love jones shit, but at that moment, I would take anything to fade that bitch out.

"Where the fuck is the good music, Monica?" I asked.

"Girl, you better choose one of those; that's all I have. I'm not into that bumpy-bump kind of music. Turn to the XM station and find the music of your choice," Monica said.

"I hope to see some good looking men in this mall; at least, better looking than the ones at that bar last night. Philly's not doing too good in the men's department, at least not for me."

"Girl, please! You have only been here for two days. Cut it out, Fatima. You kill me sometime, you know that, right?"

"I hope there's some good looking men in there my damn self," Dee chimed in.

As soon as she started talking, I pressed 'play' to drown her ass out. I don't know what it was about her. *She rubbed me the wrong damn way the first time I met her, and shit hasn't changed. She's still rubbing me the wrong way,* I thought as I rolled my eyes and looked out the window.

When we arrived at the mall, I decided to go to Frederick's of Hollywood and get something that says "come get me", or "I know you like what you see" to wear for Khalief. I picked up a couple of pieces to wear for him and a few other pieces just to add to my collection. Monica also picked up some items. I didn't see Dee buy a damn thing. I promised Monica that I would keep it cool, so that's what I did. We did a little sightseeing and I realized Philly is really a beautiful place.

*****

When we got back to the house, I had to talk to Monica just to make sure she was doing the right thing by having a threesome with Dee.

"I know you say that's your girl, but trust me, I would never steer you wrong. Something is up with her. Not to mention she thinks she's the shit, too, with that ugly ass mole on her face. She need to have that shit removed like yesterday," I said with disgust.

"Alright, Tima, calm down. I hear you, but she's been helping me since I've been down here. No, she's not in our inner circle, but until I get acquainted with other people, she's all I have. Besides, she hasn't done anything wrong to me yet."

"Whatever you say, bitch. But mark my words; she's a trifling hoe. But I will not say another word about what's her name. To be honest with you, she's taking up too much of my energy."

The rest of the night went well. We hung around the house and Ron put some chicken and steak on the grill. After dinner, we watched Kevin Heart's *Laugh at My Pain.* His little ass is so funny. This was a relaxing, much-needed trip, and now, I was looking forward to seeing Khalief. I was anxious to know what our day and night would be like.

*****

My flight arrived on time. When I walked out, there he was, as promised. He stood there looking like he knew what was about to go down.

"Hi, sexy." I hugged him tightly.

"Hey, babe." He hugged me right back and then kissed me on the cheek. I guess he was trying to be a gentleman. A little tongue wouldn't have bothered me but I'll let him lead for a little while, then I'll go in for the attack.

"How was your flight?"

"It was great. No turbulence at all; just a smooth flight. Thank God for that!"

As we walked to the parking lot, I was looking for his Benz, but to my surprise, he was driving a charcoal colored Range Rover. It was beautiful. I loved my new X5, but this was nice. It had me a little jealous.

"Oh, wow! I like this."

"You do?" he asked, sounding somewhat condescending.

I don't think that's how he meant it, but that's how it came off.

"I know I didn't call or text you yesterday. I just wanted you to have some 'you-time' and chill with your girl. I didn't want to seem like a stalker," he said.

"I understand! I wanted to give you some space as well. I wanted you to get your mind right and be focused for your second glance at all of this right here," I said laughing.

"Before I drive too far, are you sure you want to spend your day with me?" he asked.

"Yes, I'm sure. I'm a grown ass woman. I don't need to second-guess myself when it comes to spending a day with or without someone," I said.

"Good, because I'm looking forward to enjoying the rest of the day with you. We can pick up right where we left off," he said, looking over at me as we sped down the highway.

"I feel the same way." I smiled back at him, and thought of my lingerie I had picked up from Frederick's of Hollywood. He had no idea what I had in store for him.

When we arrived at his apartment, he opened the door and allowed me to step inside before him. On the table, inside a beautiful crystal vase, were a dozen beautiful long-stemmed red roses. Next to the roses, was a card with my name on it, and a bottle of red wine. He picked up the card and gave it to me.

"The roses are yours as well," he said.

"Wow! They are beautiful, Khalief. And they smell so good, too." The sweet scent of the roses made his living room smell like a florist.

I opened the card and read it. It's been such a long time since I'd received a card from a man and I loved it. I was so excited, I felt like I had little butterflies on the inside. I walked over to him and kissed him gently on his lips. His lips were nice and soft.

"Thank you, Khalief; this is so beautiful. You have definitely made my day."

"You're welcome, babe. I think this is the start of something big," he said.

"I'd like to go take a shower, if that's okay with you. Sometimes those plane rides can make you feel so yucky," I said.

"No, problem. Take your time. I'll be here waiting for you, unless you want me to come join you…"

I looked at him seductively, with my finger slightly in my mouth.

"Next time, naughty!" I said as I walked towards the bathroom with my luggage in my hand.

He had no idea what was about to go down.

In the shower, the hot water felt so damn good against my skin! My muscles felt nice and relaxed. *There might be a lot of aerobics going on tonight*, I thought as I dried off and put on my new teddy and red stilettos. I put on my favorite Jadore' perfume. Not too much, just a dab here and there. I walked into the living room and saw Khalief sitting on the couch with his head down listening to some music. He was surprised when he looked up and saw me standing there. He was speechless.

"Damn, baby!" He sprang up from his seat, staring at me.

I placed both hands on my waist and stood there biting gently on my bottom lip. *Damn, did Taraine just jump into my body? This is totally unlike me. This is definitely starting to feel like a Taraine and LaQuan moment*, I thought. *But it feels good, I feel sexy, and for the first time, I think I'm going to switch roles and let him be the aggressor.*

"Do you like what you see?" I asked.

"Yes, I do!" He grabbed my waist and started to kiss me passionately.

He caressed my breast, then… I felt his nature rise. He backed me against the wall, lift up one leg, and began teasing my Kat. He had her purring. It felt so nice, and I was ready to give in.

I unbuckled his belt and unzipped his jeans. We continued kissing harder, more passionately. He thrust his entire manhood up against me.

"I want you bad, babe," he whispered against my ear.

I couldn't take it any longer.

"Take me then!" I groaned.

We tongue-locked and stumbled towards his bedroom. He laid me on his bed, spread my legs apart, and next thing I knew, he was tonguing my Kat. He did it just the way I like it, too. I grabbed his head and glided him deeper inside of me.

"Baby, I'm about to go there," I moaned.

That didn't stop him. He kept teasing her and tasting her — taking me there, until I felt myself release and let go all my loving. I had his hands in mine and I squeezed them so tightly, enjoying every moment.

After I released, I pulled him up towards me. He came up and began pulling off my teddy. Then he began kissing my stomach and working his way towards my breast. He gently sucked on my nipple as I lay there—moaning from the pleasure of his tongue and lips. He kissed me seductively on my lips, teasing me. He had me ready to beg for it. Usually, I'm just ready to get my fuck on, but I decided to relax and go with it. I was so open and so ready to give in to this man without a second thought. I reached for his dick. It was long and thick. I caressed it with my hand a couple of times, and then I just slid it in. At first, it got the best of me; he was definitely packing. So I just wrapped my legs around him and enjoyed it. We kissed and caressed one another. We made love like there was no tomorrow, and he took his time with me. He made sure I was satisfied. We tried every position imaginable, some I didn't realize I could get into. I knew I was flexible, but not that damn flexible. This man had me twisted—mentally and physically, and I was loving every minute of it. Our love-making was the best experience of my life. My heart was racing from the adrenaline rush. I laid on top of Khalief listening to his heart beat. It raced just as fast as mine. He brushed his finger through my hair, relaxing me even more.

*That was beautiful,* I thought to myself as I closed my eyes and continued lying on top of this gorgeous hunk of a man. *If I'm dreaming, I don't ever want to wake up. This feels too good to be true.*

I woke up to an empty bed. I got up and went into the living room. I found him in the kitchen. The table was set up so beautifully - wine glasses, china, my roses and two lit candles.

"Hey, babe! he said as I walked towards him.

I smiled at him, I felt myself glowing. I was definitely impressed. At this very moment, he had me exactly where he wanted me.

He pulled my chair out for me to have a seat.

"I'm impressed," I said.

"You were sleeping so good, so I just decided to make dinner. Oh, that's another thing you will learn about me. I love to cook!"

"What did you make?"

"I made lasagna."

"Okay," I replied, raising an eyebrow. "It smells good, but let me see how it tastes! I'm very honest and I will tell you if it's nasty," I said with a straight face.

"I expect you to be honest, but trust me, you're going to love it! Anybody that really knows me, know how I get down in the kitchen. I'm a chef, babe!" he said.

I tasted the lasagna and it was delicious! The wine was nice and mellow. *He knows how to make a queen feel special,* I thought, taking a sip of my wine.

We ate and chatted. We even fed each other. He put on some music and we danced our way back into his bedroom, where we made love for the rest of the night. I just closed my eyes and hugged him tightly, as he stroked me nice and slow – I enjoyed the beauty of our love-making. We were one and this definitely caught me off guard, but this time around, I was glad I didn't fight it.

*This one right here is a keeper!*

\*\*\*\*\*

"Damn, Taraine! I need you to wake up out of this coma. I need you right now. I need to hear your response to what I just told you. I'm in a very vulnerable position right now and nobody would understand this better than you," I pleaded. "I love you so much, Taraine!" I hugged her tightly. "Keep fighting. And when you're ready to come back to us, we will all be here waiting, showing you all the love you deserve."

As I continued talking, I could have sworn I felt Taraine move a little. It felt as if she was trying to break out of a shell, but didn't have enough strength.

*Fatima, I heard everything you said, and I'm so happy for you. Maybe Khaleif is the one for you. You sound so happy. I'm still trying to fight my way back to you guys, but I will never give up. I was trying to give you a sign. I'm still here, so please don't give up on me.*

"Khalief and I are meeting up tonight. So when I come back to-morrow I should have some more news for you. I'm not going to leave here without being me. So, with that being said, you know I don't mean no harm, but, bitch… it's time for you to wake the fuck up. You wanted the attention; you got it. I love you and I'll see you tomorrow." I laughed and kissed my girl on her forehead.

# I'm Still Here

## Toraine

*Well, God, I'm still here fighting and I know it's all because of you. I just want to wake up for my family, I miss them and they miss me. I guess in due time, right? That bitch…oops, my bad, God. That chick Sidora has to be dealt with.*

Just knowing I could hear what was going on around me made me believe I would come out of this. I am a child of God and I have faith.

"You still in that damn bed with your eyes closed? All right, April fools is over. You can stop playing these jokes on us." Shantae laughed.

*You're so stupid, Tae. I miss your nasty ass. I bet you're still out there being God's gift to both men and woman,* I thought as she kissed me on my cheek.

"I know if you could talk, you would say 'ewe, don't kiss me. I don't know where your lips been,' Shantae said as she mocked my voice. "I would do anything in this world to hear you say that right about now. I was suppose to meet Kelly's ass up here, but I see she hasn't gotten here yet. I told Debrah and LaQuan if they need help with anything to let me know. I spoke to the little princesses and, of course, they are missing their mommy. I see I have to be a pest. That's the only way you're going to get your ass up, huh? I ain't come here to do no crying. I know you don't want to hear that. I do believe you can hear me. It's just so sad you can't respond back. I just really came here in hopes that you had come back to us physically. Kandi and I are still together and I'm in love with this chick. We told Fatima about it and she's been acting real funny. I don't know how she feels about us being together, but at the end of the day, I really don't give a shit how she feels. This is our life and our choice. I never judged her on any of the decisions she's made when it came to her relationships. I still love her crazy ass. She just needs to respect my lifestyle. This is my life, and my relationship. I'm going to do me, no matter how people feel. The only thing I want is for my girls to be there for me if Kandi's ass decides to act up – the same way I would be there for ya'll. You guys are my life!

I can't wait until they take these damn bandages off your head. You know how you are about your hair and how you need to be divafied all day long. Kandi is exactly the same way. I love all that, I think it's so sexy. I'm not going to lie, Tee. I am a little worried. She tells me she has stopped doing that escorting bullshit, but something seems a little off with that whole situation. Maybe I'm being a little extra, somewhat paranoid. But you know me, I like to stay two steps ahead of it all."

*It sounds like she already got you where she wants you, Tae. I don't know why you let her move in after one date. Don't you think that was a little too soon? You guys should have dated for a little while just to get to know each better. I guess it's a good thing I'm lying here unable to talk. You probably wouldn't want to hear what I have to say. Only time will tell between you and Kandi, but I wish you guys the best of luck.*

"Tee, you wouldn't believe I haven't looked at another chick or man since I've been with her. I did ask her if she was interested in hooking up with Mike, but she said no. She fears that when she's not around, me and him would still be hooking up. Maybe if I was with her a couple of months ago – when I was living the carefree life – then she would have had something to be worried about. Shit, I'm living the loyal life now! I'm on some brand new shit. I bought her a nice diamond watch. I hope she likes it," Shantae said.

*Oh wow, bitch! You really are open. You got it bad. I understand, you have to do what you have to do to keep what you got. You know if the girls were here, they would be getting on your open ass right about now. I say live your life; you only get one. I'm laying here stuck inside my own body, but I know God has a plan for me. I miss communicating with all of you guys. I miss hugging my kids and making love to my man.* I felt myself choking up.

"Are you crying, Tee? See, I knew you could hear me," Shantae said. Let me wipe your tears. Good thing you don't have any make up on. You would be looking crazy from the mascara right about now, and you know I'm no good with that make up shit. But I'd rather see you looking crazy than to never see you at all. That's all I want you to do, Tee –fight and fight hard. You're much stronger than this coma! Well, I'm going to take my ass home, but I will be back soon. I don't know what's going on with Kelly, but you know how she is with her disappearing acts. When I come back tomorrow, I'll let you know if she liked the watch or not. Shit, her ass better like it. I spent a lot of money on it. Love you, Taraine. We get it now. I know you're fighting; you just need to fight a little bit harder," Shantae kissed me on my forehead before she left my room.

A couple of minutes later, I could hear movement in my room, but no one said a word. I didn't feel a slight touch on my hand or face. I didn't feel any poking on pulling – all I heard was movement. The aroma of fresh flowers breezed across my nose. I heard movement again as it seemed to get further away from me. Then there was silence.

*Whatever your plan is, God, I wish you would tell me because this is a lonely place to be in. I'm not sure how long I can go on like this. I feel like I'm losing my mind.* And then I heard Kelly.

"Oh my God!"

That was all I heard as the scream and cry came rushing towards me.

"I'm so sorry. I'm so sorry," Kelly sobbed.

*I know you're sorry, but where has your ass been all this time? I've been up in this hospital for months now, and this is the first time you've been up here to see me,* I thought as Kelly continued crying hysterically.

"Taraine, when they told me you were in a coma, I just couldn't seem to bring myself up here to see you. I didn't want to see you like this, but the guilt started eating me alive. I'm so sorry, Taraine; you know I love the shit out of you. I'm just lost for words. Who would want to do this to you? If it's who I think it is, we are going to get that bastard. Rell is not getting away with this, if it turns out his stalking ass is the one that did this to you. He should have been the man you needed him to be and you wouldn't have left his dumb ass. I promise you today, if I find out it was Rell, I am going to kill that motherfuck-er myself," Kelly said angrily.

*Oh, Kelly, it wasn't Rell's punk ass. You guys are searching in the wrong direction. I wish I could communicate with you guys, and let you know who did this, but don't worry. I will get the strength to open my mouth to tell all of you what happened to me. When I catch that bitch, she is going to regret the day she ever walked through my door and violated me. She is going to pay for taking me away from my family and friends. That bitch probably laid back thinking she left me for dead. Yeah, she thinks she got away with murder, but she doesn't know I'm a fighter, and I will come back with a vengeance,* I thought as I listened to Kelly sniffle and cry.

"Tee, so much has happened to me. I lost custody of the kids. The courts granted Keith full custody, but that's okay. That motherfucker manipulated the judge with all his lies and deceit, but it ain't over until it's over. I will have my babies back with me soon. He's doing all this bullshit to me just because I don't want him in my life. If I was fucking him every night we wouldn't be going through this court shit. I slipped a couple of times and gave him some pussy because I was horny, but once he realized I was serious about not taking him back, he started running back and forth to the court telling a bunch of lies. He is a straight up bitch! I made a huge mistake when I slept with him, but trust me, that shit will never happen again."

"I've been doing temp jobs here and there to make sure my rent is paid. I found a nice cozy three-bedroom apartment in Long Island. I needed to get as far away from Keith as possible. Every time I leave for work, I feel like I'm being watched. It could just be my imagina-tion, but my intuition tells me it's Keith in the cut stalking me. I bought me some mace, and trust me, I will use it if I have to. I miss going to our little spot Sugarcane. I haven't been there in a minute. I decided to wait for you guys, but I damn sure miss their Mojito wings and I've been dying to get some. I heard the shrimp roti is banging, so I got to try that the next time we go. I know LaQuan is hurting seeing you like this because it's killing me. The devil is so damn busy, but he's fucking with the wrong people. Every time something good is going on in ya'll life, here he comes with some other bullshit trying to steal your joy. You need to have a little radio in here to stimulate your mind. I'm going to bring one when I come back. I'm just glad you're not dead, and I'm not saying it to be mean. I'm just saying since you're in a coma there's still a chance for you to come back to us. But there is no coming back when you're dead. People stay in a coma for a long time; then one day, a miracle happens and they come out of it like they were never in it. I'm nobody's psychic, but I know that's exactly what's going to happen. I don't think God is ready for you yet," Kelly said.

"Look at your nails. Damn, I don't like this shit. When I come back, I'm going to bring my kit and hook you up. I should pay one of them Chinese chicks to come up here and give you a mani/pedi, but that's okay. I'll do it myself. We should all come up here together and have a session. I know your ass would wake up then, especially once we start telling you all the bullshit going on in our lives."

*I already know some of the shit everybody's going through—both the good and the bad.*

"Besides trying to get my kids back and working, I've been seeing a couple a guys. Nothing to my standards, but hey, just some friends to keep my mind occupied throughout all the shit going on. One guy, he drives a cab. I know, I know. Yes, he's a cab driver. At least he has a job, but besides that, he is an asshole and it's time for him to go. I was using him whenever I didn't feel like driving to work or driving to the city to go to family court," Kelly said.

*You fucking with a cab driver? I guess he must be fucking you real good, but a cab driver, Kelly? Come on!!!*

"I know you're probably thinking why am I fucking with a cab driver? Well, he gets me to my destination when I need him and he's very genuine at times. The sex game is alright, but I figured I could teach him as we go along. The first time we fucked, he was making all this damn noise. I wanted to tell him to shut the fuck up. He was breaking my concentration." Kelly laughed.

"Nah, Joseph is cool. He thinks I'm too aggressive. He says I want to be in control of everything. I told him to take the lead and I will follow—that's what a real man would do. But check this out, he still lives with his mother! He claims she is sick and he is just there to take care of her. He ain't paying no rent, so why shouldn't I spend his money? He wants to get between these thighs, ok cool. But it's not for free, so with that being said, where you taking me tonight? What are you buying me? Oh, this bracelet is real nice. You want me to cook dinner tonight? No problem. What time are you taking me grocery shopping?"

"Tee, you know I don't have time to be playing with these idiots. I'm doing them the way they do us. Fuck that! Whenever I don't feel like being bothered with his ass, I let him know I'm not in the mood, and I'll call him when I am. He can't do shit to me. All he can do is deal with it. Take me as I am or leave me the fuck alone. Keith got me so paranoid. I think I'm afraid to let someone else into my life. I don't want to ever go through the bullshit I went through with Keith with anybody else. My children are the most important people in my life. I want them back with me and I'm going to fight until that happens. Everything else is put on the sideline. I'll be back tomorrow to make you look like the diva you are. Love you!" Kelly said, then she kissed me and left the room.

# Emotional Roller Coaster

## Taraine

Lying here in this paralyzed position, hearing my own thoughts for Lord knows how long was beginning to drive me crazy.

*What day is it? How long have I been lying here? What time is it? Did I miss my girl's birthday? This is killing me, I want out of this damn coma.*

I grew angrier by the second. Every chance I got, I used all the strength I had to to try and open my eyes or to move my hands or legs.

*It would mean everything to me just to see my kids' faces and to look into my husband's eyes. This is not working out for me, not at all, but I know it's all in Your plan. I wonder what my husband is doing. I know he loves me with all his heart, but let's face it — he's only human. I know he's missing me like crazy, but I also know he's lonely. Did he find someone else to take my place? Why haven't I heard his voice in a while? Why haven't I felt him stroking my hand and asking me to wake up for him? He's gone. I could feel it in my soul. I know he got tired of waiting on me to come out of this coma and he decided to move on and find someone else. Everyone needs someone to love and to feel that love in return. I can't blame him for moving on and finding another woman, but damn. It hurts like hell. Please, God. Just make sure that whoever she is, she respects and loves my family. My little girls mean everything to me. Make sure she is good to him because LaQuan is a great man; we were great together, but he can't be at a stand-still for the rest of his life. Please, God. Just make sure they are all okay. When I wake up, I know my family will reunite and become one once again.*

Suddenly, I heard voices singing in unison.

"Happy Birthday to you, happy birthday to you, happy birthday dear Taraine, happy birthday to you!!!!!!!!!!!!!"

*Wow, today is June 22. It's my birthday. That means I've been stuck in my own head for almost a year. Hearing my baby girls yelling 'happy birthday, mommy' is killing me. Awh, how I wish I could just grab them, hug them, and squeeze them real tight. I miss my babies! This is so over-whelming. I love my family, and I'm ready to be with them. I deserve to be with my family. I can't take this any longer!* I began to scream inside from the frustration built up inside of me. I knew no one could hear me, but it felt so good to get it out.

"Happy Birthday, Tee! You're supposed to be up and out this bed by now. What's up with that? I know you're tired of me getting on your nerves! Well, that's why you need to wake your ass up. Kelly is on her way; she's going to give you a makeover. You will be looking fierce for your b-day. Speaking of the devil, her ass just walked in," Fatima said.

"Hey, divas!" Kelly called out. "How's my girl? Happy Birthday, Tee!"

Although I couldn't see anything, I could hear movement rustling around me.

"I'm just going to make room, so Kelly can get you all divafied for your birthday," Fatima continued.

"Oh, yeah. I'm about to make you glamorous, chick," Kelly chimed in.

I felt little brushes and touches across my cheek and some tugging on my hair.

*These bitches were doing me up. I guess some things will never change. I love my divas to death for trying to keep me sexy while I lay here comatose.*

I felt myself getting choked up again. I was on an emotional roller coaster with plenty of things going through my mind.

*Where is my husband?*

I didn't hear his voice at all. I know my mother was there because I heard the girls call her continuously. They didn't call her 'Grandma' or 'Nana'; they were calling her 'Mamo'. I was happy to hear them calling her, but I wished it was me they were giving all their attention to. I'm grateful to my mother for taking good care of them. She adores them and I know they adore her as well.

*Where is my man?*

LaQuan always made sure he was the first to do everything. He didn't want anyone to wish me a happy birthday or give me gifts before he did. So why didn't I hear him say happy birthday to me? Better yet, why haven't I heard him say he had infinity love for me? Most of all, why haven't I heard him recite *Phenomenal Woman* to me? I felt like my heart was in my throat; it was racing uncontrollably. I had all these thought going through my mind all at once. In my mind, I could see him kissing and hugging on some woman, but I couldn't see her face. He was telling her how beautiful she was. They were slowly undressing each other, right before my eyes.

*Don't they see me lying here? That's so disrespectful of you, LaQuan.*

They didn't care; they continued making passionate love to each other. I still couldn't see her face. She got on top of him, riding him the way I did. This was more than lust; they seem to be in love. After they were done, she laid her head on his chest.

"You're my everything, LaQuan. Nothing will ever tear us apart," the familiar voice said.

LaQuan stroked her face gently. "I love you, Sidora!"

*No, no baby. You can't love her. She did this to me!* My heart instantly raced faster, and I couldn't breathe. The monitor at my bedside beeped incessantly.

"What's wrong, Tee?" Fatima yelled nervously. "Kelly, go get the doctor — something is wrong with Taraine. Hurry up! Please!"

I heard everyone crying and screaming for the doctor. Suddenly, everything went dark. I felt hard compressions on my chest. I began to breathe with the help of the oxygen mask that was placed over my face. I could hear the doctors talking around me as they used medical terms I didn't understand. I heard the doctor clearly state that I needed plenty of rest and that I was putting a lot of stress and strain on my heart. He told the nurses to check on me frequently.

*What the hell does this doctor mean I need plenty of rest? I've been resting for almost an entire year.*

"Damn, Tee. You can't keep scaring us like this. I didn't know what was happening to you. It was a scary sight to see this happening to you and I don't care to witness it again. Maybe all of this was just a little too much for you today. I'm sorry, Taraine. We all just wanted to make you feel special. We're going to leave and let you get some rest like the doctor suggested. But I will be back to check on you and I promise not to get on your nerves. Love you!" Fatima said.

# And Baby Makes Three

## Fatima

Khalief and I were in love. We were together 24/7 and I finally had the courage to tell Karl the truth. I was tired of ignoring him; he didn't deserve that type of treatment. He was a good man; he just wasn't the man for me. We ended it on a good note. He was disappointed, but he handled it well. I always thought Karl would be the man to change me. I must admit, I did change a little, but we were still on two different levels. He was on the 'let's slow it down' type of level and I was on the 'let's get it on and popping' type of level. Karl lived the good life, he traveled a lot and was able to meet, mix, and mingle with new people, so I'm sure it's only a matter of time before he finds the right one. Not to mention he was getting up there in age. I know they say you're only as old as you feel, but the things I loved to do he just wasn't into anymore. I love going to dinner, the museum, and to the movies, but I also loved to shake my ass and get a little rowdy from time to time. I'm on a new journey in life now, and I'm enjoying the travel. The adventures on this ride is remarkable.

Even though Khalief and I were both from NYC, we were both Boston Celtic fans. Khalief surprised me a couple of times with tickets to a game. We both love to gamble, and one day he called me and told me to get dressed; we were going to Las Vegas. Once there, we both hit the roulette table and went in big. His motto was 'scared money don't make money'. I loved that about him! That shit turned me on. We were two of a kind and we were in love.

I gazed out the window and smiled at the thought of Khalief. My concentration was broken by my cell phone ringing loudly.

"Hey, babe. I'm on my way. Do you need anything?" Khalief asked.

"No, I'm good! Just get here as fast as you can; I've been missing you all week," I said.

Khalief had been out of town on a business trip and was on his way back. I was anxiously awaiting his return; I was missing him like crazy. I'm not much of a cook, but I did make my famous baked ziti. I was so anxious to see him and couldn't wait to give him some great news. I had just finished a nice long bath and slipped into one of my seductive pieces with a pair of my stilettos with the gold heels. This was just one of the things that would make him rise to the occasion. Just thinking about it gave me chills.

*Damn, I love me some him!* I thought as I checked myself out in the mirror.

Suddenly, I heard keys jingling in the lock and he was coming through the door. It was time to put my acting skills to the test. I giggled my way to the door.

*Get it together, bitch,* I thought as I walked towards the living room.

When he finally got the door opened he stood there looking as if he was about to have an asthma or anxiety attack! His chest was rising and falling fast and hard.

I smiled and gestured to my surroundings. "Welcome to the house of seduction. Enter at your own risk!" I said, giving him the 'come and get it' smile.

He walked in and closed the door. He looked down at the whip I held in my hand and smiled.

"They call me Ms. Seductress and I am ready to give you the most exciting and fulfilling ride of your life, sexy," I said.

I circled him, and when I reached the back, I lashed him gently on his ass. Now, I'm not into the S&M shit, but I know how to role-play. I can be anybody I choose to be. I think I must have turned into a nymphomaniac white chick because I found myself ripping off his shirt, popping buttons and breathing all heavy. *Wait a minute, black chicks don't do this shit! Let me take a moment, regroup, and do this shit right.* I grabbed his face from the side and tongued him down. By that time, he just took charge of my little game of seduction. He had my toes curling up in my stilettos as he kissed me gently on my neck. He knew that was my soft spot, and he knew he had me.

*Hold on… this is clearly not going the way I planned at all.* But it felt so good, I just had to let go and let him have his way. We never made it to the bedroom, but we surely did bless the couch.

Khalief laid on top of me as I caressed his back up and down.

"I missed you so much, baby," I said.

"I missed you too, babe. Being away from you for a week was killing me and it got me to thinking. Maybe you and I should move in together," he said.

"Are you serious?" I asked. "Well, we can't live here; it's too small."

"Babe, why do you think my apartment is too small? Is it because you need a room for all your clothes and shoes?" He laughed. "By the way, the gold heels you're rocking are hot; you are sexy as hell, babe. You had me damn near ready to catch a stroke at the door."

We both started laughing

"When I say it's too small, I'm not saying it to be judgmental. Don't get me wrong, I love your apartment. It's very nice for a bachelor. I do need a room for my shoes and clothes, but so do you, Mr. 'I stay fresh every day'. Most importantly, I think it's better for us to get a three-bedroom for our new baby," I confessed, winking and smiling.

Khalief didn't react; he just lay motionless, never moving from his original position.

"Um…hello? Did you hear what I just said, boo? I am having your baby."

"Damn, we were so careful. What happened, babe?" he asked softly, his voice barely a whisper.

I looked at him about to go in.

"What the…" I began before he cut me off.

"You're about to have my baby? Damn," he said again, looking at me with tears in his eyes. "Babe, you just made my day – my life!"

I got up and wiped the tears from his eyes.

"So, I guess these are happy tears, huh?"

"Yes, babe. They are happy tears. Thank you!"

"No, thank *us*, babe. This was a team accomplishment. We did this together," I said.

"I guess we need to start looking for a three or four-bedroom like you said, babe." He smiled.

"We sure do, but right now, I'm going to fix me something to eat. I'm with child!" I said, rubbing my stomach.

I rose from the bed and he gently swatted me on my ass. I looked back at him.

"I love you!"

"I love you too, Khalief; now let's eat. The mom-to-be and baby needs nourishment."

After we ate, we sat down watched some TV and discussed our plans for the future.

"So, when did you find out you were pregnant?" Khalief asked.

"Two days ago. I was brushing my teeth and started feeling nauseous. My breakfast tasted bland and everything smelled disgusting. So, I stopped to get a test on my way to work. I was so anxious to find out if I was pregnant; my ass couldn't wait until I got home. I took the test and it was positive. I made an appointment for the Ob/GYN. It's next week, so we can go together and find out what's going on. Khalief, this is my first pregnancy, and even though I can't take the morning sickness, I am so ecstatic about it. I hope you are just as excited as I am, Khalief."

"Yes, babe. I am very happy. My little man is going to look just like me."

"Your little man? Don't you mean *my* little *diva* is going to look just like *me*? She's going to come into this world giving attitude," I said crying tears of joy.

"I never thought this would ever happen to me, Khalief. Boo, you just don't understand what is going through my mind right now. My girls have their families and husbands or lovers. I just accepted the fact that it might just be me – and maybe a little Yorkie. Then here you come and knock my ass up! What makes me happy about being pregnant is the simple fact that you're just as happy as I am. You didn't ask me stupid shit like if it's yours or not, and you didn't ask me when was I going to make an appointment to get an abortion.

We're on the same page and it feels good. This is definitely the best day of my life, Khalief. I got you and I got our little angel growing inside of me," I said, reaching over and kissing him on his cheek.

"Did you tell your girls yet?"

"No, I didn't tell them yet. The situation with Taraine is so painful to all of us and we all miss her so much. Maybe if I go talk to her and tell her my good news she will wake up. After going to see her on her birthday and seeing her body shake uncontrollably broke my heart. She may have had a mild heart attack, but it wasn't strong enough to take her completely from us. She's a strong woman, Khalief!" I said as I began to cry. "I want my cousin back. This is killing me; I don't want to lose her. Her babies need her here. They are growing up so fast and they miss their mommy so much. I'm going up there soon to see how she's coming along and then I'll give her the news. I swear, when I talk to her, I believe she can hear every word I am saying. And she's probably cursing my ass out in her mind. All I do is pray for her, love. She's a fighter and I know she will come out of this and be there for me during this pregnancy. I don't want to run around telling everybody my good news. I would rather wait until we go to the doctor and he confirms everything," I said.

"I got you, babe. Whatever you want to do, I'm with it. It's all about you, me, and the baby makes three." He rubbed my belly and smiled. "Just know that I got your back and I'm always going to hold you down. This is the product of some good loving," he said, rubbing my belly again. "And as of right now, the proud daddy needs some good loving from its beautiful proud mommy. Can I get that?"

"You damn right. You can get that and then some, but let's take this to the bedroom," I said pulling him off the couch.

Once we got into the bedroom, it was on again. Khalief made love to me like never before. I felt his love from all angles. I was just as ecstatic as he was as we kissed passionately until I began tasting the salt water in my mouth from his tears. I gently wiped them away as my own tears began to flow.

"Thank you, babe. I promised to make this the best experience for both of us."

"I know you will, love," I said, wrapping my legs around him and enjoyed every inch of love he was giving me.

*****

I was awakened by the smell of bacon. I got up and went into the kitchen, where Khalief was making us breakfast. He had such a glow on his face; you would think he was the one carrying this baby. It touched my heart to see him like this.

"Good morning, boo; you're up early," I said.

"Yes, I woke up a little earlier to make you breakfast. I'm so happy, babe. I couldn't get much sleep, so I watched you sleep, and decided to get up and make you breakfast. Your news got me feeling a little queasy inside."

"Queasy?" I laughed.

"Yes, queasy - and don't tell nobody I said that," he said, looking at me with a straight face.

"I promise I won't tell a soul," I laughed. *Except for my girls,* I thought.

Breakfast was delicious. Khalief likes his eggs sunny side up. One glance at them damn eggs and it was over. I rushed from the table, to the toilet, and everything I had for breakfast came right back up. I didn't want to seem like a spoiled brat, but this was all new to me and I began crying. Khalief came up behind me and rubbed my back gently, telling me everything was going to be alright; this was all a part of the process of becoming a new mother. *Yeah, of course you would say that - you're not the one throwing up your guts up,* I thought. I had to give my man an 'E' for effort. Some other motherfucker probably would have just yelled down the hall and asked if I was okay. I guess I was just being a little emotional. *I just need to shake it off,* I thought. So I laughed as Khaleif helped me off of my knees. He gave me a cup of water and wiped my face with a damp cloth.

"I got you, babe. I told you I was going to make this pregnancy a great experience for both of us."

"Thanks, boo!" I said, hugging him real tight. "This might be a rough road, love. I just hope you have lots of patience," I said.

"Yes, I do! I may not be feeling what you're going through physically, but I want to hold your hand every step of the way, okay."

"Yes!" I said smiling.

"It looks like this baby already turning Ms. Aggressive into a Ms. Softy," he said laughing.

"I think you're right, but I will toughen up. I can't let anyone else see my soft side. Trust me, I'm still a bitch."

"So, what you want to do today?" he asked.

"Not too much, but we can start looking into getting a bigger apartment."

"Apartment, babe? Nah, I was thinking more like a house," Khalief said.

"Now that's what I'm talking about, love. Time to step our game up. I love you, Khalief. This is going to be great," I said, hugging him tightly.

# You Only Live Once

## Shantae

"Damn, Kandi. I can't stand to see Taraine suffering like that. The fucked up part about all of this is they haven't even found the motherfucker yet. I wonder if these detectives are doing their job or are they just bullshitting around."

"Does it seem like she's getting any better?" Kandi asked.

"No, and yesterday was her birthday. We were singing happy birthday to her and all of a sudden, she started shaking and her machine started going crazy. The doctors rushed us out of the room to work on her. They said she had a mild heart attack. I know I'm not a doctor, but I never heard of someone having a heart attack while being in a coma. But come to think about it, I never knew anybody who was in a coma. It's just so sad. I question why God would put her through all of this. Just when everything was going so well, the family gets a head-on collision. LaQuan looked so stressed out. Just seeing him like that brought tears to my eyes. He walked in the room, said a silent prayer, and walked out. He misses her so much and it shows all over his face. He is a wonderful husband and a great father. I know plenty of men who would have left her and the girls a long time ago."

"All we can do is continue to show her love and support. Pray that she comes out of that coma and be a stronger woman than she was before the incident occurred," Kandi said, running her fingers through Shantae's hair.

"Why don't we go out to the movies or go get a bite to eat, maybe going out for a little while will ease my mind."

"Sound good to me, but I'm not really in the mood for the movies today. I'm waiting for the movie 'Stripped by Love' to hit the theaters. That shit is going to be good!" Kandi said.

"I know right. The previews got me hyped and there's a lot of good looking women in that movie."

"Um, excuse me?" Kandi snapped.

"I'm just playing; you know I only got eyes for you."

We decided to go to Sammy's in City Island. Everybody goes there, and I loved their seafood. We ordered our food and chatted while we waited. I watched this guy admire my lady from afar. I'm quite sure he didn't realize we were together, so I didn't take it to heart. What bothered me most was the fact that he was courting some other chick but still had the time to watch mine. The chick he was with was giving him all of her attention. I guess he thought he had it like that! *These men kill me; if only he knew. If I was available, I would take his chick right from under his eyes,* I thought as he continued to gaze our way.

Kandi and I both looked at each other and laughed. We ignored his ass and enjoy our drinks and appetizers.

"You look so hot tonight, you know when we get back home it's on, right?" I said.

"I know that's right. I don't want to hear no shit about you being so tired. You talk a good game until I knock your ass out first round," Kandi said.

"We'll see when we get home," I said.

"Well, why wait until we get home? We can get things started right here, right now," Kandi said.

All of a sudden, the stalker who was watching Kandi from across the room came walking towards our table.

"How you ladies doing tonight?" he asked.

He had a deep, seductive voice, similar to Barry White. He was very handsome. I would do him my damn self if I wasn't into Kandi hard body.

*I know one thing – he better stop checking out my girl or I'm going to have to check that chin with the one-two punch,* I thought.

"I'm fine!" Kandi giggled.

*Hold up. Is she checking him out in my face?* I thought.

"As you can see, I'm on a date." He nodded in the direction of the female he was with. "But I had to come and say something to you. I know you noticed me checking you out. I can't let you leave without giving you my number," he added, watching Kandi.

Kandi looked at me and shook her head. "No, it's okay. I'm good," she replied, still making eye contact with me.

"I know you are good. You are also fine as hell. Since you won't take my number, I'm going to pass it to your home girl." He put the card in my hand. "Tell your friend to call me."

He grabbed Kandi's hand and kissed it, winked at her, and told her to call him. We looked at each other.

"You like what you see? I couldn't help but notice you checking him out," I said.

"No, I wasn't, Tae. I was looking at you the entire time," Kandi said.

"Let's see," I said, looking at the paper he handed me. "His name is DeShawn – and check this out – he left his cell number and his house number. Do you want to call him?" I asked. "You know he was fine, Kandi. Just be honest with me," I said.

"Why are you starting? Did you see me say anything to him? No, you didn't!" Kandi rolled her eyes and continued. "Did you see me give him any eye contact? No, you didn't, so why are you bugging out right now? Are you upset because he said something to me and not you?" Kandi asked with an attitude.

"No, but just by your reaction, I know you're feeling like he could have been one of your clients," I said.

"Are you fucking kidding me? I know you're not saying all this because of what I use to do in my past!" Kandi yelled as she grabbed her bag and walked out the restaurant.

"Come here, Kandi!" I yelled, throwing the money on the table before running after her. By the time I reached the car, she was fuming.

"What's up? Why did you storm out the restaurant like that?" I asked.

"First of all, where do you come off disrespecting me like that? I told you I was done with escorting. If you don't believe me, that's your fucking problem. You're the one who decided to take the fucking number. What's up with that?" Kandi asked. "Did he look good to me? Hell yeah. And if we weren't together, would I take his number? Hell yeah! Would I fuck the shit out of him? Hell yeah! Did that answer all the fucking questions you had in the back of your mind? I hope so, because as of now, I'm brushing this shit off and I'm no longer having this discussion. Do me a favor, Tae. Please don't say a word to me while I'm driving home. I want to get there safely and furthermore, I'm not in the mood for any more of your bullshit tonight. Thank you so kindly," Kandi snapped.

All I could do was look at her and think, *you better be glad you're sexy as hell, Kandi. Yeah, your ass is lucky.* I kept quiet the entire ride home. I know I was wrong and I know I had pissed Kandi off, but hey, that's what I do. I pissed people the fuck off with the way I react to shit. If I want to know something, I have no problem asking them whatever I need to know – even if I came off as a bitch.

We finally made it home safely and she went straight into the bedroom and closed the door. I sat in the living room on the couch feeling slightly out of place, but I didn't know Kandi would take it this hard. I decided to grow some balls and go into the bedroom. I lay behind her and stroked her soft black hair. That was one of the things I loved about her; she had long beautiful hair.

"I'm sorry, baby," I apologized compassionately. "I didn't think you would get so offended by what I asked. I thought you would throw some smart-ass remark towards me, like you usually do. I thought you would tell me to kiss your ass or shut the fuck up. Once you stormed out the restaurant to the car, that's when I knew I had overstepped my boundaries."

Kandi still didn't respond to me. This made me feel like something more was going on than that little episode we'd just gone through. Suddenly, she turned towards me.

"Don't let my past fuck up our future. If you don't want this relationship, let me know so I can get the fuck out of your space and we can both move on. To be honest with you, I don't know what or *who* you did before we got into this relationship. I only know what you told me. And you were spreading it wide and laying it low your damn self. I just got paid for what I did and I was getting paid well. Did I enjoy the extra money? You damn right I did. We're all still struggling in this economy we live in today. I was always safe. I made sure I protected myself at all times. Do I feel bad about what I did? No. Would I do it again? I can't answer that right now, but if you had asked me that hours ago, the answer would be no. I wouldn't go back to escorting. I thought I was in a beautiful and secure relationship with a down-to-earth person I adored. Well, maybe I was wrong, Tae. And maybe you're not the woman I thought you were. Should we really be in this relationship?" Kandi asked. "As a matter of fact, give me the number – maybe I'll call him since that's what you think of me!" Kandi yelled as tears streamed down her face.

"Do you really want the number, Kandi?" I asked. "You know what? Since you're being so *extra* about the situation. Take the number. I dare you to call him," I said, passing her the number.

"I will call him, Tae, but when I'm ready to, not because you said so," Kandi said with attitude.

"Fuck you, Kandi!" I screamed, storming out of the bedroom.

*This bitch must be crazy,* I thought as I made my way back into the living room and sat on the couch. *She's sexy, but she's not all that...please!* The more I sat there, the more I thought about losing her.

*I don't want to lose her, and the sex is kind of crazy, but she didn't have to come at me like that. Well, then again, I did play her in regards to her past. No, fuck that. Fuck that. She's wrong and I'm right.*

I went back and forth in my mind about who was right and who was wrong. I knew I was wrong, so I decided to give her some space and give myself a little bit of time before making it up to her in the morning. *One thing for sure, I'm not sleeping next to her ass tonight! I might wake up with a dagger in my heart. Damn, fucked up my night of romance,* I thought as I took it down for the night. *I'm not crazy. When you piss a woman off, you better sleep with one eye open and that's exactly what I'm going to do.*

*****

I woke up to the sound of keys locking the door. By the time I got up off the couch, Kandi was driving off. I tried to call her cell phone, but she sent me to voicemail.

"Call me, baby," I said on her voicemail.

I knew in my heart she wouldn't call back; she could be so stubborn at times. I went into the bedroom to make sure she hadn't packed all her shit up. Everything was still in its place, which made me feel a little better. Then again, Kandi had enough clothes in her other apartment and she could maintain without anything she had at the house. I was bugging out and anxiety was coming on strong. I needed to release this stress, and she was gone. *Damn, what the fuck did I just do?* I asked myself.

I decided to take a shower, get dressed and go get some much needed advice, or at least an ear to listen. I drove around for a little while just to get my thoughts together and found myself in the parking lot of where I should have gone in the first place. I made my way to the room, sat in the chair, and began to cry. Usually, I'm not a crier, but as I looked at my cousin lying in her bed so peacefully, I became overwhelmed with emotions. I thought about all the craziness I had just gone through. All the fighting and arguing at times is just unnecessary. That bullshit with Kandi last night was uncalled for. My cousin would do anything to just to be able to see her family again and I'm out here acting like a complete ass. I grabbed her hand and stroked it gently.

"Hey, Tee. I know it's been a couple of days since I've seen you. I wish you were up and available to give me some advice right now. I need you; we all need you to be honest," I said as I laid my face in her hand. "I am really feeling Kandi, but her past has got me afraid to look towards our future. You know I'm secure and all that good shit, but at times, I wonder if she's off doing that escorting shit just to put extra money in her pocket, or maybe she's doing it because she wants to be with a man from time to time. I'm just a little confused right now, Tee. I am fucked up mentally."

"Last night, we went out to dinner and this dude was checking her out. He was nice looking. I even said *DAMN* to myself. He stepped to Kandi to introduce himself and gave her his number. She refused to take the number, so he gave it to me for her. I did kind of feel jealous at first, but then I thought she's a good looking woman and men come on to her all the time. The funny thing about it was this dude was already there with some other chick and he still was damn near undressing my girl with his eyes," I said.

"So, I questioned her and asked her if she was feeling him. You know how I get at times, my mouth can be real reckless. She felt disrespected, so she got up and left the restaurant. She said what she had to say to me before she went to bed. Then she got up first thing this morning and left without saying a word to me. I know I was wrong, Tee, but when I tried to apologize to her she came at me sideways, I mean, she let my ass have it," I admitted as I held on to Taraine's hands, hoping she would squeeze it.

*Yes, Shantae, you were wrong, but at this moment – while I'm lying here stuck in my own head – I really don't care about that. You guys are living as you should be, but my husband gave up on me. On top of everything else, he's fucking that bitch that put me in this coma to begin with. I saw it and I felt it, Tae. He didn't even show up for my birthday. I heard everybody tell me happy birthday except my husband. It seems like he never comes to visit me anymore. So to be honest with you, Tae, I don't care about your little 'break up to make up' situation you and Kandi are going through right now.*

"Tee, I have to fix this, and I know exactly what to do. You know how I get down, and you know I'm open to any and everything. I just hope she'll go along with the plan; that way, we can both release this unwanted tension on both our parts." I paused. "Okay, Tee. I'm going to go, but I'll be back to tell you if my plan worked out or not. I love you always and forever," I said kissing her on her forehead.

*I love you too, Shantae.*

*****

When I got home, Kandi was in the tub. I knocked on the door before walking inside. She was laid back relaxing, looking as if she was trying to collect her thoughts.

"Hey, baby!" I said.

"Hey, what's up?" Kandi said nonchalantly.

"Can we talk?" I asked.

"Yeah, we can talk, but I would rather do it when I get out of the tub, if you don't mind. I'm almost done." Kandi said.

"Alright, I respect that," I replied, closed the door to let her finishing with her bathing.

I went to put the Rosé I bought on ice, just to give it a little chill. I placed the dozen roses I bought her on the bed with another wrapped gift beside it, which I knew Kandi would love. Then I just waited for her to finish bathing.

When she came into the room, saw the flowers and gift on the bed, her eyes lit up. I could tell she was surprised but she was trying to act like she wasn't impressed.

As she walked closer to me to me, I picked up the roses and said, "Baby, I apologize for being an ass. You know how I get at times. I was wrong and I want to make it up to you, if you will let me," I pleaded, my voice barely a whisper.

"I think I could do that," Kandi said as she sat on the bed. "I just want to let you know I love you and I'm not doing anything other than what's right. I'm very happy with you and I don't feel the need to indulge in the escorting game. I just need for you to let it go and trust me."

"I trust you, baby; sometimes I just let my imagination run wild," I said.

When she opened the box, I could tell she was happy with what she saw. It was a diamond bracelet and matching earrings.

"They are beautiful, baby," she said, reaching over to hug me.

"There's more," I said handing her another box.

Kandi opened up the next box and it was filled with all types of lingerie.

"Awh, shit! I love it, especially these," she said, holding up a fish-net bodysuit. "These are banging; they are just what I've been looking for. Thanks, boo. I see you know how to make a lady feel good after you made her feel so bad. Kandi pouted, then smiled. "At least you admitted to being wrong. You're so sweet, but please don't get it twisted. You better make sure it never happens again," Kandi said aggressively.

"I promise it won't ever happen again, but I just wanted to run something past you. I'm not going to lie, Kandi. The guy at the restaurant was kind of hot and if I was still fucking dudes right about now, he would definitely be first in line."

"Yeah, he was kind of hot. Anyway, what did you want to run by me?"

"We should tag his ass!" I said.

"What the fuck do you mean 'tag him'?" Kandi looked totally baffled.

"You know what the hell I'm talking about," I answered, looking her straight in her eyes.

"I don't know, Tae!" Her brow furrowed. "Are you strong enough mentally for this?" Kandi asked.

I nodded. "Hell yeah, I'm strong enough. Let's add some spice to what we already got going on."

"I don't know if that's a good idea, especially when you already question if I'm still escorting. It could stir up some unwanted drama." Kandi studied her, uncertainty showing in her eyes.

"Why?" I questioned. "Don't you trust yourself, Kandi?" I asked. "Let's have some fun! It won't hurt either of us because we would both be agreeing to do it," I said.

"I guess you're right, Tae. If you're down without bringing it up later or having any preconceived notions, then I'm with it," Kandi said.

"Okay, so call him and talk to him, but let him know straight from jump the reason you're calling. That way, he won't be confused or try to hit you up later," I said.

"I'm going to ask him if he wants to hang out with us tomorrow night. I want to talk to him first to see what he's about. I'm not trying to be hooking up with some type of serial killer," Kandi said laughing.

I laughed with her. "Yeah, you're right! "So call him now to see what he's all about. If that motherfucker sounds like he got issues, tell his ass to kick rocks. You hear me, baby? Or do I have to repeat myself?" I asked. "If he sounds like he got issues, bye-bye, don't even waste our time."

Kandi nodded, then picked up her phone and dialed the number. "Hey, Deshawn. How are you doing? This is Kandi, the woman from the restaurant last night."

"Oh, what's up?" he said. "What made you decide to call me? Tell your home girl I said good looking out. I owe her one."

Kandi looked at me as I was trying to figure out what he was saying.

"Put him on speaker phone," I said.

"So, how you doing, Kandi?" he asked.

"I'm doing well!"

"You know I was watching you the entire time you were at the restaurant, right?" he said.

"Oh really? Well, how disrespectful was that? You were already there with someone, so why would you be watching me?"

"Oh, she's no problem. I'm not held down to one particular woman. I like to go out and have fun. I don't have any children, I have a pretty good job, and I take good care of whoever is around me," he said. "So, when are you going to let me take you out?" he asked.

"I was thinking maybe we can go to a club or maybe a sports bar," Kandi replied.

"That sounds good to me, sexy. When can we make this happen?" he asked.

"Tomorrow night is good for me, but there's a catch. Due to the fact I really don't know you, I would be more comfortable if I bring someone with me."

"Who? Your sexy home girl who passed you my number?" he asked excitedly.

"Yes, my sexy home girl!"

"It's all good; the more the better," he said.

"All right, hun. So I'll hit you up tomorrow to be sure of the time and then we will take it from there."

"Okay. I look forward to seeing that beautiful smile of yours."

I could tell he was smiling.

"Great, hun. See you tomorrow night! Enjoy the rest of your night."

Kandi hung up and looked at me. "Are you really down for this?" she asked.

"Yeah, I'm down! Let's just get this all out of our system. When we meet up with him, if we have any weird vibes about the situation, then we'll just have drinks and leave his ass there. Then we'll come home and handle our own business. There's nothing wrong with having a little fun, just as long as we're both on the same page," I said.

*****

We both dressed in our very best. Kandi is more flashy when it comes to fashion, but I definitely can turn heads with my couture as well. We decided to meet up at the Denim Lounge. It's nice and cozy there; the lighting is just right – not too bright, not too dark. The drinks are always on point, never watered down, and most importantly, it's operated by BITCHES! *I love it!* Deshawn thought he was coming out to mack with my girl, but he was in for a surprise.

About 15 minutes went by and he finally walked in. He looked even better than he did at the restaurant. He spotted us and headed in our direction.

"Here he comes, Kandi. Let's turn his ass out!"

Kandi nodded her head in agreement. "Let's do it."

"Hey, sexy!" he said, walking up on Kandi and kissing her on the cheek.

"How you doing?" he asked as he reached for my hand.

" It's Shantae!" I said.

"How you doing, Shantae? Thanks for getting your girl to call me. I owe you!"

"What we drinking tonight?" he asked.

"I think I want to sip on some Moscato tonight," Kandi said.

"Yeah, that sounds good to me," I said.

"Okay, that's what's up," he said as he called the bartender over to order our drinks.

"So, ladies," Deshawn said, smiling. "Tell me a little about ya' selves."

"You first," I said.

"Cool, I'm Deshawn. I live right here in BK, I'm single and I love to mingle. No children, which means no baby mama drama, and I'm an accountant. I like to live drama-free, stress-free, everything-free. I'm not with all the bullshit. That's why I let women know from jump I'm dating until I find that special someone, and I haven't found her yet," he said.

"That sounds good. But now tell us about the real you!" I said as I winked at Kandi. We both laughed.

"What you mean by that?" he asked. "This is the real me; there's no baggage tagging along behind me. What you see is what you get. I look good and I make good money – legal money. I'm not confined in nobody's jail and I ain't got no baby mama drama. I'm doing me and I'm doing it well. If I did have any kids, I wouldn't have no problems letting ya'll know about them. I would be a damn good father. That's just me. I'm good at everything I do!" he said.

"Oh shit! I hear that. It all sounds good," I said.

"Tell me about you, sexy," he said, looking in Kandi's direction.

"Well, first of all, you can stop calling me 'sexy'. I told you my name is Kandi. I don't have any children yet. I have my own business. I have my BA in Sociology and I'm working on my Master's. I appreciate you calling me sexy, but I love it when my baby says it to me," Kandi said, smirking.

"Oh, so you have a man already. I'm sorry, sexy – I mean, Kandi. I should have asked you that when we spoke," he said.

"You're right, you should have, but we can't go back in time now. Let's just keep it flowing," I said.

"So, what about you? Are you taken as well?" he asked looking in my direction.

"Well, just like you, I'm also drama-free. I have one son, and no, I'm not with his father. I make good money as well. I love to party and have fun! I'm God's gift to both men and women, and by the way, Kandi is my girl," I said, winking at him before kissing Kandi on her lips.

Deshawn looked at both of us, but he wasn't fazed by it at all. He actually looked like he enjoyed it.

"Get the fuck out of here!" he said with a big smile on his face. "Why did you agree to meet up with me, Kandi? Was this some kind of joke?" he asked.

"No, it's not a joke! We have a proposition for you!" I said.

"Oh yeah? What you got in mind?" He smiled.

"Well, we were thinking maybe the three of us could have some fun together," Kandi said.

"What kind of fun?" he asked.

"Come on, now. You're not stupid, Deshawn. We want to have a threesome," I admitted.

"I'm down!" he quickly replied, still grinning. "So, when is this threesome supposed to take place?" He looked from me to Kandi.

"Tonight," I said.

"I'm ready," he replied, looking in Kandi's direction.

Kandi looked at me and mouthed, "Let's turn this motherfucker out."

We gave him the directions to our home and left the bar. Once we arrived, I told him to make himself comfortable. Kandi got him a beer and then she made a drink for the both of us. She looked kind of nervous, so I asked her to step into the bedroom.

"Baby, are you sure you want to go through with this? All of a sudden, you're looking kind of nervous."

"I'm good! Are you sure you want to do this, Tae? Because once we start there's no turning back. I don't want any regrets or bullshit from you later."

"I'm good, baby. And trust me, there won't be any regrets and no bullshit from me," I said as I passionately kissed her lips.

We tapped hands as I said, "Let's get his ass."

"Bring him into the bedroom," I said.

Deshawn walked into the room as if he was Mr. Cassanova. I just looked at him, then at Kandi. You could tell she knew exactly what I was thinking, which was – let's bring his ass down…all the way down.

*****

I'm sure he thought he was going to be able to handle us, but we proved him wrong. He was lost in the moment as we took him to ecstasy. This was probably a fantasy he'd been dreaming about since he was a teen. He loved watching Kandi and I make love to one another and I love watching him turn her out. I got the opportunity to see how she rocked her client's world; she definitely had an alter ego. At the end of the day, it was all in fun. I love every bit of it and I'm sure they did, too. He was definitely good at what he did, and I wondered if Kandi was thinking the same thing. *That's really not important,* I thought as I lay in bed in between the both of them. No matter what, I had fun, and let's face it…you only live once.

# Sistas

## Monica

"What's up, Dee? I want to know if you'd like to take this ride to Brooklyn with me this Friday," I said as I sat at my desk, hoping Dee would say yes. I really didn't want to drive alone.

"Hmmm…it sounds like a plan, Monica," Dee said. "What are you going to New York for?"

"I need to go see my family and check on my girls. I haven't seen my best friend in a minute. I feel bad for missing her birthday, so I need to go and check on her – make sure she's okay. I haven't seen her in weeks. This move I made took a lot out of me and I forgot about all the important people in my life in NY," I said sadly.

"Are you bringing the boys along?" Dee asked.

"No, they can stay home with their father. This is my weekend. I'm doing me!"

"That's what I'm talking about," Dee said "Why does Fatima come at me sideways? She gives me a lot of attitude and I don't know why! It's not like she really knows me. She don't know a damn thing about me," Dee said angrily.

"That's how Tima is. I respect and love her to death because she is real. Deep inside, she's a beautiful person, but when she feels a certain way about something or someone, that's it. It's hard to change her mind, so don't worry about it. Are you going to see your family while we're in NY?" I asked.

"Probably not, but I'll see how I feel once we reach the city."

"So, we'll leave right after work on Friday."

"That's cool! I will be ready! I need a break from Philly anyway," Dee said.

"Great! I'll talk to you later!"

*****

"Babe, don't forget, I'm going to New York on Friday!" I said.

"What you mean 'you going to New York on Friday?' Why am I just hearing about this now?" Ron asked.

"Let's not go there, Ron. You know I had made plans to go to the city this weekend. When was the last time I checked on my girl, Taraine? I didn't even go out there for her birthday. Not to mention my mother, who is out there on her own. So please, don't bring your BS my way, not tonight."

"So, I guess you're taking the boys with you?" he asked.

"You guessed wrong. No, I am not taking the boys with me. They are staying home with their daddy to do some male bonding. That's how it's going down. They can go with me on the next trip. Me and Dee will leave at 6 p.m. on Friday right after work."

"Well, I feel like you're up to no good!" he said with an attitude.

"Like I said, I'm not doing this with you tonight. There's no need for you to get all paranoid. Don't get crazy, it's only for the weekend. I need to check on my loved ones. I pray they are all doing okay. I definitely pray Taraine is doing much better than the last time I saw her. I feel really bad that I haven't been to see her in a while."

Ron just looked at me and sucked his teeth.

*So typical,* I thought to myself. *I guess he won't be talking to me for the next month or so.*

He looked at me and sucked his teeth once more.

*Oh well. You can be mad at me all you want, but I'm still going to NYC this weekend, and the boys are staying home with you,* I thought.

"Good night!" I said, kissing him gently on the cheek and turning my back on him. *In other words, you can kiss my ass with that nasty attitude of yours. I'm use to it!*

*****

By 6 p.m., me and Dee was on the road jamming to Mary's "My Life" CD, definitely a classic.

*'If you looked at my life, you'd see what I see….la di da dada. Life can be only what you make it…'*

*Damn*, I thought to myself as I sang along with Mary. *She is so right. You have to make every moment count because shit changes all the time. Nothing stays the same and no one is promised tomorrow, so we have to live life to the fullest. My girl Taraine is in a coma, her babies are without their mother, and LaQuan is without his wife.*

"What's up, Monica?" Dee asked. "It looks like you were in deep thought."

"I was, girl. This CD got me thinking about life. How we have to live every moment like it's our last. I was thinking about my best friend, well, she's more like a sister who's been in the hospital for almost a year. It's just too much…too, too much, girl." I said as a tear rolled down my cheek.

Then the next song came on and got me hype.

*'I don't know what I would do, do without you, you bring me joy…'*

We were back to jamming and cruising. Before you knew it, we were hitting the Holland Tunnel. It felt good to be home; there's nothing like NYC. We had plans to hit up the good spots tonight. Starting with the Denim Lounge. I love that place, and it's own by a woman.

"Divas running shit in Brooklyn," I said.

We stopped by my mother's to check on her, freshen up and drop off our luggage. My mother was so happy to see me. She hated the fact that I moved to Philly, but she understood I had to live my life the way I chose. It was 10:45 p.m. and she was already in bed. I knew she would be. She worked hard every day to make ends meet. I laid on the bed next her and talked to her about Ron and the boys. Her eyes looked heavy, so I decided to let her get some rest.

"We'll hang out tomorrow, Mommy. Maybe we can go have brunch. I'm going to let you get some rest. I'm going out with the girls tonight," I said.

I called my girls to let them know I made it to Brooklyn and was ready to mingle. We all agreed to me up at Denim's.

Denim Lounge was popping. The bar was nice and two women were bartending. They had the drinks flowing and they were on point – not watered down. Dee was all smiles. You could tell she was feeling this spot.

The girls finally started coming through. Fatima walked in and she was all smiles. She was glowing and happier than I had seen her in a while. Then Shantae walked in right behind her with Kandi and our friend Diamond. Diamond and I go way back. We went to the same high school. She was kind of stuck up, but I loved her to death. I always thought her and Shantae would end up together, but shit didn't go as planned.

"Hey, divas!" I yelled, as my girls approached. We started hugging and kissing each other as if we hadn't seen each other in years. "This is my girl, Dee. She's from Philly! She took the ride with me to keep me company."

"Hey, Dee!" All the ladies said, greeting her warmly, all except for Fatima. Even with her glow she still managed to look at Dee sideways.

"Hey, Fatima. How are you doing?" Dee asked.

"Fabulous!" Fatima answered sarcastically.

"What's up, ladies? What are we drinking tonight?" Shantae asked.

Everybody ordered their drinks. When it was time for Fatima to order hers, she asked for seltzer water with lemon. We all looked at her like she was losing her mind.

"What's up with you, chica?"

"What you talking about, Monica?" Fatima asked.

"What's up with the seltzer and lemon, are you feeling okay?"

She started laughing. "Oh, I knew I had to tell ya'll bitches something. Oh yeah, I'm pregnant!" Fatima shouted.

Everybody stopped and stared at her.

"What!" They all yelled, the shock apparent on each of their faces. "Congratulations, girl!" they echoed, showing Fatima so much love.

"You finally did it, huh, chica? I can't believe you're pregnant. Karl finally trapped that ass, huh?"

"Stop playing, bitch. You know Karl has been out of the picture for a minute."

"Nah, I'm just playing. I'm so happy for you and Khalief. How does he feel about you being pregnant?"

"Oh, he's so happy! You would think he's the one carrying the baby. He spoils me to death and I love every minute of it," Fatima said, smiling.

"How far along are you, mama?" Kandi asked.

"I'm about 10 or 11 weeks pregnant, but I'm going to have a sonogram next week, so I will know for sure," Fatima said.

"What you want a boy or a girl?" Monica asked.

"I want a boy. Then again, I want a girl, but as long as we have a healthy baby, that's all that really matters."

"We really have a reason to celebrate now. I wish Tee was here celebrating with us," Shantae said. "Congrats to you and your baby!" Shantae said.

"Yes!!!!!!!!!!!" The ladies cheered and clicked their glasses together.

"Has anyone been to the hospital today to see Tee?" Monica asked.

"I haven't been up there in a couple of days, but she was pretty much the same the last time I saw her. It just hurts me so bad to see her lying there like that and it's nothing you can do to help her. It just kills me, but I know God is going to pull her through this. He's just giving her a much needed vacation, that's how I look at it. We should all meet up there tomorrow and have a girl's session," Shantae said.

"Yeah, I planned on going up there tomorrow anyway, so we can meet up around 12 noon. Okay, let's not get all sad, we are going to celebrate Fatima's pregnancy and we will also celebrate and pray for Tee to get well," I said.

"I love my sister-girls. We will always be united. Our love for one another over rules everything. Divas forever, baby! We love you, Tee, always and forever. See you manania!" Fatima said as we raised our glasses and toasted to life.

We continued laughing, chatting and having a good time. The DJ started playing Biggie's song "Juicy" and that got us going. We made our way to the dance floor and got it in!

*'It was all a dream! I use to read word up magazines…'*

We had a beautiful time together at Denim's. The drinks and the music was on point. Before we knew it, it was 3 a.m.

"Okay, ladies. I'm heading to my mother's house. I will see you bitches later at the hospital. Love you guys, muah!" I said as me and Dee headed out the lounge. Fatima and the rest of the ladies stayed. They probably stayed until the lounge closed.

I dropped Deed off in the Bronx so she could visit some of her relatives. She probably didn't want to sit at the hospital with us all day anyway, especially with Fatima making her feel uncomfortable. If Fatima doesn't like someone, they would definitely know it.

When I reached the hospital, I realized I was the first one there, which was good. It gave me a little bit of alone time with Taraine. Once I looked at her, I automatically started crying. It hurt my heart to see her still lying here like that after all this time. She looked so peaceful, as if she was just in dreamland without a care in the world. That's what they usually say about dead people; the sad part was, she wasn't dead. I pulled the chair up close to her bed as I held her hand tight, hoping she would just squeeze it one good time.

"Hey, Taraine. I'm here! I know it's been a while, but I just got myself situated in Philly, so this was the perfect time for me to come back home," I said, still rubbing her hand. "Your hands are still nice and soft. I miss talking to you, Tee, and I definitely miss calling you for advice. I'm just waiting for you to decide you're ready to open your eyes and come back to us. I wish I knew what was going on in your mind while you're in this coma. Is it all black or are you in dream land? I wish you could just squeeze my hand and let me know you hear me, that would make me feel so much better."

I looked down at my hand but nothing happened.

*I hear you, Slim Boogie, and I'm still here holding on, responding to everyone who talks to me. The one thing that drives me crazy – besides being stuck in my own mind – is no one hears me. I don't question why God has me stuck in my own head, or maybe I do, Slim Boogie. I don't know what the hell is going on, but it does get scary and lonely at times. I'm just patiently waiting, and continuously praying that the day will come and God will give me the strength to come out of this situation. Please believe, I miss you guys just as much as you guys miss me.*

"I'm supposed to meet the rest of the girls here. I guess they're on their way. We all hung out at the Lounge last night. Tima gave us the good news about being pregnant. I never expected to hear that from her; it was definitely a surprise to me. I can't imagine Tima with a baby, but you know that baby will be well cared for, even if she has to hire a live in nanny." Monica laughed.

"I rode up here with my girl from Philly, her name is Dee, but I dropped her off in the BX. We are going to have a session here with you today. This wasn't really the place for her to be, but when you come out of this coma and you come visit me in Philly, you will meet her. I hope you like her, but Tima can't stand her for some reason. You know she don't have no problem expressing how she feels about someone," I said with a sigh.

"Feels about what?" Fatima said as she came walking through the door.

"You know exactly what I'm talking about, chica. I was telling Tee you're not feeling my girl, Dee."

"Oh please! That bitch ain't worth my time," Fatima said, reaching down and kissing Taraine on her forehead.

"Monica decided she wanted to start hanging with this chick, Dee. When I met her ass a while ago, I wasn't feeling her. When I went to Philly, I still wasn't feeling her ass. I'm always going to be on point with everything and everyone around me; it's just something about that bitch. Everybody knows how I get down. If I love you, I love you with every part of me, but if I'm not feeling you, I want no part of you. Anyway, we are here to shake shit up, Tee. I know you're just punishing us, Tee, but that's okay. We're going to drive you crazy, leaving you no choice but to want to come and join our session."

"Yes, we are here to shake shit up. But honestly, Fatima, you didn't even get to know her. How do you know if you like her or not?" I asked.

"Monica, you know I have a good judgment of character. When it comes to your girl, the glass is crystal clear. I can see right through that bitch and I know she's phony. She might have pulled the wool over your eyes, but trust me, that bitch is twisted. Just watch your back, that's all I'm saying. You need to also remember I can't fuck her ass up right now if she tries to hurt you. I'm with child, so you better be on point," Fatima said as she rubbed her belly and smiled.

"You hear this chick, Tee?" I said as I continued rubbing gently on Taraine's hand.

*You know how Fatima is, Slim. Wow how I wish you could hear me. You know Fatima always says what's on her mind, whether we like it or not. And nine times out of ten, she's usually right. If she's telling you something is up with your girl, just be careful.*

"Did you speak to Kelly? Because I haven't heard from her in a minute," Fatima said.

"No. I haven't heard from Kelly in a minute. You know how she is. Here today, and tomorrow she's playing them disappearing acts," I said, and we both starting laughing.

"You should call her and tell her to bring her ass up here, but you know she probably won't answer her cell phone," Fatima said.

"You're right; straight to her voicemail. Hey, Kelly, it's Monica. Call my cell when you get a chance, or if you can, come up to the hospital. We're having a girl's session, so get your ass up here. Hope to see you soon," I said, ending the call. "So, what's up with LaQuan and the girls? How are they doing?" I asked.

"Well, he's about the same; missing Taraine like hell, but he's a great dad and Deb has been great for them as well," Fatima said.

*I felt myself becoming very emotional. It's hard for me not to be with my husband and my two little princesses. I felt like my heart was racing, my throat was tightening up on me, and I was having a hard time breathing. If my sisters really wanted to do something for me, please get him away from that bitch, Sidora. She's the one who shot me and he doesn't know it. She taking my Daddy away from me and there's nothing I can do to stop it. Damn, I wish you guys could hear me and feel my pain. I don't deserve this! Why are you doing this to me, God?* I started crying on the inside and I guess I started to shed tears.

"Don't cry; it's okay, Tee! We are here for you. We're just waiting for you to come back to us, baby girl. We miss you so much, and we will always be here for you," I said.

"Yes, boo. You know I miss my sister." Fatima began crying. "I know she has to hear us. Why else would she be shedding tears? That's why when I come to see her, I always talk to her and tell her my problems because I know she gives me a piece of her mind. I just can't hear her. I can definitely feel her. Her love is everywhere, and I'm at peace because I know she will come back to us."

*You damn right, I'm going to make my way back to my sisters and my family. You guys seem like a complete mess without me.*

"What's up, ya'll?" Shatae said as she and Kandi walked into the room all smiles.

"You guys look happy, and as usual, you're always late. I guess somebody was getting it in," I said.

"Shut up, Monica; you're so nasty. I don't see Kelly's ass here yet. I tried to call her but it went straight to voicemail, so I just left a message letting her know I was on my way up here. Hopefully, she will show up," Shantae said.

Shante turned to Fatima."What's up, prego? Any morning sickness?"

"No, not today. The morning sickness is not as bad anymore," Fatima replied.

"You lucky. My boys gave me hell," I said.

"I pray it's over with for the rest of my pregnancy. I'm not with all that throwing up and shit. Khalief says he feels sick all the time. I feel bad for him, but better him than me. But you know how men are; they can get a simple cold and act as if they are dying. I think it's all in their head," Fatima said.

"Cuz, I know you missed me!" Shantae said reaching down to kiss Taraine.

"There you go! If she misses anybody, baby, I can guarantee you it's me," Fatima said.

"Whatever!" Shantae said.

"So, what's up, bitches? What's been going on since I've been gone? I know we couldn't really chat much last night. Why are you so quiet over there, Ms. Kandi?" I asked.

"Nothing, mama. I'm good; in a great place right now with this chick right here. We're just exploring and living life," Kandi said.

"Wait, what you mean by *exploring*?" Fatima asked.

"That word sounds a little too suspect, especially when it involves Shantae," I said.

Kandi laughed shyly as she looked in Shantae's direction.

"Kandi, why are you looking at Shantae?" Fatima asked.

"No reason," Kandi said.

"Ya'll bitches are hiding something."

*Call em' out, Fatima. How I wish I could pick their brains, but I know Tima – she got this. Damn, I miss my girls so much.*

"So, once again, what's the 411, bitches?" Fatima asked.

"Damn, you are so noisy," Shantae said. "We had a threesome. Are you happy now?" Shantae asked.

"Hell yeah!" Fatima said. "Let's get this conversation started, and don't hold nothing back because you know my nosey ass wants to hear everything."

As soon as she was about to start telling us the good news, a loud voice boomed through the room.

"HELLO, BITCHES!!!" Kelly greeted as she came busting through the door. "I miss ya'll!" She hugged and kissed everyone, leaving the best for last. "I love you, Tee, and I just wanted to let you know you're the best bitch of them all. I see you're still playing possum, but it's all good. I'll just go along with your little plan. I brought my makeup kit; you will be divafied once again." Kelly said as she pulled the make-up out of her bag. "When I walked in, you ladies looked like there was some real good shit being discussed. Don't stop on my account; let me in on the gossip."

"Actually, Shantae was about to give us the scoop," Fatima said.

"Give them the scoop on what?" Kelly asked.

"Well, since ya'll bitches dying to get all in my business, I'll just let ya'll know. Kandi and I had a threesome," Shantae said.

"That's all? Shit, that's your specialty. Was it another youngin you decided to use this time?" Fatima asked.

"No! It was actually a man," Shantae said.

"A who?" I asked.

"A man, and a sexy ass man at that!" Shantae said.

*I don't know why ya'll acting all surprise. She already told us she was God's gift to both men and women. Well, God, I may not be able to respond to them the way I would like but I see nothing has changed. They better be lucky I can't talk because I would gladly give all of them a piece of my mind, especially Shantae's stuck up ass.*

"You were down for this threesome, Kandi?" Fatima asked.

"I thought you were shy and sweet. I guess things changed, huh?" I asked.

"No, nothing's changed. You know how them shy and quiet girl get down. Shit, to be honest, they are the freakiest freaks," Fatima said, laughing.

"Don't try to get on my baby," Shantae said. "She's not that same little girl ya'll grew up with. Just like neither one of ya'll are the same as when ya'll were younger. Who knows what kind of skeletons ya'll bitches got in the closet."

"I'm just asking if Kandi was forced into your crazy ass world; don't get all uptight with me, Tae," Fatima said.

"So anyway, we met this guy at a restaurant. He was trying to hit on Kandi, and to make a long story short, he got two for the price of one. He thought he was going to turn us out, but he ended up getting turned out. By the time we finished with his ass, he was ready to give up his car and the deed to his house." Shantae said.

We all laughed.

"I was thinking about having a threesome myself," I said. "I was thinking about asking Dee to join me and my husband in a threesome. When the time came, I got nervous and I reneged on the idea of bringing someone into my personal space. Ron and I have been doing pretty well since moving to Philly and I didn't want to do anything to destroy that. He was a little upset when he found out I was coming to NY, but I told him I was going to check on my girls and family and I wasn't changing my mind. When I get home, his attitude better be correct. I'm a changed woman, ya'll. I'm in control of my feelings, my happiness, and most importantly, I'm in control of me. I told him either we ride together or we ride apart, but I'm going to live a stress-free life. He goes through his moments when he decides not to talk to me for days. When I get home, he'll probably try it again. But once I give him the 'enough is enough' look he'll change that shit quick, fast, and in a hurry. He even goes deep sea diving on me. I don't ever have to beg for it anymore. Satisfy me or else someone else will do the job. It takes two to work at having a strong relationship."

"That's right!" Kelly said, giving me a high five. "Stand your ground and fight for your marriage if you think it's worth it. So, you decided not to have this threesome, but did you ever just think about rocking with the girl?" Kelly asked.

"Actually, I did. When Tima came out to see me, she was just so opposed to Dee and I think that's what really changed my feelings towards her. I just decided to keep her as my Philly bitch. To be honest, I was probably going through a phase, and I'm too damn old to be going through a phase like that," I said.

"Well, where is she?" Kelly asked.

"I didn't think she would feel comfortable coming here with us. Especially with this bitch, Tima, throwing shade. To be honest, this is our thing. We don't need no extra's in our clique. This is more than enough. You know it can't be too many women interacting at one time. It's sad to say, but it's true," I said.

"That's for sure!" Fatima said.

"She hung with us last night at the Lounge," I said.

"What lounge?" Kelly asked.

"Denim Lounge," Shantae said.

"Oh, ya'll heffah's was hanging out last night and nobody called me? I see how all ya'll bitches be getting down," Kelly said.

"Now you know you don't answer your phone," Monica said.

"Why don't you ever answer your phone? What got you so occupied?" Fatima asked.

"My life has been a drag and I'm still trying to fight for my kids. Still dealing with these no good ass bastards who act like they're the shit but don't have a window and well… you know the rest. How you living in the projects but you're driving a Range Rover, or you're still living with your mother and you're pushing 40? Come on! Really? I don't know. Maybe it's just me. They say you get what you ask for, but damn, I don't think I was asking for a bunch of lowlifes. It has to be some good men out here somewhere," Kelly said, reaching in her bag and pulling out a high-lighted china doll-cut wig and placing it on Taraine's head. "There you go, diva. You're working that wig, bitch. I'm loving it. Now you looking like yourself; the way you would look if you wasn't up in this damn place."

"What's up with the investigation, are there any leads on the motherfucker who did this to her?" Kelly asked.

"No, but they better catch his ass before LaQuan does because he is pissed the fuck off," Shantae said.

"I know he is pissed off. Taraine is his life. They survived so much just to have some jackass come along and take that away from them. He needs to get the death penalty," Fatima said. "But I don't think they do that here."

*If only you guys realized it was not a HIM, but a HER! And the sad part is that HER is with my man and she's probably setting him up. She said she was coming for him, but since he wasn't home, she had no problem taking me out. She's going to kill my husband and then my girls will be without their dad as well. That bitch has to pay for putting me here. I wish I was able to tell you girls what really happened so you could put a stop to her seducing my husband. Don't you guys wonder why he's not up here? He would have been up here before any of you got here, but he's been neglecting me. He doesn't love me anymore. He is being blindsided by that scandalous, psychotic bitch. My heart is broken right now, but I'm still going to fight.*

"I'm not feeling like I'm a part of this clique anymore. Why am I the last to know everything?" Kelly said.

"Maybe because you do that disappearing bullshit on us, Kelly. You're available one minute, and the next minute, you're nowhere to be found. We can't even get you on your cell phone, but we still love you, Kells. You're still down with us, and by the way, I'm pregnant," Fatima said.

"Get the fuck out of here! You are so lying, bitch!" Kelly said with her mouth wide open in shock.

"Now, you know I don't play no pregnancy games. It's definitely true – the Queen is pregnant!"

"Awh, come here!" Kelly said walking over and giving her friend a hug. "I'm so happy for you and Karl!"

"This is not Karl's baby. See what happens when you never come around?" Fatima said with an attitude.

"Wait a minute; another surprise, huh? Well, who the hell got you pregnant?" Kelly said.

"His name is Khalief. I know him from my teenage years, and fortunately for us, we've crossed paths again. That's my baby, Kelly, and I am so in love with him and in love with this baby that's growing inside of me. He spoils me and I spoil him right back. Shit, for a minute, it felt like we were turning into Taraine and LaQuan. You know how she's so big on the black love thingy," Fatima said, brushing her hands across Tarine's cheek. "Even while sleeping, Tee, you are still so beautiful. You fixed her up real nice, Kelly."

"Every time I come see you, Taraine, I'm going to have you looking right. We know when your ass wake up, you are going to wreak havoc," Kelly said.

"You damn right, I just miss my baby girl so much. You know if she was up, I would be driving her up a wall with this pregnancy," Fatima said as tears began to flow heavily down her face. "I'm sorry, guys. I'm just so emotional right now and my hormones are out of control. I just miss my sister and just wish God would let her come back to us."

"He will, Fatima. We all have to keep praying," Shantae said.

*That's right, divas. Keep praying that God gives me the strength. I got a lot of business to handle out there, plus Fatima is going to need me more than she thinks. Ya'll know she can't raise no baby by herself.*

"So, now that ya'll had this threesome with this...um, what's his name?" Kelly asked.

"His name is Deshawn," Kandi quickly replied.

"Oh, okay. Excuse me. Don't take my head off. I don't want him," Kelly said laughing. "Well, are you guys going another round with this Deshawn character, or was one round enough?" Kelly asked.

"We're going for seconds!" Kandi said.

"Are we?" Shantae asked, with a surprised look on her face.

"We can discuss this when we get home," Kandi said.

"We can actually talk about it now. I don't keep anything from them, so why should I start now? So you want to go back for more, huh?" Shantae asked. "I didn't know you enjoyed it that much!" Shantae said with an attitude.

"I know you're not getting upset!" Kandi said. "That's the reason I said we can discuss this at home. I'm not going to argue with you, baby, not today. Let's just enjoy our time visiting Taraine. I'm quite sure she really doesn't want to hear any arguing."

"I know my cousin. She's good! I'm not fussing, I'm just trying to understand something here. You want to have another threesome with Deshawn? I thought the goal was to turn his ass out one good time. So what changed?" Shantae asked, annoyed by the whole situation.

"Baby," Kandi said softly. "Nothing has changed. It's not that serious."

"Yeah, okay," Shantae said. "I got you!"

"Like I said, baby, it's not that serious. I'm happy with you and we can just forget about it. I love you and I'm not going to risk losing us," Kandi said, walking over to Shante and kissing her on the lips.

"That's why you have to be careful when you invite others into your bedroom," I said.

"Wait, hold up! You just said you were thinking about having one with Ron and Dee," Shantae said.

"Yes, I did say that, but with sex, emotions can play a huge part, and I don't want nobody catching feeling –not him or her," I replied.

*Tell them, Slim Boogie. That's why I have to get the fuck out of this co-ma. That bitch thinks she got my damn man and she's trying to live my life with my family. Well, I'm not having it! When I get the strength to get up out of here, that bitch is mine.*

"Well, ya'll know this is not the first time I've had a threesome, but this is the first time I felt awkward about it," Shantae said.

As Shantae rambled on, Kandi got up and walked out the room.

"Damn, Tae! She got you twisted like that?" Fatima asked. "Maybe you should have waited to talk about that when you guys were alone. She seems a little embarrassed."

"She'll be alright! You know I'm just trying to be sure about what's going on. I know what we discussed, which was to break his ass up and that's it. Don't get me wrong, he definitely did his thing and he's fine as hell. So, I'm just wondering if she's looking for something more. To be honest, she was out there doing her thing and making money while doing it," Shantae said.

"What?" they all said at the same time.

"Well, let me be clear; she was escorting. Doing shit her way on her time and making good money. So, I'm a little insecure and things do cross my mind from time to time. Deshawn is a sight for sore eyes and he did lay the pipe down on both of us. He claimed that was a first for him, or so he says. If I was strickly dickly, he would be the perfect dude. So, like I said, I wonder if it's more to her madness than she's telling me," Shantae said.

"Oh wow. I need to talk to her about this escorting business; maybe I can make some extra money on the side," Kelly said.

"You are so stupid!" Fatima laughed.

"She stopped doing that escorting shit since we've been together. All the calls have stopped coming in and it's just been about me and her, but we all know shit can change in a blink of an eye," Shantae said.

"Well, I think you have a lot of making up to do tonight," Fatima said.

"Please! I'm not kissing her ass," Shantae said.

"Stop lying. You know you're going to beg and plead," I said laughing.

"Yeah, maybe you're right. I don't want to lose her, ya'll. I love that girl, that's my boo-boo," Shatae said, making a sad face.

"Here you go again. You always go through this. Maybe you need to slow down a little and not come off so vain. Okay, Ms. God's Gift to the world? If you feel she is the one, then you need to show her that you trust her and that you also trust yourself," Fatima said.

"Okay, Ms. Love Doctor. I hear you and you're right. I do need to be easy and trust her. I'll give it a try!" Shantae said.

"I'm surprised LaQuan or Debrah haven't been up here yet. You know how he feels about his Moc," Kelly said.

"Yeah, he love him some Taraine. I feel for him but he is definitely strong and he's a loving husband," I said.

"That's right! He got this room smelling like a florist. I was looking at the cards and all these flowers. The majority of them are from him. He loves this girl so much, it's a beautiful thing and I love it," Kelly said.

*Well, if he loves me so much, where is he? Flowers? I'll take the flowers when I'm dead. I haven't heard him recite* Phenomenal Woman *to me in a while. I know she's seducing my man. I just know it. That crazy bitch, Sidora! You guys should go to my mother's apartment and see what's up with him. Please, ya'll. Call him or just go see what's going on.*

"So, Kelly, how's the love life?" I asked.

"Dull and boring as hell. Right now, I have no love life! I'm just working, working and working. I'm not fucking around with these losers no longer and I mean it," Kelly said.

"You should make a trip to Philly. You might find something nice and tender out there. When Fatima came, she had some man buying her drinks at the club. That's all it was too; just a drink. I had just gone out with Khalief and he had me wide open, so anybody else who tried to get next to me was a failure," Fatima said.

"Maybe I will come out there," Kelly said.

"I was thinking about going over to Debrah's house to say hello to the girls. Make sure everything is okay over there," Fatima said.

*Now that's what I'm talking about. I should have known it would be you to hear me. That's right, Tima. You go over there and you regulate. Go see what's going on, and if that bitch is there, throw her ass the fuck out. You know how to do it, Tima. Tell that bitch to GET THE FUCK OUT!!!*

"Alright, diva, we are about to be out. I love you!" Kelly said. "I'll be back to do you up in a couple of days."

"Yeah Tee, I have to take this 4 hour ride back home, but I will be back and I know when I return, your eyes will be wide open and you will be talking shit. I love you!" I said, and kissed her on the forehead.

"Well, cuzzo, you know I love you and I'll be back tomorrow to update you on this little situation. You know you're my stress reliever," Shantae said.

"Yeah, chica. I'll be back tomorrow. I'm heading over to Deb's to see what's going on over there," Fatima said.

*I love you bitches to death. It won't be like this for long. Before you know it, we'll be doing it up real big, trust me. I feel like crying, but I'm gonna stay strong. Come back soon, divas. Smooches.*

# Overjoyed

## Fatima

After leaving the hospital, I decided to keep my word and go check on LaQuan, Deb, and the girls. Kelly decided to come along with me, which gave us some one-on-one time.

"So, what's really going on with you, Kelly, and why haven't you been reaching out to anybody?" I asked. "You know you can't fool me, right?"

"Everything is good, seriously. But I know one thing for sure, your news surprised the fuck out of me. You? Pregnant? I never saw it coming, but I'm so happy for you."

"Bitch! Don't try to change the subject, what's really good with you?" I demanded.

"Your ass don't quit, do you?" Kelly asked. "Like I said, I'm just trying to stay focused. It's hard not having my kids and I feel like my life has been turned upside down. At my last court appearance, I totally lost it and before I knew it, the judge was giving that bastard full custody."

"Get the fuck out of here! Why didn't call me? You know I would have been there for you, girl."

"I know, but I was gone mentally after that. I had lots of dark moments. It's real depressing, no matter how positive I try to stay. That bastard will get his; that's all I keep telling myself. Those are my babies and I would do anything for them; he knows that. He's just so bitter because I chose not to be with him anymore. This motherfucker went into court telling the judge all sorts of lies. He altered pictures of me with other men performing sexual acts. He did whatever he could to make himself look good and to make me look like a nymphomaniac. After they awarded him custody, his bitch ass had the nerve to ask me to take him back. At first, I was going to say yes just to be with my children, but reality stepped in, kicked me, and said, 'bitch you better get a reality check'. I kindly told him to kiss my fucking ass. I would have been a damn fool to go back to his manipulating ass. All the controlling, all the abuse –I just had enough of that shit. I deserve much better than that, so does my children. After I told him hell no, I became every bitch and hoe in the world. This is the man that they awarded my children to. Really? I want the best for my children. I am very concerned about their welfare and I will fight to get them back," Kelly said as the tears rolled down her face.

"So, do you have any visitation right?"

"I get the kids every other weekend for six hours a day. It's horrible, but I'll take whatever I can get while I continue to fight. I need to see my children, otherwise, I would completely lose my mind and you guys will be seeing me on the 5 o'clock news," Kelly said.

"Well, you know I'm here for you, Kelly. Whenever you feel like you're going to do something crazy, just pick up the phone and call me or Tae. We don't need you in confinement! You can't fight for your kids if you're on lockdown."

"I know. I miss talking to all of you girls, especially Taraine. When I think about her being in a coma it lets me know shit could be worse for me. When it comes to these crazy ass men, girl, I don't know who to trust. Every time I think I'm connecting with someone who has a little bit of sense, they turn out to be a complete ass. Where are all the good men? I'm not asking for Jesus Christ himself, but someone who can hold his own. We both can't have issues. Damn!" Kelly said.

"You're a mess, girl, but I feel you. I am so grateful to have Khalief in my life; he has brought me so much joy. I thought Karl was the one and I definitely didn't mean to hurt him, but Khalief came and swept me off my feet. We fell in love fast, and the next thing I know, I'm pregnant. When I told him I was pregnant, he was just as excited about it as I was, and now we're living together. It's crazy, Kelly. We're happy, we're in love, and now I'm with child. Who would have ever thought I would be having a baby?"

"How many months are you?" Kelly asked.

"I will be going to my first prenatal appointment next week, but I say I'm around 10 or 11 weeks. I can't wait to find out. I'm so fucking excited. I'm glad your ass resurfaced because I am going to need you just as much as you need me. This morning when I woke up, I was spotting a little. I had a slight pain on my left side, but the pain subsided and the spotting stopped. You know I was nervous for a minute, but I'm good now."

"Okay, that's good, but if it happens again, make sure you take your ass to the emergency room," Kelly said with concern.

"I will! Now let's go up here and see the little princesses," I said.

When I rang the bell, all I heard was little feet running towards the door. It was the most adorable sound to hear the girls yell, "Who is it?" in unison.

"It's Aunt Tima, babies!" I said.

LaQuan opened the door and they came running towards us.

"Hi, my babies! How are my little princesses doing?" I asked, hugging and kissing both of them. "Hey, Q, what's going on? We're just coming from seeing Taraine. You got her room smelling like a flower shop. I love it! Kelly did her up Diva style; you know how Taraine likes it. I thought I would catch you at the hospital, but when you didn't show up, I said let me come check on you. So how are you doing? What's going on with the investigation?" I asked.

"New York's Finest claim they got a lot of clues and they have an idea of who did this, but you know me. I'm not waiting on them. I hired a private investigator to get the job done. I just want them to find this motherfucker before I do. I'm just trying to stay focused for Nicera and Raine'. Deb has been a tremendous help to me and the girls as she tries to deal with her own pain and hurt. I just can't get the vision of seeing my baby lying on the ground helpless out of my mind. It doesn't matter that an entire year has passed; it still seems like it happened yesterday. I wish I would have never left her home. I should have asked her to go with me. Fatima, I don't know what I would do if I lost my baby," LaQuan said as the tears flowed heavily down his face.

All I could do was hug him to let him know I felt his pain and I loved him so very much.

"Q, you have to believe everything is going to be alright and that Taraine is going to pull through this. You know she's a strong woman, and as long as we keep her in our prayers and show her love, I believe she will keep on fighting. The love between you and her alone is one of the reasons she's still holding on. She may not be able to talk to us, to hold us, and to curse our asses out when we piss her off, but her spirit is so strong. You can feel her everywhere. She's just on a much needed vacation, that's what I keep telling myself. You have to be strong, Q, and make sure you continue to take care of your girls. They need lots of support and love as well. I'm quite sure they are missing their mother more than they can express. If you need me to do anything, don't hesitate to call. We're family, and nothing will ever change that," I said.

"I know, you're right, but sometimes it just gets too hard to bear. I want to hurt somebody bad; not just somebody, but that heartless motherfucker who did this to her. Why? Why? I'm not understanding any of this, Tima. There was no forced entry. They didn't sexually assault her and they didn't rob us, so I'm totally lost. I need to know who did this to my baby and why?" LaQuan said angrily.

"You're right, LaQuan. And that's why hiring your own investigator was a great move. They will find him. Just have faith. She will come out of this just in enough time to give me a baby shower. You know I need her around so I can nag the shit out of her. I don't know shit about being a mom." I laughed, but I was so serious.

"You're pregnant?" LaQuan asked, shocked. "Congratulations, cuzzo! That's a beautiful thing. What you want a boy or girl?" Laquan asked.

"To be honest, it really doesn't matter. I just want a healthy baby. People always say they want a girl or they want a boy, and at first, I was like that, too. At the end of the day, I just want a healthy baby that I can give all my love to."

"I'm happy for you. I know if Moc knew about this she would be overjoyed," LaQuan said.

"Trust me, Q, she knows! I still go up there and tell her everything and she gives me feedback in her own little way. That's why I know she's still here with us. She's here in our hearts. Do you ever talk to her, and out of the blue, her heart rate increases? Or you ask her a question and what she would have said pops in your head?" I asked.

"Yeah, I know exactly what you're talking about. That's why when I talk to her, I try not to cry so much. She knows I'm a strong person and she knows I have a soft side, but she needs the strength of her husband right now; not some wimp crying his heart out."

"I think the next time you decide to have a sentimental moment with her, try not to hold it in. Let it all out. Let her feel how much you miss her and need her. Let her feel your hurt and pain. Show her that all you want is for her to come back to you," I suggested.

"Okay, mom! I will do just that when I go see her later on today," LaQuan said with a smile. What's up, Kelly? Why you so quiet over there?" he asked.

"I'm good, Quan! This is just so difficult for all of us. I'm just listening to you guys and having hope. You know my girl Tee is definitely a champ but how much can one person take?" Kelly asked.

"That's right. She is a champ and she is going to rise through it all. She's got God on her side. Your mommy is a fighter, right ladies?"

"Yes!" both of the girls said in unison.

"Alright, Q., we're about to be out. I'll come by and check on the girls in a couple of days. I have to go home and cook for my man," I said, winking at him. "Love you, guys!"

"Okay, girlies. I'll see you soon. Stay strong, Quan. Call me if you need me," Kelly said, heading out the door.

*****

I made it home before Khalief. *Good, this gives me a chance to shower and cook before he gets here. I'll boil some water for the spaghetti while I'm in the shower.* As I bent down to get a big pot to boil the water in, that same little sharp pain hit me again on my side. *Maybe we'll just eat take out tonight,* I said to myself as I walked to the bathroom to get in the shower. The hot water felt so comforting as it glided down my back. The pain had once again subsided.

After my much-needed shower, I got my blanket and went into the living room to watch TV and relax. My favorite episode of *Martin* was playing; it was an all-day marathon. *Good, I could use some laughter, I thought after seeing my girl laid up and unresponsive.*

I laid there cracking up at Sheneneh as my baby came walking in.

"Hi, baby! How was your day?" I asked excitedly.

"It was good!" he said, kissing me on my lips.

"Umm, you taste good!" I said seductively.

He smiled, looking at me like he was ready to get it popping.

"You know I hate working on weekends, but I have to do it. Babies are expensive, and trust me, she's going to have the best there is," Khalief said.

"You said *'she'* like you're sure it's a girl."

"I know it's a girl. That's my little Angel Boo growing inside of you right now," he said, lovingly rubbing my belly. "I love her so much already, and I love her mother to death," Khalief said.

Khalief had such a glow! *Damn, I'm so excited for us!* I thought to myself as I stared at my man, falling more and more in love with him.

"Baby, I order take out; it should be here soon. I was going to make some spaghetti, but I keep getting these sharp pains on my left side, so I decided to take it easy and relax."

"Are you okay? Do you want me to drive you to the hospital?"

"No, I think I'm okay. I just need a little rest; plus, I have my appointment next Tuesday. I'm good, baby. Don't stress it."

"I will stress it because I want you and the baby to be okay," he said, kissing me on my forehead. "Are you sure you don't want to go?" he asked again.

"No, boo. I'm good! Trust me, okay?"

"Okay. I'm going to jump in the shower and then I'll come and relax with you. You may get some extra surprises."

"Oh really?" I said, smiling.

"Yes, really! he said, winking at me before proceeding to the bathroom.

I decided to light some candles and spread them throughout the living room. I laid a blanket and a couple of pillows on the floor to keep us comfortable. I placed some plates, water for me, and a beer for him. The food arrived and I put it in the center of my exquisite décor. I dimmed the lights low and waited for my man to come join me.

When he walked in the living room, he grinned from ear to ear.

"You are too much, babe! You know how to keep a smile on my face."

We sat down ate and fed one another. We looked into each other eyes, finishing each other's sentences, and enjoyed each other company. We're in love and it felt good.

After we finished eating, we cleared the food and lay on the pallet and watched *Martin* together as he rubbed my stomach.

"So, how was your day today, babe?" he asked.

"My day was beautiful. I went to see Taraine. She's about the same. All the girls met up at her room and we had our Diva session, just like normal. Even though she couldn't respond back to us, her presence was felt. She probably was giving all of us a piece of her mind. It was great seeing the girls. I miss them so much. They were so surprised to find out I was pregnant. They are so happy for me, for us."

"I'm happy for us, babe," he said.

He got up and went into our bedroom. He took a while and I was ready to go back there and check on him, just to make sure he didn't go to sleep on me. As I was getting up off our little pallet, he came walking back into the living room.

"Where are you going, babe?" he asked.

"I was on my way to check on you. I thought you jumped in bed and fell asleep on me."

"No, babe; sit back down and relax. Do you need anything, something to drink or some more food?" he asked.

"No, not right now. I'm good! You looking real suspect right now, what are you up to Khalief?"

Suddenly, he got down on one knee, right in front of me.

*Oh shit! I know he is not about to propose,* I thought.

"Fatima, I am so in love with you. We've been together for a minute and when it's right, you know it and feel it all over. You're pregnant and that was just the icing on the cake. I can truly say I love you and mean it from the depths of my soul!" he said.

"I love you, too!" I said as I kissed him on his lips.

He pulled a velvet red box from behind his back.

"I want us to be a family today, tomorrow, and forever," he said.

My eyes begin to fill with tears. *Oh my God! He is proposing to me. He is about to say what I've been secretly dreaming about for years,* I thought as the tears flowed faster.

He popped open the box and inside was a locket. He pulled the locket out and opened it. One side had a picture of us and the other side was empty.

"We will place a picture of the baby on the other side when she comes," he said as he placed the locket around my neck.

"This is beautiful, Khalief. I love it and I can't wait to put a picture of our baby on the other side," I said, hugging him tight.

*Oh, damn! I was a step ahead of him thinking he was going to propose to me, but it's okay. I still love my man to death. Even if he threw me for a loop by getting on one knee to give me a locket!* I thought.

He started kissing my belly. I could tell he was filled with so much joy and happiness.

"I have one question for you, Khalief. Why did you get on one knee just to give me a locket?" I asked.

"You don't like me on bended knee?" he asked.

"I'm fine with it. I was just wondering, that's all."

"I hope I didn't offend you by getting on one knee. I know usually if someone gets on one knee it's to ask for the woman's hand in marriage. I'm sorry if I sent the wrong message to you. Do you forgive me?" he asked.

"Yes, I do! I love you and nothing can change that."

"Good. So, I guess you will love me even more when I ask you if you would do me the honor of being my wife – to have and to hold from this day forward, 'til death do us part," he said, pulling another red velvet box from behind.

He opened the box and inside was the most beautiful yellow diamond I had ever seen in my life.

"I'll ask my queen again. Fatima, will you do me the honors of being my lawfully wedded wife?" he asked.

"Yes, yes and yes!" I screamed as I stuck my hand out for him to place the ring on my finger. It was a perfect fit.

"Khalief, you have made me the happiest woman in the world. No, let me rephrase that, you have made me the happiest bitch in the world. I love you!"

He looked at me and shook his head.

"Well, you're my bitch and I love you!" he said as he kissed me gently on my lips, down to my breast, and then down and all around my belly until he finally reach my jewels.

It was all said and done after that. We made love over and over again; it was a beautiful night. It all felt so good, it felt like my life was just beginning and everything was finally going my way.

I was awakened by the pain in my side once again. This time, the pain was getting sharper. It was beginning to bother me and scare me at the same time. *Why the hell was I having these pains? I can't wait until Tuesday,* I thought as I got up to use the bathroom. I wiped and checked to see if I was spotting, but everything was clear, so I felt a little less worried. *Damn, I wish I could call Taraine and ask for her opinion. I really don't want to disturb Deb; she has been like a mother figure in my life since my mother died, who was also her sister. I miss my mother so much and I know she would have been so excited for me. I could see her now, singing and dancing, pretending to be her favorite singer, Whitney Houston. I guess they are both in heaven singing and dancing together,* I thought as I wiped the tears from my face. *Rest in Peace, Betty Boop. That's what they called her, but she was my shining star.*

*Oh, God! I pray that everything is going well with my baby,* I thought as I rubbed my belly. *This is our first baby and we are both overwhelmed and overjoyed about bringing this new baby into the world.*

I laid next to Khalief and continued to pray. I decide not to wake him. I didn't want to worry him for nothing.

Before I knew it, the pain had stopped once again. I kissed Khalief on his cheek and dozed off peacefully. *I thank you, God for all my blessings!* was my last thought as I drifted off to sleep.

# Two Can Play That Game

## Shantae

"How long are you going to carry on in this silent mode, Kandi? Do you think it's something cute about that? If you have something that you need to share with me, let's hear it. I don't know why I'm going through this. The whole entire weekend you gave me this fucked up attitude, so let's talk!" I snapped.

Kandi said nothing as she put on her shoes, picked up her car keys, and walked out the door.

*Alright, hottie pants. Two can play that game,* I thought to myself as I grabbed my cell phone and looked through my contacts. I found the name I was searching for and pressed call.

"Hey, what's up?"

"I was calling to see if we can meet up. I would like to see you. We can meet up by the Promenade, if that's alright with you, in about an hour. Okay, see you there," I said and hung up the phone.

*Okay! She wants to play games? Well let's play. I'm tired of being kicked in my face. Women these days don't want you to ask them a damn thing, but feel it's okay to ask you 21 questions. I'm going to be a lipstick lesbian today!* I thought as I got ready. No jogging suit and sneakers today; its jeans and stilettos. Oh, and let's not forget the lip gloss. "I can get sexy, too, Ms. Kandi," I said out loud.

I arrived at the promenade a couple of minutes late and my friend was there waiting.

"Hey, boo," I said, walking over to Deshawn and kissing him on the cheek.

"Damn, baby, you look good. I almost didn't recognize you. You are fine as hell," he said.

"Boy, please. I'm the same woman you were getting it on with a couple of weeks ago," I said, even though I was looking seductively-sexy. "So, how are you, what you been up to?"

"Nothing much, just hanging out with my boys after work. You know, the regular shit."

"I hear that! Do you want to walk or sit and chat?" I asked.

"We can sit and talk for a little while," he replied.

"Why are you smiling?" I asked.

"I'm smiling because I'm shocked; you look like a totally different person. I mean, you looked nice before, but now you are so fucking sexy. I was kind of twisted after we did our thing. Ya'll had me floating for a minute, but gravity pulled me back down and my head is clear now. All I can say is *damn!* You got me reminiscing and feeling like it just happened last night," he said. "So, what's up? Why did you ask me to meet up with you?" he asked.

"I just wanted to see you – mix and mingle a little. Why, was I wrong for calling you?" I asked.

"No, that's fine with me. I'm glad you called. Where's your girl, Kandi? How is she doing?" he asked.

"She's good. You haven't heard from her?" I asked.

"Nah! I texted her a couple of times, but she never responded." He sounded disappointed.

*Oh wow, she really wasn't fucking around with him. Damn, I'm always fucking up. I guess I will be kissing some major ass tonight,* I thought.

"So, do you want to go get something to eat? There's a nice restaurant a couple of blocks from here," he said.

"Sure, that sound good. I'm starving anyway," I said.

At the restaurant, the food was pretty good and the conversation was even better. Things ended on a good note. So... I'm trying to figure out how I ended up naked in his bed. Oh, I remember, that damn Tequila!

After we ate and had a couple of drinks, he asked me if I wanted to go back to his house and watch a movie. I agreed, but I knew damn well we were not going to watch a movie. The only movie showing was the one we ended up making.

When we got to his house, he pulled out a bottle of Moscato and put it on ice. We sat in the living room and he poured me a glass. I sipped on it, and before I could put the glass down, we were tongue locking.

*Bitch, what the fuck are you about to get yourself into?*

He started massaging my breast, then he pulled them out of my bra and started sucking on them. He undressed me as he walked me down the hall into his bedroom, leaving a trail of my clothing behind us. He gently pushed me on the bed and turned me over. He pulled a bottle of massage oil from his closet and started massaging me from my shoulder down. When he got to my ass, he really put in work. Then he turned me over on my back and massaged my breast. He licked around my belly button and then he continued going all the way down to my tunnel with his tongue. The threesome we had was just another experiment under my belt, but the last time I was with a man had to be when I was with my son's father. But Deshawn felt so good, this felt so good. I felt like I was in a fucking time warp. Was I going back to the days when I loved only men? I felt kind of weird and a little confused, but I was enjoying every moment. He was laying the pipe down which was usually my job. I never thought I could feel this way, at least not when it came to a man. I was the one who laid it down when it came to my girls and they were always satisfied.

He pulled me on top of him and I handled my business like a real bitch would. I had his ass moaning and calling my name, something that did not happen during our threesome. Damn, I still had it. I began to ride that horse as if it was my prize possession.

"Damn, baby. You really took me there just now," he said.

I just looked at him and smiled.

"That shit was good as hell," he said, trying to catch his breath.

"I know, right!" I said as the guilt began to kick in.

What felt so good was so bad! I knew this was not supposed to happen.

*Why did Kandi have to ignore me this morning? If she had stayed and talked to me like a real woman, I wouldn't have been here with Deshawn. I would have been home getting it on with her,* I thought.

"So, what now?" he asked as he turned over and looked me dead in my eyes.

"What do you mean 'so what now'?" I asked.

"I want to know where we go from here. Are you and Kandi in a serious relationship or is it something ya'll are trying out?"

I didn't know how to respond to that because at that very moment I was lost. I was confused and I didn't know what was going on with me and Kandi.

*You have gotten yourself into some more bullshit,* I thought.

"To be honest, Deshawn. I'm not sure where we will go from here."

"Well, maybe I can help you make that decision."

"Wait a minute. Hold up! You were not trying to push up on me in the restaurant. You were hitting on Kandi!"

"You're right, but you saw her reaction. She wasn't trying to holla back. I told you, I even texted her a couple of times and she never hit me back. That told me she wasn't interested, and I respect that, so I stopped. Like I told the both of ya'll, I'm cool and laid back. I like to date and have fun, but if I find the special someone, I'm down with being in a monogamous relationship."

"I feel you, I think we should talk and text and try to get to know each other better. How does that sound to you?" I asked.

"I'm cool with that, sexy," he said.

I got up to get dressed. I needed to get my ass home. I had business to handle. *I don't know how I ended up here, but I'm glad I came,* I thought as I smile looking down at his sexy ass.

It looked like he could read my mind because he was smiling right back at me.

As I drove home, everything that just occurred played over and over in my mind. Sad to say, but I got chills the more I thought about it, which was a good thing.

"What the fuck is going on?" I shouted as "I Should Have Cheated" by Keisha Cole began playing on the radio.

"I should have cheated? Bitch, I already did," I yelled at the radio.

When I got home, Kandi was not there, so I got undressed and got in the shower. While I was in the shower, I heard movements going on which meant she was home. My heart was racing and I was feeling guilty as hell for what I had done. If she still decides not to talk to me, then I will just give her some space.

I get out the shower and went straight into the bedroom. I could hear her in the kitchen. I put on a tee-shirt and some boy-shorts and made my way into the kitchen.

"Hey, baby. What's up?" I asked.

She didn't say a word. She didn't give me the time of day.

*It's all good!* I thought as I poured myself a glass of wine and took my ass right back into the bedroom. Even though I was feeling guilty about what happened today, I was still in the moment and I wasn't going to let Kandi's sweet and sour ass ruin it.

I picked up my phone and text him to let him know I made it home safely.

He text me back saying he had a great time with me and asked when could he see me again. It took me a moment to respond, but then I realized this bitch was still acting shitty, so I texted him back letting him know we could meet the next day.

He text back: **Ok, I'll call you around 3.**

Then I texted back: **Ok, have a good night.**

I finished drinking my wine and didn't have a care in the world. I wasn't even feeling as guilty as I did earlier, probably due to her fucked up attitude. I finished my wine and called it a night.

*I have plans tomorrow and I'm not going to let her spoil it.*

*****

I woke up and turned over to realize Kandi wasn't in the bed with me. *Did she even sleep in the bed at all?* I wondered.

I got up and went into the living room. She was nowhere to be found. I looked at the clock and it said 7:48 a.m.

Oh well, my day must go on. I made me some coffee and went back to bed. I had plans that surely didn't include Kandi, so I might as well get some more much needed sleep.

My cell phone woke me from my sleep. I looked and realized it was Deshawn calling.

"Hey, what's up? I'm coming out today, so I'll see you around 4 o'clock," I said.

I got up and started going through my closet. I decided to rock my red and black form fitted dress.

*He thought I was sexy yesterday, just wait until he sees me today; his jaws will drop. I will be smelling so edible, too!* I thought as I dabbed my favorite perfume on my neck, Delicious by Donna Karan. Then, I glazed my lips with the crystal clear gloss by Mac. I looked in the mirror and even I fell in love with myself. "Damn, you are a sexy bitch when you want to be," I said as my alter ego, Jazzmine, took over. *I almost forgot I could look this good,* I thought as I blew a kiss at myself in the mirror.

I grabbed my clutch and my car keys and headed towards the door. It was going on 3:30 p.m. and Kandi hadn't called me at all. I had no clue as to where she may have been. *Well, two can play that game! Maybe I will just spend the night out and return in the morning to get ready for work,* I thought. I was wrong for the way I came at her in the hospital, but now she's taking this shit a little too far. I'm all about living life to the fullest and I'm going to do just that, with or without her.

I rang the bell and Deshawn came to the door. He opened it and he closed it back quickly.

I started smiling because I knew, at that very moment, I had him right where I wanted him.

He opened the door again, this time, with a huge smile.

"You're just full of surprises, huh?" he said.

"What do you mean by that?" I asked, laughing. I knew damn well what he meant by it. He was shocked by my glam look today.

"You look beautiful. I need to change. I thought we were on some chill shit today."

"You don't have to change, baby. You look fine just the way you are."

"Are you sure?" he asked.

"I'm very sure."

"Okay, let me grab my keys. So, what do you want to do today?" he asked.

"Well, I have two tickets to a play in the city. It starts at 7 o'clock, if you're interested. We have time to go to dinner and then we can go see the play. Are you down with that?" I asked.

"I've never been to a play. That was never my thing, but I'm down to try anything with you, sexy," he replied.

I had originally bought the tickets as a surprise for me and Kandi, but things had changed abruptly and I'm going to get my money's worth.

Dinner was just great and the play was really nice. I'm not really into all that singing during the play and neither was Deshawn, so we found ourselves tongue-locking throughout most of the play. I wondered if the people sitting next to us or behind us were turned off or on. It really didn't matter who was next to us; the way we carried on you would have thought we were at a private screening.

Before we knew it, the play was over. We walked slowly to his car holding hands as people watched. They probably assumed we were together for years and were deeply in love, and it'd only been two days.

*Jazzmine, bitch, you are a hot mess, girl,* I thought as I got into his car. *But hey, like I always say, I am God's gift to both men and women.*

We drove back to his place.

"You might as well get comfortable. I can give you a tee-shirt if you like," he said.

"Sure!" I said.

We relaxed and watched the game. The Miami Heat was playing the Chicago Bulls. I wasn't into basketball at all, but it didn't matter because the TV was watching us.

Before I knew it, we were intertwined into one another hard and heavy. He had me up against the wall as he thrust every inch of himself inside of me. I felt good all over. He turned my head gently to the right and started kissing me gently. His mouth tasted sweet and salty as his sweat dripped all over me. He was giving it to me good and I loved it.

Before I knew it, it was five in the morning and I was drained from all the fucking we had done last night. I really didn't want to get up and go home, and that's when Shantae stepped back into the game.

*Bitch! Stop being a hoe and get your ass up. There's money to be made. It's all about the Benjamins, baby, and you can't make that laying here,* I thought.

I got up and got dressed. He got dressed as well and walked me to my car.

"This weekend was great. I hope this is not where it all ends," he said.

"No, it's not. I had a great weekend as well, and I definitely look forward to seeing you again."

We kissed as if we were never going to see each other again, then I slowly pulled back.

"I'm not ready for this to be over, call me!" I said as I got into my car.

*****

I walked into my house and I knew instantly she was not there, so I decide to walk throughout the house and my instincts were right. I decided to give her a call, but it went straight to her voicemail.

"She can't be serious!" I said deciding to leave a message.

"This weekend has been awkward for the both of us. I don't know exactly what you want from me. I'm not going to pretend this is not bothering me because clearly it is. I would rather have a conversation face-to-face with you. Just know that I love you and whatever you decide you want to do, I will respect that, but I will no longer continue with the bullshit. So, please call me, but until then, have a great day. I Love you!" I said before hanging up the phone.

I got up and got my things ready for work.

*Life goes on no matter what. I'm going to see if she calls me back. If not, I will continue to spend time with Deshawn,* I thought as I headed to the shower to get ready for work.

# Twisted
## Monica

"Dee, did you have fun in the city?" I asked.

"Yes, Monica. I had a blast, even with Fatima being around. I know she can't stand me, but your other friends were nice. I should have stayed with you on Sunday because my family visit wasn't a good one at all. They act as if they didn't want to see me. It's all good. I was never close to them anyway; it was always about me and my man."

I was surprised to hear her say something about her man because she never really talked about him. I had never met him, so I was beginning to wonder if he even existed.

"Well, when am I going to meet your man?"

"Soon," Dee replied.

"Okay, I can't wait. I should have brought you to the hospital with me. We had our little ladies' session, or venting session, as we say, but whatever it was, it was much needed," I said.

"How is your friend doing?"

"She's still in a coma. It's so sad. A motherfucker shot her and left her for dead. That's so fucked up! And it hurts me to my heart to see her like that, but they're going to catch his ass. That motherfucker better hope her husband doesn't catch his ass first. He is going through it right now. They were inseparable. It's just so sad anyway you look at it, Dee. When he does get caught, he better pray he doesn't go into Fatima's jail. If he does, he will definitely regret the day he ever violated Tee like that. My friend Kelly came and made her fierce. She still looked hot, even though she's not here physically. We prayed over her; it was so uplifting. We all believe she will come out of this. She is one of the strongest women I know. Both her and her husband have been through hurricanes, tornadoes, and tsunamis, and they still overcame it all. They are definitely survivors and their love for one another definitely gets them through it all."

"I'm sorry this has happened to your friend. I feel bad for her and I don't even know her. I'll pray for her as well. So, when are you going back to New York?" Dee asked.

"I'm not sure, maybe in two weeks. Why? You trying to roll out with me again?"

"You know I'm down, but I won't be going to see my family; that's for sure. They can love me from a distant, phony motherfuck-ers!" Dee said, angrily.

"Okay, sounds like a plan. You're finally home, and now I need to get home to my boys and my husband. I know he was missing me over the weekend. See you bright and early in the morning," I said as Dee got out of the car.

When I reached home, I saw it all over my boy's faces just how much they missed me as they hugged and kissed me at the door.

"Hey, baby. Did you miss me?" I asked Ron as I kissed him on the lips.

He didn't respond.

"I know you're still not upset because I decided to go away this weekend. You have got to be kidding me!"

"Why?" he said angrily.

"What do you mean 'why'? First of all, this wasn't no 'let's go par-ty' weekend. You do remember my mother is still in NY and so is my best friend, who to this day, is still holding on for dear life. I come home and you still have a fucking chip on your shoulder. You need to let it go, Ron. Unless you want mommy to come live with us."

"I didn't say all that!" Ron shouted.

"Oh, I see you respond quickly to that one. I missed you, baby, and I didn't want to come home to argue. Can't you just find it in your heart to let it go and let's just enjoy the rest of the night together? You, me, and the boys – is that alright with you?"

"Yeah, it's alright with me!"

"Good, because I missed my Jamaican stud," I said, giving him another kiss on the lips. "Find the Monopoly game so I can take all you guys money and properties," I said, laughing.

After we ate dinner, we enjoy the rest of the night playing games with the boys until we tired them out. Then it was time for some grown up action. I needed to relieve some stress and my husband was definitely learning how to become the stress reliever.

*****

After work, I decided to go over to Dee's house. She didn't show up for work, so I wanted to make sure she was all right. The way she talked about her family and boyfriend had me a little suspicious about her. Maybe Fatima was right about her, but I needed to do some digging to see what skeletons she was hiding in her closet.

I rang the doorbell, but got no answer. I called her phone but still no answer. I walked back to my car and looked toward her house before I pulled off. I noticed her standing in her doorway. She was looking as if she had been in a fight. Her hair was everywhere and her clothes were dangling off of her body. *Maybe she was doing the wild thing and I had disturbed her,* I thought as I got out of the car and walked back towards the door.

"Hey, girl. What's up? I was just about to pull off and go home. I'm sorry for dropping by unannounced. I didn't want to go straight home. Ron pissed me off, so I needed to go cool off."

I was lying through my teeth. Ron and I were doing just fine. I was just being nosey and trying to figure this chick out.

"Really?" she asked. "Are you guys still fussing over the trip to New York?"

"Yes, and other shit. He's just in one of those moods. Do you have company? If so, we can talk tomorrow."

"No, I don't have company. I was just lying down watching TV. Come in."

I walked into her house and it was a complete mess. I wanted to turn back around. I found a little spot on the sofa and sat there hoping nothing climbed on me. She had pictures, letters and newspaper articles all over the place.

"What's all this, girl?" I asked.

"Oh, that's just some old letters and pictures from my man," she said.

"Letters? Is he in jail?"

"He was in jail," she said. She picked everything up off the couch and floor then took them into her bedroom.

"So, where is he now?" my nosey ass asked.

"He couldn't be here right now. Not by choice, but I fixed everything the best I could. You see, people are jealous and a lot of people hate on him real bad; it's so sad. He was my protector, he loved me to death. We were supposed to get married, but people found a way to put a stop to that. Jealousy is a motherfucker; it's a horrible and contagious disease," Dee said angrily, shaking her head.

"So, he broke off the wedding?"

"No, I just told you. Hating ass, jealous ass motherfuckers put an end to it, but we'll be together in holy matrimony one day," Dee said as fresh tears began to flow.

"That's right, girl. Never give up. Whatever is meant to be will be, regardless of who tries to destroy it."

"I never give up on anything," Dee said.

She continued mumbling under her breath as she looked at the picture in her hand. I couldn't understand what she was saying. I started feeling a little uncomfortable, but then again, she did look like she was in a lot of pain. She looked deeply hurt.

"Is that him in the picture?" I asked, getting up to look at the picture.

It was a picture of him and her kissing. He kind of looked familiar from the side, but I could only see half his face.

"Awh, you guys look happy."

She started crying hysterically.

"Don't worry, Dee. He will come around and you guys will get married as planned."

To be honest, she didn't seem mentally stable. She had a weird look on her face. I didn't know if I should be worried for her, or myself, so I decided I needed to make an exit.

"Well, Dee, I'm going to head home, but I can stay longer if you want me to."

"No, thanks, Monica. I'm okay. I'm going to go lay down, but I will drop by your office tomorrow," Dee said sadly.

"Okay, that sounds good. Maybe we can go out and eat after work," I said, walking to the door.

She didn't even bother to walk me to the door. She just sat there and continued to stare at the picture of her boyfriend.

*Damn, I think Fatima was right. Something is terribly wrong with that chick,* I thought as I walked to my car. *She could just be really missing her man! Damn, I hope she will be all right, but she definitely didn't look like the Dee I had befriended some years ago.*

As soon as I got in my car, I called Fatima, but she didn't answer.

"Hey, girl, call me when you get this message. I got some shit to tell you. I think you might be right about Dee. I just saw some craziness from her ass today. I will tell you about it when you call me. Love you! Bye."

\*\*\*\*\*

During my lunch break, I decided to call Dee to see if she was all right and if she wanted to go out to eat after work. I felt a need to do more investigation on this chick.

"Hey, Dee. What's up?"

"Hey, Monica. I'm good, girl. What's up with you?"

I looked at my phone because she sounded back to normal, as if yesterday never happened.

"I'm good. I was calling to see if you want to go out and get something to eat after work. Nothing fancy, maybe the Olive Garden."

"Sounds good to me, girl. To be honest with you, I'm starving now, but I can hold out for a couple hours more.

"I was worried about you last night. So, how are you doing today?"

"I'm okay. Sometimes I just snap from all the hurt I'm feeling.

*What the fuck she mean by 'snap'?* I thought.

"Well, don't snap too hard if you want to get your man back."

"What you mean 'get him back'? I still got him. He ain't going anywhere. That's my baby. I love him and he loves me right back."

"I hear that," I said, looking at my phone once again.

*I wonder if this bitch is bipolar. Maybe I shouldn't go out to eat with her after all. Damn, what the fuck is up with her? I know I don't know too many people out here, but I don't want to be connected to some psychotic bitch. If she continues acting as if she has some major issues, I will definitely have to leave her ass alone. I have plenty of true friends; losing her as an associate won't make me lose any sleep,* I thought.

"Okay, so I'll meet you in the lobby at 5 o'clock."

"Cool!" Dee said.

*****

"Girl, I'm starving," Dee said as she looked at the menu. "I think I'll get the chicken Parmesan. My baby use to love that."

"When is the last time you saw him?"

"It's been a while, but like I said, haters are the root of all evil. They can't keep us apart – not for too long. He will always be in my heart, I'll see him soon."

"I would love to meet him. Maybe we could go out on a double date."

She didn't respond. She just continued staring at the menu.

"Yeah, I think I'll get the chicken Parm."

*Okay!* I thought to myself. *She is definitely not playing with a full deck of cards.*

I ordered shrimp Alfredo. As we waited for our food, there was such an awkward feeling in the air. I had enough of this chick, but while were sitting here I might as well dig deeper into her twisted mind.

"How long was your boyfriend locked up?"

"He was locked up for a minute because of some bullshit. He was set up. You can't trust a motherfucker these days – everybody trying to do them and protect their necks. They always wanted what we had. I told him not to go to New York, but he told me he was offered a good hustle out there and he wanted to see if it was for him. If things went well, we would move to New York, which I wasn't too happy to hear. After a couple of months, I guess things weren't going too well, so he called and said he was coming back home. Next thing I knew, I get a call telling me he's locked up. I completely lost it. But later, I received a letter and he let me know all the shit that went down. My man told me he was set up, so he came up with a plan. You know how it goes when it comes to plans – sometimes it goes well and sometimes it just don't go the way you expected it to. They even tried to set him up in jail – fucking bastards. One thing about my man is he always kept me on top of shit and he trained me well. If something was to happen to him, he gave me orders for any and every situation. That's how it was for him and me. I ride for my man, you feel me, Monica?"

"Yes, I feel you, girl. Well, when you guys get married, I hope I'm invited."

She spaced out once again, as if she didn't hear a word I said about her getting married.

*Damn, you never really know a person,* I thought, shaking my head.

"Girl, I'm stuffed. That was good. I guess I'll take my ass home to my three handsome men."

*Oh, damn. Why did I just say that?* I thought. *I don't think she heard me anyway, she's in her own little world.*

"Dee, you ready?"

"Yeah, girl. I'm ready. Where's our waiter so we can pay this damn bill?" Dee yelled as she scanned the entire restaurant in search of our waiter.

"Don't worry, Dee. I got this one," I said as Dee continued searching for the waiter with frustration written all over her face.

*I'm glad we drove separately because I surely wouldn't want to ride home with her crazy ass,* I thought.

"Okay, Dee. I'll call you later; get home safe," I said, getting into my car.

When I got in my car, I tried to call Fatima's ass again, but still no answer.

"Girl, call me back," I said frustrated. "I got some shit to tell you. Call me back, heffah."

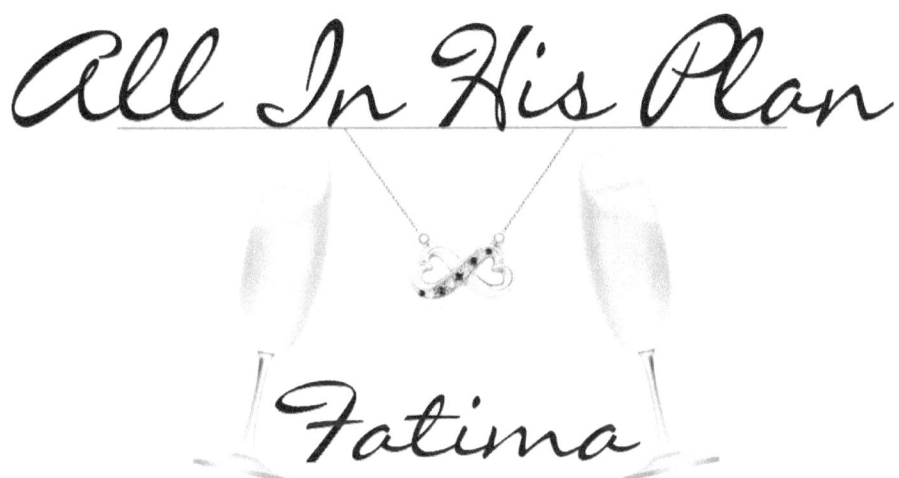

# All In His Plan

## Fatima

When I woke up, I was still feeling the same pain on my side. I'm so glad my doctor's appointment was today.

"Good morning, babe!" Khalief said as he kissed me on my forehead.

Good morning, Khalief. The pain on my side has returned. I hope the doctor will tell me the reason for why this is happening. I pray everything is okay," I said nervously.

"I'm sorry to hear that, babe. Why didn't you wake me up? I would have taken you to the ER. Do you want me to go to the doctor with you today?" he asked.

"No, I think I'll be okay, but I do want you to come with me when I have my sonogram, okay, my love?" I said smiling.

"Anything you want, anything you ask of me, you know I will do, my future wife and mother of my first born," he said as he brushed his fingers through my hair.

Damn, he was turning me on, and even though I was in pain, my body still knew how to react to his gentle touch. It felt good that everything was falling into place and we were deeply in love. It seemed like I finally found that ONE, whatever that means. Better late than never, I guess.

"I love you so much; both you and the baby mean everything to me. I never thought I would meet my match and here you come, out of nowhere. They say opposite attracts and I am definitely a believer. I always left the 'falling in love' thing to my girls. I knew I could love someone deeply, but I never thought it would happen like this. You made me feel so brand new and beautiful inside, more than just a good fuck. I feel so blessed and I am so excited and overjoyed. I can't wait until the day I become your wife. You mean the world to me and we're definitely going to make it," I said, looking deep into his eyes, and for the very first time, didn't question my feelings or thoughts.

"I know we will make it," he said as he began to sing while rubbing my belly. *'You are everything and everything is you.'*

All I could do was smile as the tears filled my eyes. I was in love and happy, but at that very moment, I was nervous and afraid due to the pain that seems to be getting worse by the minute.

Khalief got up to take a shower and I got up to find something comfortable to wear to the doctor.

I reached the clinic half an hour early. There were so many bellies of all sizes, and I was excited and anxious to get where they were.

*So, that's how I will look in a couple of months,* I thought as I waited for my name to be called.

I finally heard someone call Fatima Edwards. I got up and was taken to the back to be weighed and asked a bunch of questions.

I wondered how much weight I gained. I didn't even look at the scale and I prayed she didn't say it out loud. Then, the nurse proceeded to check my vitals. After I was done, the nurse sent me into a room to see the doctor. Dr Mac was nice looking. He was Taraine's OB/GYN, and if he was good enough for her, then he was good enough for me.

"Good morning, Ms. Edwards."

"Hi, Dr. Mac," I said shyly.

*Me? Shy? Now you know I must be going through some hormonal changes,* I thought.

"So, how is everything going?" he asked as he looked through my chart.

"Well, Dr. Mac, I know I'm pregnant, but for some reason, I keep having these sharp pains on my left side. And I was spotting a couple of times."

"Oh, I don't like the sound of that," Dr. Mac said. "Undress and put the gown on from front to back and let's see what's going on," he said, walking out the room giving me some privacy.

I began to undress. The more clothing I took off, the harder my heart pounded. I was scared and wondered why he said he didn't like the sound of that.

The doctor gave me a few minutes before re-entering the room with a nurse to assist him.

"Lie down on your back and put your feet in the stir-ups."

I did exactly what he asked me to do. I tried to relax, but my heart was pounding as if it was trying to punch its way through my body.

He placed the gloves on and squeezed the cold gel onto his fingers. He inserted his fingers gently inside of my vagina and felt around.

"How long were you bleeding, Ms. Edwards?"

"I would just spot every now and then, but it was never heavy bleeding."

After he finished, he told me to get dressed and come to his office.

I was just hoping for the best and trying not to stress myself out with negative thoughts. I know stress was not good for me or the baby.

I got dressed and proceeded to his office. I sat down and waited for him to tell me what was going on.

"Well, Ms. Edwards, it looks as if the baby is trying to abort itself."

My heart dropped.

"What?"

"I'm putting you on bed rest. No lifting, no sexual intercourse and no stress. Try to drink plenty of liquids, I don't want you to do too much of anything."

"Will my baby survive?"

"Yes, the baby can survive, but there's a very high chance of you miscarrying. That's why it's very imperative for you to follow my instructions. Go home and relax. I want you to come back tomorrow, sign in, and go upstairs to the sonogram department, so we can see what's going on with the little bambino."

"Okay!" I replied, trying to sound as if I was really okay.

But I wasn't okay. I was scared as shit. As I walked to my car I began to shake. I was nervous and confused. The doctor said there was a chance I could be miscarrying. I didn't want to hear that; my heart couldn't take that type of news.

I got into my car and began praying. In the mist of praying, I began crying.

"Oh, God! Please, please, please don't let me miscarry. I love this baby growing inside of me so much and she's hasn't entered the world yet. My baby, our first born... I can't lose her. I just can't, God," I prayed.

*Okay, okay, bitch. Get a grip. He said no stress, and if I want to bring this baby to full term, I need to follow the doctor's orders and calm the fuck down. Should I call Khalief and tell him what the doctor said? No, I'll just wait until he gets home. He doesn't need to be stressed out while working,* I thought.

I took a deep breath.

*Inhale*

*Exhale*

*Inhale*

*Exhale*

*I got this, God. I know you got me, right?* I looked up to the sky and crossed my belly. *Yeah, you got me. No matter what happens, I know it is all in your plan.*

I started the engine.

"Relax, relate, release," I said as I took a deep breath and slowly pulled off.

*****

As soon as I got home, I put on my pajamas, poured me a big glass of orange juice, and headed straight to my bed. Everything the doctor said played over and over in my mind. Tears filled my eyes as my heart began to pound. I grabbed the remote control and flipped through the channels. Maybe I could find something to make me laugh. It seemed like everything was about pregnancy test or showing pregnant women.

*Ugh… I need a movie to watch.*

I came across *Baby Boy* which was one of my favorite movies. *I will watch this until I fall asleep,* I thought. The movie didn't distract me at all because I was still deep in thought about what took place today. A beautiful baby girl's face continuously flashed across my mind as if she was born already. She looked just like my grandmother, Florie, who had just recently died from cancer. I just knew my baby was meant to be and I would do whatever it took to carry her to full term.

I closed my eyes and begin to pray once again, "I believe in you, God, and I know my baby will make it. I know I will carry my Angel Boo to full term; that's what I'll call her until she's born. Then Khaielf and I will give her a beautiful name with meaning." The tears flowed, but this time it was tears of joy. *I am focused and I know everything will be alright.*

*****

The touch of Khalief's lips kissing mines woke me out of my sleep.

"Hey, babe. How did it go today at your doctor's appointment? I called you a couple of times but I guess you were sleeping."

"Yes, I was drained, baby – emotionally and physically," I said, sitting up in bed.

"What do you mean?"

Before I could even get it out, I just grabbed him and hugged him.

"The doctor said the baby was trying to abort itself and the best thing I could do is get plenty of rest, stay off my feet, and drink plenty of fluids. I don't want to lose our baby, Khalief," I said as I cried hysterically on his shoulder.

"I got you, babe. We're not going to lose the baby. I'm here. I got you. I'm going to take care of you; whatever you need me to do just tell me. You have to calm down and relax. As a matter of fact, let me lay here next to you and let's talk," Khalief said, wrapping his arms around me.

"Well, I have to go back tomorrow for a sonogram and I need you to come with me."

"I'm there, babe; you don't even have to ask. I should have gone with you today, that was wrong on my part. I apologize for that."

"You don't have to apologize; you weren't wrong. I just got some news today I wasn't expecting. I just don't want to lose my baby, our baby."

"We'll be all right; me, you, and the baby."

"Yeah, she's my Angel Boo," I said smiling.

"*Your* Angel Boo?"

"No, she's *our* Angel Boo."

"Well, how do you know it's a girl? I thought you wanted a boy," Khalief said.

"All I want is a healthy baby, but today, I just knew it was a girl. Don't ask me how, Khalief, but I just know it. I feel it all over."

"Okay, well you and Angel Boo need to get some rest. Are you hungry?"

"No, I'm good. I don't have an appetite. I just want you to lay next to me until I fall back to sleep. Can you do that for me, baby?"

"You got it, babe. I love you. Everything is going to be all right. Just relax," He said, kissing me gently all over.

*****

The next morning, we both got up and headed to the doctor for the sonogram. The ride there was so quiet. I guess we were both nervous and didn't know what to say to each other.

As soon as I signed in, the nurse took us straight to the room. I undressed, put on a hospital gown, and tried to relax.

*Here we go again,* I thought as the nurse put that cold gel on my stomach and moved the plastic tube in circular motions, looking at the monitor. I lay there watching Khalief watch every movement the nurse made. We were both waiting for her to show us our baby. She started shaking her head slowly.

"I don't see any movement," the nurse said.

"What do you mean you don't see any movement?" Khalief asked.

"Well, let me take a look vaginally."

She put a condom and some lubricant on the scope and then she slid it gently into my vagina. Once again she shook her head slowly.

"I don't see any movement and there's also no sound of the baby's heartbeat."

She pointed at the monitor to show us what she was looking at.

"There should be some type of movement from the baby in this area. There's the sac, but there's nothing going on there. I'm sorry to tell you this, but you miscarried."

I turned to her and said okay, but I went numb on the inside. I didn't want to believe she just told me I lost my baby.

*Oh, no! I think she did something wrong,* I thought.

I looked at Khalief and his eyes were red. She gave me some wipes to clean myself off. I got dressed as Khalief waiting for me in the next room. While getting dressed, I realized this wasn't a dream; this was reality and my baby was gone. As I began to button my pants, I paused for a moment and found myself sinking to the floor as the numbness subsided and I felt my heart pound. I began crying uncontrollably. The nurse came back into the room and found me on the floor in a fetal position. The nurse opened the door and asked Khalief to come inside. I saw his lips moving, but I couldn't hear a word he was saying.

"My baby is gone, my baby is gone," I said over and over.

He hugged me tightly as I watched his lips say it's going to be all right.

"Please, Ms. Edwards. Calm down. I'm sorry for your loss. You and your husband can try again, but you can't stress yourself out."

"I don't want to try again. This was our first baby. I never thought I could get pregnant and it finally happened and God took her away from me. My Angel Boo is gone. I prayed and asked HIM to bring my baby to full term and HE didn't. Why are you punishing me, God? What did I do to deserve this?" I screamed.

Khalief grabbed my hand and gently pulled me up off the floor. He held my hand and walked me out of the room. We walked inside of Dr. Mac's office and listened to him explain what had happened.

The sac was still in my uterus and I was going to need a D and C procedure to remove it. Then Dr. Mac gave me an appointment for the following morning at 7 a.m. My heart was heavy; all I wanted to do was sleep and wake up to find out this was a dream – a horrible nightmare and my Angel Boo was still growing inside of me, healthy and strong.

The drive back home was dreadful. There was no communication, no music or anything; just the sound of both of our heartbeats. A fifteen minute ride home felt like an eternity. Khalief held my hand as we walked into our home. I went straight to the bathroom, pulled off my clothes, and got into the shower. As the water glided down my back, I leaned on the wall and cried silently, sliding midway down onto the tub floor. I felt violated, but in a different way. I could no longer hold it in as I began to cry hysterically. The water was no longer falling on me, when I looked up, Khalief was holding out his hand for me to grab it. He wrapped the towel around me and dried me off. He wiped away my tears and gently kissed me on my fore-head down to my nose and then my lips.

"I'm here, babe," he said as he walked me out of the bathroom to our bedroom.

He pulled out a pair of my pajamas and dressed me. He got a hair clip off the dresser and wrapped my hair the best way he knew how.

I laid down in the fetal position and Khalief laid right behind me, wrapping his arms around me.

"Everything is going to be all right, Fatima. I am here for you and I'm never going to leave your side. You hear me, babe? Never."

I heard every word he said, but couldn't respond. I felt as if something was stuck in my throat and it was choking me slowly. My body was numb and my baby was gone.

*She slipped away without me ever getting to know her,* I thought.

"I'm going to make you some chamomile tea. That will help you relax and sleep a little better," Khalief said.

I nodded my head 'yes', but I didn't want no tea, I wanted my ba-by. I wanted to know she was still inside of me and that I was going to carry her to full term.

*What did I do to deserve this? Why did you take my baby, God? I just don't understand why?* Everything was going through my head, from the men I had been with to how I partied.

*Was it because I was so aggressive and had the 'I don't give a fuck' atti-tude? What was it? Why did you choose to take my baby? This was going to be the complete package for me... my new beginning,* I thought as the tears just flowed heavier and my heart raced faster. I sat up in bed because I was finding it hard to breathe as I tried to grasp for a little bit of air. It's obvious I was having a panic attack.

Khalief came into the room and he glided me towards the edge of the bed. He began rubbing my back in circular motions.

"Breathe in and out, baby; relax, relax," he said as he turned my face towards his. "You have to calm down, babe. I, too, just found out I lost my firstborn. I don't want to lose you as well."

"I know, Khalief, but it just hurt so bad. I don't understand why? My very best friend, my sister is in a coma and now I lose my baby. I just can't take it. I really can't, Khalief. I need to go see her! Can you take me to the hospital? I really can't drive like this. I just need to go talk to Taraine right now," I said.

"I thought you were going to try to get some rest?"

"I was, Khalief, but I just need to go and see Taraine right now. I need you to take me to see her, please."

"Okay, if that's what you want. Get dressed and I will drive you to see her."

"Thank you, baby."

*****

When I walked into the room, Taraine was lying there so peacefully. I sat next to her and just held her hand. She still had the wig on that Kelly put on her, but somebody took the makeup off.

"Hey, Taraine. I was hoping to come in here and find you wide awake. I wanted to hear you ask me what took me so long to get here. Tee, I miss you so much and my heart is broken. You're here in this hospital stuck in a coma and today I just learned I lost my baby. I just don't understand, and even though Khalief has been wonderful, I just wished you were here for me. I know you would tell me how to get past this.

*I'm so sorry you lost your baby, Tima. I know it hurts like hell, and yes, I wish I could be there with you physically to help you get through this loss. If anybody knows pain, it's me. God will heal you in due time. He is the ultimate healer, but you have to believe that. Just like I know he'll bring me out of this coma when he feel it's time.*

"I know if you were here you would tell me to lean on Khalief and accept his support and give him support as well. I feel kind of selfish because he lost his baby as well. I just feel so empty inside and I feel a little lost," I said as I wiped the tears away.

*You guys will be comforters to each other, just like Laquan and I were. You said you have a great man! Well, you need to love and appreciate him; appreciate the connection that you have with one another. Your baby is in heaven with our maker, you have to have faith, Fatima, and your baby will come back to you when God is ready.*

"I love you so much, girl, and I'm glad I came here because I feel a little better. I told Khalief I needed to come see you. You are my heart, my world, and I need for you to come back to me. I may sound selfish, but that's how I feel. I'm going to go home and grieve with my man because he lost his baby, too. I know that's what you're probably telling me right. Tomorrow, I will have a D and C procedure to remove the sac, so we'll see what happens after that. I guess the healing process will begin. This is so crazy, Taraine. Even though the sonogram says I lost the baby, I still have all the symptoms of being pregnant. I wouldn't wish this pain on anyone, not even my worst enemy. I'm sorry I came here and put everything on you, but you know you're the only one who could calm me down. I'm going to go home and try to get some rest. I'll be back soon. Love you forever, Taraine," I said as I kissed her on the cheek.

*I love you too, Fatima, and I'm so sorry about the lost of your baby. Things happen for a reason and if you're meant to have a baby, God will bless you with one.*

\*\*\*\*\*

I got in the car and kissed Khalief.

"Thank you for driving me here to see Taraine. I really needed to talk to her."

"No problem, you should know by now that I would do anything for you. I just want you to be all right. I want us to be all right."

"We will be all right; we'll take it day by day. I just want to apologize to you if I made you feel left out. I was just soaking in my own pain and I didn't acknowledge that fact that you had a loss as well. I just hope you're able to forgive me."

"Forgive you for what?"

"For losing our baby. Maybe it's something I did wrong. I don't know, but I just feel so bad. Maybe I should have gone to the doctor a lot sooner. When I first felt the pain in my side, I should have gone straight to the emergency room."

"Baby, let's be clear on one thing; it is not your fault. You did nothing wrong, believe me. I'm hurting as well, but I refuse to let you blame yourself. It wasn't time; that's what I tell myself. You called her your Angel Boo, right?"

"Yes!" I said smiling.

"Well, Angel Boo is in heaven; it just wasn't her time to be with us. Things happen for a reason, but we will try again once the doctors say it's okay. I'm not going anywhere; you are stuck with me for life. Is that okay with you?"

"Yes, it is!"

"I know women have the maternal thing and I could never experience that, but I do hurt. Trust me, we will get through this together, one day at a time. How is Tee doing? I would have gone with you to see her, but I knew you needed some personal time with her," Khalief said.

"She is still the same, but I can feel her every time I'm near her. She's still there, she's just living in her own world right now. I'm just waiting for her to open them beautiful eyes and say 'I'm back, bitch and I know you've been getting in a lot of trouble while I was on sabbatical'," I said laughing at the thought.

"I just can't think about it, it's just too much to take. Now I have to prepare myself for this procedure tomorrow. I'm so grateful to have you in my life. I know it's going to take some time to heal, but we'll do it together," I said, looking out the window, trying to hold back my tears.

*****

We arrived at the hospital at 6:30 a.m., and the procedure began on time. All I remember is being in the operating room and the nurse's assistant strapping me down to the operating table. They gave me anesthesia through the intravenous. They told me to count backwards from 10, and that's all I remember. I woke up in the recovery room feeling slight dizzy, but most of all, completely empty. My symptoms were gone and so was the last part of my baby. The tears flowed once again as I looked up at the ceiling in a daze. The nurse came by to check on me.

"How are you feeling, Ms. Edwards?" the nurse asked.

"I'm okay," I said, even though I was lying through my teeth.

*I just wanted my baby back. I know we will try again, but it still hurts. It hurts like hell. How can I go on? How can I get through this pain? I don't think I ever will,* I thought as I lay there feeling lonely and confused.

# Sexually Connected

## Kandi

*Fatima needs me right now; she is hurting so bad. My babies need me right now. I know they are missing their mommy. LaQuan really need me; he is being seduced by that bitch, Sidora. I thought our love was strong enough to withstand anything, but I guess I was wrong. I'm just trying to figure out why you want to keep me in this predicament, God? What is the lesson in all of this? My family and friends need me and you're the only one who could make that happen. I'm fighting as hard as I can and I'm still here in the comatose state. I can hear everything going on around me, but I can't respond. This is so unfair.*

I heard someone walk into my room but they didn't say a word. They just sat next to me, rubbing my hand. A few moments later, they began to cry.

"Hey, Taraine. I don't know what brought me here, but I'm here for some strange reason. The last time I came here it was just a complete disaster. Your cousin showed her ass and it hasn't been the same since. Shantae really thinks she God's gift and she is really giving me her ass to kiss."

*Wait! I recognize the voice. It's Angela, or Kandi. I think that's what Shantae said she calls herself now. Damn, what did my cousin do now that has you crying hysterically? I can tell you're hurting, Kandi, but why?*

"I told Tae I didn't want to have a threesome with Deshawn. Sometimes when you indulge in certain types of sexual acts, it may cost you your relationship, and that's exactly what happened. We haven't spoken or conversed with one another since the altercation here at the hospital. I love your cousin so much, but she's got issues and I just don't have the time or patience for the bullshit or disrespect. The fucked up part about it is if I wanted to be with him, I could have. He was coming on strong at the restaurant and I ignored him, but she's the one who kept pushing for a threesome and she got exactly what she wanted. I guess the line of work I did on the side made her suspicious of me all the damn time. That's what I did by choice, but I wasn't trying to catch feelings for any of them. At the end of the day, they were just my clients. I'm sorry I came here with our issues. You were always a great listener, even when we were younger. We lost contact as we got older, which is sad because now that I'm back in the picture, this is not how I wanted to see you –lying here motionless. You have always been a fighter, so I know you will find the strength to come through this. I just need to find the strength to figure out how to deal with your cousin before I do something I damn sure don't want to do," Kandi said.

*You guys are too much. I was shocked to hear you and Tae were an item and that you changed your name, amongst other things. Shantae feels she is Ms. Lovergirl and that's never going to change. If she does change, it will be surprising, I thought as I listened to Kandi cry uncontrollably. Wow, she must really love Tae. I wish Tae would stop using and abusing these women. I think she just needs to be in a relationship with herself because that's who she's really in love with, herself. Damn, Kandi. I wish you could hear me because I would tell you to RUN FOR YOUR LIFE. My cousin is too much, but I love her to death and I got her back no matter what.*

"I will be back to see you soon, Taraine, and hopefully, I'll have some good news to tell you. Love you, mama. It's time for you to come out of that deep sleep," Kandi said, kissing Taraine on the cheek.

I stood waiting for the elevator and thought about all the shit that occurred between Shantae and me. None of it was good. The more I thought about it, the more pissed off I became. I pulled out my cell phone and decided to make a call.

"Hey, baby. How have you been? I'm good. I was here at the hospital visiting a friend of mine and you crossed my mind, so I decided to call you. What's up when can I see you? Yes, tonight is good for me. So, I'll see you around eight. Later!" I said with a smile on my face.

*****

*When I got to the house, Shantae wasn't there. That's okay. I am going to enjoy myself tonight and this is not business, it's personal,* I thought as I looked through the closet for something nice to put on. "Yes! This will definitely work," I said as I laid my outfit across the bed. "I'll take a little nap, and then it's on tonight."

I slept longer than I wanted too, when I woke up it was a quarter to seven. Tae still hadn't come home, but it was all good. I got in the shower, got dressed, and left the house leaving my scent of Chanel lingering. I looked good and I knew it. There's nothing better than a great pair of stilettos to give you that extra push that says 'Bitch, you are working it'.

I looked at my phone to get the address to my destination. I looked in the mirror to make sure the lips were looking good enough to taste. I winked at myself. "Let's do it, mama, and do it well."

*****

I rang the doorbell and stood there in my sexy 'come get me' pose as the door opened slowly.

"Hey, handsome," I said as I kissed him on the lips and walked inside the apartment. It was nice and cozy just right for a bachelor. "Are you happy to see me?"

"Yes!" he replied.

"Why do you look so shocked? I must be the last person you expected to see."

"Actually, you are," he said.

"I know you have been calling and texting me, and yes, I have been ignoring you, but I was going through some personal issues at the time," I said, walking up closer to him and pushing him on the couch. "Do you forgive me?" I asked.

"Yes!" he said.

"So, what are you waiting for, baby? Let's have some fun. That threesome we had was just a little taste of all I could deliver. Plus, I was sharing you with Shantae. Now, I got you all to myself. Don't you want me as much as I want you, Deshawn?" He looked at me like a deer caught in headlights.

"Yes." He moaned as I kissed him gently on his neck.

Deshawn tried to play hard to get, but once our clothes were off, there was nothing but pure magic taking place as we rocked each other's world. He definitely had more to offer than what he gave during that threesome. Maybe he was just too excited at that time because he was experiencing the male ultimate fantasy. Tonight he was giving me the best that he had, and I enjoyed every minute of it. We didn't even make it into his bedroom as we both reached our climax right there on the couch. We were stuck holding one another tight, breathing heavily as sweat covered both of our bodies.

"Damn, baby. I loved that," I said as I laid on top of him listening to his heart beat.

"That was crazy," he replied as he rubbed my ass in circular motions.

We both sat up on the couch.

"I didn't see this coming at all. What made you call me today?"

"You have been on my mind for the past couple of days. I finally got the courage to call you and… here I am. Why? Is that a problem?"

"Hell no! I'm glad you called; better yet, I'm glad you came. You just surprised the fuck out of me, for real," DeShawn said.

"Why are you so surprised? You were trying to get with me, right?"

"Yes, but you acted as if you weren't interested."

"It wasn't that. I was just in a bad situation."

"So, are you still in that bad situation?" DeShawn asked.

"Yeah, kind of, but I have to live my life. I can't let a person's issues hold me back. I wanted something and I went after it, and I'm glad I did. Because, honestly, you are a great fuck," I said, winking at him.

He looked at me as if hearing he was a great fuck was nothing new.

"You did your thing too, Kandi. I'm glad you changed your mind and decided to hit me up. So, what happens from here, Ms. Aggressor?" he asked.

"Whatever you want to happen," I said, looking at him seductively.

*Damn, I released all my stress out on him and it felt good. I wish it didn't have to come to this, but hey, you get what you ask for,* I thought as I had flashbacks of what just went down. He was definitely holding back the night of our threesome. He was nice on the eyes and had pretty white teeth, too. When I first saw him, I thought he was just alright, but looking at him now, he was the total package. Nice chocolate complexion, fit body, about 5"11, and he had a beautiful smile. Damn, he had me turned on again and I was ready to go for round two.

Round two was even better than round one. He had me thinking hard because I was really enjoying myself a little too much. This would really hurt Shantae and put an end to our relationship, but it was too late to turn back now.

*Now, I need to show him how I really get down; make him fiend for me more and more.*

He was drenched in sweat and so was I.

"Why don't we take this to the shower?" he suggested.

"Sounds like a plan, just show me the way."

Before I knew it, we were sexing each other in the shower as the water poured down on both of us. It was like something out of a movie and I acted out every scene. This was no client of mine who I just came to blow off get my money and leave. This was real emotions, real satisfaction, real enjoyment, and it I loved it.

"We got it in just now, handsome. I think I worked up an appetite, I'm starving," I said.

"We can order some take out if you like," he said.

"Yes, that sounds good. I know I just burned off a lot of calories today," I said, smiling.

"Do you want to lay down and watch TV while we wait for the food to come?"

"Yes, I'm down. We can watch TV or a movie; or better, yet we can make our own movie," I said as I looked at him and licked my lips slowly.

He started flipping through the channels and came across *Basketball Wives*.

"These chicks are out of control," he said.

"Yes, they are, and I love every bit of it; especially Evelyn. That bitch is crazy, I can hang with her any day." I laughed.

"So, what's up? Is this just a one-time fuck or are we kicking?" Deshawn asked.

"I don't know about kicking it; let's just say we're sexually connected."

"Sexually connected?" he repeated.

"Yes, sexually connected. In other words, friends with benefits. You are a good piece and I would like to keep seeing you. If that's alright with you." I said.

"Baby, I'm with that," he said with a slight smirk.

Our food finally arrived. We ate, talked, and fucked for the rest of the night. I woke up and looked at the clock, it was 4:00 a.m.

*Oh, well, I might as well stay until the morning. It's a little too late for me to hit the streets and I'm comfortable right where I am,* I thought. I didn't have anything to go home to anyway. The damage was already done, so fuck it. I looked at Deshawn and smiled until I dozed back off to sleep.

# Fight or Die Trying

## Taraine

*I wonder what day, month, or year it is.*

It was too quiet; I didn't hear any communication – no sound of footsteps or nothing. It was just too damn quiet and it was driving me crazy. I felt lonely and hurt. *Where was everybody? Why is there no one here to see me? I don't know what's going on and I wish someone would come and say something.* Then I heard the sweet sound of joy.

"Hi, mommy!" Raine' said.

"Shh, Raine', mommy is sleeping," Nicera said.

Just hearing them made my heart skip a beat.

*Hi, my babies! I miss you so much and mommy loves her baby girls.*

Then I heard the sound of my mother Deb.

"Come here, Raine'. Come give your mother a kiss," Deb said.

"Okay, Mamo," Raine said.

Nicera started calling her that when she was learning to talk, so I guess Raine' followed in her big sister's footsteps.

"I can reach her by myself; I'm a big girl, Mamo," Nicera said.

"Yes, you are a big girl but you have to be careful, okay?" Deb said.

"Okay, Mamo," Nicera said.

I could actually feel Nicera's wet kisses on my cheek. I tried to lift my hand to feel her, but nothing happened. I tried to turn my head in the direction her voice was coming from, but still nothing. This was so frustrating.

"Don't you think it's time for you to wake up and get out of that bed? You got things to do; you got these girls to raise and a husband who is miserable. I'm tired, Taraine, and I know you didn't come this far to let some punk man take you out like this," Deb said.

I could hear the sadness all in her voice.

"LaQuan is trying to stay strong for these girls, but I see him breaking down slowly but surely," Deb said.

*How is he breaking down if he's running around with that bitch that shot me? How could my family and friends allow this to happen? That's what's keeping me alive, besides my girls. That bitch won't win; she's not taking my place. She doesn't have what it takes to walk in my shoes. I'm his one and only, even if he's being manipulated by her conniving ass. No one can ever take my place, ever.*

"I spoke to Fatima. She's trying to hang in there. Losing her baby really broke her heart and she needs all the support she can get. I don't want to lose you, Taraine. I need you to come back to us. We all want that!" Debra said as she began to cry.

"Mamo, you crying?" Raine' asked.

"No, baby. Grandma is okay," Deb said.

*I wish I was up and focused enough to see this. I've never seen my mother shed a tear; she was always the strong one in the family. I have to find my way back to you; this is too much and I'm not ready to leave ya'll yet. My heart hurts for Fatima and I know she needs me.*

"Your girls are getting big. Nicera will be starting school this year and I'm quite sure she wants her mommy and daddy to take her on her very first day. The girls helped me pick out this beautiful charm for you. It's a charm in the shape of a heart with a cross on the back. I put a picture of the girls on the inside; this is their good luck charm for you. They want their mommy back. LaQuan wants his wife back and I want my beautiful, but stubborn, daughter back. LaQuan will be here later on. He had to go talk to the investigators to see if they're getting any closer to finding the suspect," Debrah said as she wiped her eyes.

*Well, they need to search in the backyard because that's where that bitch is. You guys are so busy trying to find this so-called man when it's really a woman. This bitch is around my girls smiling in their faces playing mommy. I'm their fucking mother, me and only me!*

"Well, I'm going to take the girls home now, but I will be back tomorrow. Maybe I will catch up with one of your doctors to see what's going on with you. Maybe when I come here tomorrow I will be able to look into your beautiful brown eyes. I miss you so much. I need my friend and I need my daughter, so please find the strength to fight, please. I love you and I will see you tomorrow," Debra said.

As my mother left with the kids, I heard her talking to someone, but couldn't quite hear who it was.

"Hey girl, I'm back. I'm going to fix your face up again and I brought you a different wig," Kelly said as she pulled another wig out of her bag. "This one has highlights. I was going to put some eyelashes on you, but I don't want to glue your eyes shut by accident. I know one thing, whenever you decide to come back to us, you'll be looking fierce, bitch. I'm going to give you the smokey eyes today, and when LaQuan sees you, girl. Um....um....um," she said, shaking her head.

"So, let me tell you what's been going on. I really think I'm starting to lose my mind. I came out of my house and walked to my car and who you think was lurking behind the fucking tree? Yeah, you know it, Keith's dumb ass. That motherfucker is pushing me to the limit. First, he takes my kids and now he's being a fucking creep. That motherfucker will never get to smell my panties, let alone my goods. I get unknown calls to my house and my cell phone. That was the fucking point of me moving as far as I could because I was trying to get away from his ass. When the kids come with me for the weekend, they tell me he questions them. 'Who was at your mother's house? What was your mother doing? Who was your mother talking to? What did your mother have on?' Now, Taraine, you know that shit is ridiculous. And I'm starting to have nightmares about his ass. I'm afraid to be in my own home alone and I'm afraid to go outside. I'm thinking about going to get a permit for a gun. I'm not going to live in fear. All I want is my children back and I'm willing to do whatever it takes to make that happen. You know we are fighters; you're in here fighting for your life. You got that will and that drive you just didn't give up and die. You are my inspiration for real, girl, and I love and respect you so much. You have been through so much and you're letting these motherfuckers know it ain't over until God says it's over," Kelly said.

"I remember how hurt you were when you couldn't find LaQuan. Then you found out you were pregnant. It was such a sweet and sour time for you, but you found a way to keep going. You made the choice to keep Raine', even though you thought LaQuan may have been dead, but something deep inside of you let you know he was still alive. I adore the type of relationship you guys have. He loves you so much and he is a genuine gentleman. I love him and I'm glad you found each other," Kelly said, rubbing Taraine's cheek.

*I'm glad I found him, too, Kelly. But I think I'm losing him. I don't hear him talking to me or singing to me the way he use to. She tried to take my life and now she's trying to take my family. I feel like I lost him, Kelly. Because I'm here and I can't fight for him. He said he would always be here for me and now he's turned his fucking back on me. He fell out of love with me for some crazy ass chick. She's crazy, Kelly, and he just can't see it because she is there comforting him and making love to him. She could never love him the way I did. I can't wait until he finds out she's the one who put me here. Do you think I should forgive him for this? Do you think I could ever love him the way I use to? I can answer that my damn self, Kelly. Yes, I would forgive him because I love him with all my heart and I know he loves me. He's just in a bad place mentally. I wish you could talk to him, Kelly; you guys have a good relationship. Tell him I am fighting for us and I will find my way back to him. Please, Kelly. Help me – help us.*

"Oh, diva, you are looking fabulous lying here. I can't wait for cuzzo to see you, he is going to fall in love with you all over again. True love never dies. That's what you always told me. You and LaQuan have definitely taught me that. I never thought I would have had that with Keith. He was too controlling and so was I. That's why we bumped heads all the damn time. He creeps me out, and it's getting worse. I brought some mace, but that shit don't work on gorillas. That's why I need to go ahead and get this gun permit. You know the fucking police are against me, so you know they're not going to protect my ass anyway. I have to protect my damn self. He is trying to manipulate the kids and he has them thinking I don't want them to be in my life. That's some bullshit. You know I love my kids to death. I loved them so much I was just going to give in and get back with him just for the sake of my kids. How could I give in and go back to a user, an abuser, and a manipulator? He started calling my job and harassing my coworkers. He even cursed out my supervisor. Why couldn't this judge see right through him? I'll tell you why, because she's bias and she feels because he's a man going to court to get full custody of his kids, that makes him special. I told that bitch let me see you live a day in my shoes with this man, just one day judge. That's when she got highly upset with me and threatened to throw my ass out of her courtroom. This motherfucker is Dr. Jekyll and Mr. Hyde, and you know this to be true, Tee. But because I couldn't control my emotions in court, the judge felt disrespected by me. Fuck that bitch! And please believe me when I tell you I'm going to fight for my children until the day I die," Kelly said angrily.

*I know you will fight for your babies, Kelly, but please don't go out there and do anything crazy. He is not worth it, and your children need their mom. Trust me, they need you. I would give anything to have the opportunity to wrap my arms around my girls and my husband. Please stay away from Keith. I think you should go get you an order of protection. The next time you see that motherfucker behind a tree, call the fucking cops. Please, just call the cops.*

"I'm so fucking angry, Taraine. I know if you were able to respond to me, you would tell me exactly what I need to hear. I am so stressed out and I really need my girls, but everybody is going through their own situations and I don't want to put my drama on anybody else. I will be back tomorrow to redo your makeup. Maybe I will bring a couple of wigs for you to try on. I should go ask my stylist to come and size you up for a lace front wig. You think that's over doing it? Yeah, I think so. We'll just stick to the regular wigs. I'll see you tomorrow and I promise I won't come to complain, but you need to come back before I fall off the deep end. Love you forever!" Kelly said as she left the room.

# My Angel

## Fatima

"Babe, I can't allow you to lay here like this. You are really scaring me, babe. Please tell me what I can do for you to make you feel better," Khalief said.

"There is absolutely nothing you can do for me. Oh wait! Can you bring me my baby back?" Fatima asked.

"If I could I would, Fatima. And she was *our* baby. I hurt just like you do."

"I doubt that very much. Did you know what morning sickness felt like? Did you know how it felt to have something precious growing inside of you and then, all of a sudden, it's not there any-more? Why didn't I go to the emergency room when I started having those sharp pains? I should have gone with my instinct, but I ignored it, and it caused me to lose my baby. I killed my baby and you will never feel the pain or guilt I feel, Khalief. She's gone because of me. Don't you understand that?" I asked as I cried uncontrollably with my face in my hands. "Do you know how it feels to lay on that table, feel that cold gel on your belly, and then hear some nurse tell you there's no heartbeat? My baby is gone. She slipped away right before my eyes. She's gone, Khalief – gone, gone, gone. Oh God, my baby is gone and I feel so empty and lost. I killed her; it's my fault and I don't deserve you," I said, sitting up in bed.

"You can't blame yourself for the loss of our baby, and yes, I hurt too. I don't know what it feels like to carry a baby. You're right, but I do know I was happy and I was in love with the thought of being a father. I was curious about how she would look. Would she be as beautiful as her mother and have your beautiful brown eyes and perky lips, or would she look like her daddy? So believe me when I tell you, Fatima. I'm hurting and it kills me to watch you like this. I love you and we need to support one another," Khalief said, grabbing Fatima's hand.

"Well, guess what, Khalief?" I said as I pulled my hand away. "I don't want your support and I don't deserve it. As a matter of fact, I don't deserve you. You should leave."

"You can forget about that. If you think I'm leaving you or leaving us, you're wrong. You got me confused with some other heartless man."

"Well, if you won't leave, then I will," I said as I quickly got up off the bed and made my way towards the door.

He grabbed me and wrapped his arms around me, hugging me tightly. I could feel his heart beating against mine.

"I can't take this, baby. I know I should be strong, but I don't know how to be. My first pregnancy... I was so happy and excited and all that is over."

"Get dressed and come with me. I want to show you something," Khalief said.

"No, I don't feel like going outside, Khalief. I look terrible, I feel terrible and I don't want anyone to see me like this."

"Please baby, trust me; it will be all right. Just trust me," he said, extending his hand out to me.

I brushed my hair back in a clip and threw on some sweats. We got into his car and he drove us to a park near the Brooklyn Bridge. It wasn't a big park, but it was beautiful with plenty of flowers and huge trees. It was beautiful. You could feel the peace and calm in the air.

He told me to pick a tree. I saw a baby tree that was just beginning to sprout; spring was definitely in the air. We walked toward the tree and he began digging a little hole. Then he pulled out his picture from the sonogram which only showed the sac. He placed it in the hole and he also placed a pink ribbon that said Angel on it. We got on our knees as we held hands and prayed silently. I began shaking and Khalief wrapped his arms around me and held me tight.

"It's okay, babe. She's in a better place and you know your grandmother is spoiling her as we kneel here and pray. She wouldn't want you to live like this. When it's our time, HE will bless us with a baby, but until then, we need to let Angel rest in peace and just know she will always be with us. She is our hearts," Khalief whispered.

I took off the charm he brought me and I placed it in the hole with the picture.

"You will always be in my heart, my Angel, until we meet again. Love you always and forever," I said as the tears rolled down my cheeks.

Khalief covered the hole with dirt and place some flowers he pulled from the garden on it.

"We will never forget you, baby. You will always be in our hearts," he said.

He helped me up from the ground and held me tight.

"I love you, Fatima; it doesn't end here for us. I still want to get married and work on having another baby. We will be fine, but I need you to focus and know that things happen for a reason and this was not your fault. I don't want you to hide your pain. I just want you to accept the loss. We are just right for one another and I'm never going to let you go. We are going to heal, rebuild, and focus on getting married," he said as he wiped my tears away.

"You're right, Khalief. I know I said I was okay, even though I wasn't. To be honest with you, I'm still not okay. Doing this memorial here has eased my heart just a little. You bringing me out here made me realize why I fell in love with you. I'm so sorry if I hurt you when I tried to push you away. When I'm feeling down or missing my baby, I will come back here to have a moment with her, my Angel Boo, *our* Angel Boo," I said, kissing Khalief gently on the lips.

Khalief knew how much I love Five Guys restaurant, so he stopped there so I could get my hamburger with the works; jalapenos, mushrooms, Swiss cheese, Mozzarella cheese and so much more. When I got home, I just wanted to dig into that hamburger, but my appetite still hadn't returned. I finally decided to listen to my voicemail and realized Monica had called more times than usual, which told me something was up. I felt I was now able to have a conversation about my loss without completely breaking down so I called her back.

"Hey, Monica. What's up, chica?"

"I'm good. Just calling to check on my girl. I knew you needed space, but you know me. I was going to call until I reached you," Monica said.

"I'm doing a little better; trying to heal mentally and physically. I was a complete wreck this morning, but thank God for Khalief. He's doing his best because you know how I can get."

"Yes, I do, but to be honest with you, Fatima. It's to be expected. People take death differently and you guys have to grieve in your own way. Just know that I'm here for you. Did you get the Cornelia's I sent you?" Monica asked.

"Yes, they are beautiful. I love them. Thank you. I just don't understand, Monica. Why did this happen to me?"

"I don't know, Fatima, but everything happens for a reason and maybe it just wasn't your time."

"I hear people saying that shit all the time and I hate it. *Everything happens for a reason.* What was the damn reason? That's all I would like to know. What was the reason?" I asked angrily.

"I can't answer that; only God knows. The one thing I do know for sure is if you and Khalief are planning on trying to conceive again, you need to find a way to relieve all that stress. Focus on the positive things going on in your life right now. Did you guys come up with a wedding date?" Monica asked.

"Actually, we didn't. I was trying to see what was going to happen with Taraine. I don't want to do anything without my girls," I said.

"How is she doing?" Monica asked.

"I haven't been up there in a couple of day." I said.

"I will be up there in the next two weeks. I'm hoping and praying she'll be up by then," Monica said.

"What's up with your girl, Dee?" I asked.

"Girl, I think you were right. Something is definitely up with her. One minute she's cool, and the next minute, she's looking weird and acting crazy. I wonder if this chick is bipolar," Monica said.

"Oh, now you think she's bipolar, but when I was telling you something is up with her, you didn't want to hear me. It was just something about her that rubbed me the wrong way. I still can't figure it out, but I know she's got some issues and you need to be very careful around her."

"I'm not stupid. I've been keeping my distance when it comes to her, but I have to keep my eye on her crazy ass. She's always talking about her man, but I never see him or ever heard her holding a conversation with him over the phone. I went to her house and she looked discombobulated and erratic. You know I got out of there fast, but not before I tried to check out some shit she had lying around. I met up with her the next day and she still seemed far gone. Ever since then, I kept away from her ass. Even at work, I do my best to keep my distance. If that bitch comes at me on some crazy shit, I'm fucking her ass up. You kept telling me something was wrong with the chick, but you know how you are and at times. I can be very naïve," Monica said.

"Well, you know if you need me to come down there, I will. I am full of rage right now and I need somewhere or someone to let it all out on."

"I know you will, girl, but I need you to take care of yourself and heal your mind and body. I will definitely be up there to check on my girls soon. Have you heard from Kelly?"

"No, I haven't heard from her. She doesn't know I had a miscarriage or anything. I don't know what's up with her, but you know how she is with us. Monica, I never knew I could feel pain like this and you know I'm tough as hell. My heart hurts and I'm just aching all over. It's not right... this shit is just not right. I've had plenty of dreams about my baby since having the miscarriage. She looks just like my grandmother, hazel eyes and all. I had another dream, and in this dream, my grandmother was sitting in a rocking chair holding her, and my grandmother was waving bye to me," I said as my heart began to race.

"Girl, you know that's your grandmother Sis, and she's letting you know in some subliminal way your baby is okay. You know your grandmother loved everybody and everyone loved her just as much. Sis will give your baby all the love and attention she needs," Monica said.

"Yes, I know my grandmother is taking care of her. I'm still trying to understand why. Although, I know I will never get the answer to that. I call her Angel Boo. I'm never going to forget the experienced I had during my pregnancy. Even if it was only for a little while, I was still overjoyed by it all. I was in love with the thought of carrying a baby inside of me for nine whole months. I'm so thankful for Khalief, Slim. He tries his best to keep me grounded and I know he was sent into my life for a reason. I tried to push him away, but he let me know he wasn't going anywhere. He is the one, Slim, and I'm ready to accept that." I started crying again.

"I miss my girls so much. You're gone, who know what Kelly's ass is up too and as for Tae, her ass is probably in some kind of love triangle, as usual, and Taraine is getting her beauty sleep. I think all that has gone on in the past year has humbled me and has changed my attitude about life. Well, Slim, I just wanted to let you know I love you, I miss you, and if you need me, don't hesitate to call; especially if that bipolar bitch tries to bring any drama your way."

"I hear you, but like I told you, I got this. She ain't that mother-fucking crazy. As they say you have to keep your enemies close. She's not my enemy, but she got some issues, so I have to watch her more closely. I'm glad I didn't invite her ass into my bedroom. I don't know what the fuck I was thinking." Monica frowned and shook her head.

"That's why I told you to think long and hard about that one. There's other ways for you and Ron to get some excitement going on in the bedroom. Buy some toys, some whips and chains." I laughed.

"Now, I ain't buying no whips and chains, but you're right. There's other ways to get it going in the bedroom. He's just so stiff and afraid to try new shit. I wish he would just relax, let go, and take charge, but we'll see.

Who the fuck is ringing my bell this time of night?" Monica said.

"It's probably the psycho!" I said, laughing.

"It better not be. What would she be ringing my bell this late at night for? Hold on let me look through the side window," Monica said as she tiptoed to her window. "Girl, you're right; it is her, but she looks normal right now," Monica said.

"Of course she does. When you're bipolar you can switch them lights off and on at any time. If you know like I know, you better leave her psychotic ass out there. Is Ron home?" I asked.

"Yes, he's upstairs with the boys. I'm going to see what this chick wants."

"Okay, but you better keep your eyes on her at all times. I'm telling you, Monica. Don't turn your back on that bitch."

"I won't, talk to you later," Monica said.

# Three's A Crowd

## Shantae

"What's up, Kandi? How long are you going to act up?" I said on Kandi's voicemail. "It's been a minute and nothing has changed. If we're going to carry on like this we might as well end this. I have been calling you for the past couple of weeks apologizing to you and you continuously ignore my calls and my text. If you don't want to be bothered, do us both a favor and come get your shit. It's obvious that you have moved on, so let's not prolong this any longer."

"If she don't contact me after today, I'm going to pack up all her shit and take it to her my damn self," I said, looking in the refrigerator and then slammed the door.

Suddenly, my phone rang.

*Yeah, I figured she would call after that last message,* I thought as I looked at my cell phone, but then I realized it was Deshawn calling.

"Hey, baby. What's up? I'm sorry you haven't heard from me. This has been a very busy week. Sure, I would love to go to the Knicks game. Okay, I'll be ready at 5. See you then," I said.

I wasn't really a Knicks fan, but he offered, and I was going. *I'm not going to sit around and wait for that chick to come to her senses. I don't care how sexy she is,* I thought to myself as I looked in my closet for something to wear.

"What the hell do you wear to a basketball game?" I said to myself as I continued to look through my closet.

"This will do," I said as I pulled out a velour sweat suit. I would be comfortable and still look good at the same time.

Deshawn arrived right on time, and of course, I wasn't ready.

"Give me five more minutes, please."

That five minutes turned into fifteen minutes. I had to make sure the hair and face was flawless. I walked out my door, got into the car, and gave him a juicy kiss.

"You look nice, baby. And you smell good, too," Deshawn said.

"Thank you. Sorry for making you wait, but I can't go to the Garden looking like I threw on anything," I said, smiling and winking at him.

"That's okay, we have time. The game starts at 7:30, but you know how traffic is in the City."

"Yeah, you're right, but don't I look good? I'm reppin' us to the fullest, right?" I said.

"Yes, you're looking real good. You can make it up to me after the game," he said.

"I got you. Trust me, I got you. I hope you can handle what's coming your way."

"I can handle anything you try to hit me with. I'm all for the challenge."

"So, let me ask you this. How did you really feel the night we had the threesome?" I asked. "You know what they say – a threesome is every man's fantasy, and nowadays, it's a lot of women's fantasy as well. Most even prefer excluding the man," I said, laughing.

"I enjoyed it. I'm not going to lie. Do I need to continue having threesomes? Not really. I've experienced it, I loved it, and now I can check it off as something I wanted to do in my lifetime."

"Was that a fantasy of yours, to have a threesome, but with two other women?" he asked.

"Yes, it was. I loved every minute of it."

He looked at me with his eyes wide open as if he was shocked by my answer.

"Why are you looking at me like that? Don't act like you wouldn't enjoy watching three women getting it on," I said.

"Of course I would enjoy it. Damn, Shantae, you're so blunt with your shit."

"You know you enjoyed that night. Do you think you would want to try it again?"

"No, not really. I'm trying to get to know you a little better one-on-one without any interruptions," he said.

"That sounds good to me. We'll see what happens," I said, winking at him. "So who's playing against the Knicks tonight?"

"They're playing against the Heat."

"Miami Heat! Get the fuck out of here. My cousin would go crazy if she knew I was going to watch the Heat play. She loves herself some Dwayne Wade. Let her tell it, that's her second husband," I said laughing.

"I had two extra tickets, too. If she could get there by 7 she can have the tickets," Deshawn said.

"Wow, that's so generous of you. I wish she could meet us down there as well, but unfortunately, she's in a coma."

"Sorry to hear that, baby. How did that happen?" Deshawn asked.

"Some bitch ass broke into her apartment shot her in the chest and in the head. That motherfucker didn't even rob her for anything. It's so scary and it's so sad that this has happened to her. I can't even imagine what was on her mind when the bastard held her life in his hand. How can someone feel the need to pull the trigger and decided to take her life? Little does he know, my girl survived. She may be in coma, but there's still hope. She has been through so much in her life, and in the end, she was always the one standing. One thing about my girl Tee, is that she is a survivor. Even after everything she's been through she's holding on for dear life. We all just say she's taking a much needed vacation, and she will come back to us when she's ready," Shantae said solemnly.

"Did they catch him?"

"No, it seems like everything is moving in slow motion when it comes to her case, but her husband stays on their asses. If LaQuan catches that motherfucker before the detectives, it's a done deal. I don't want to see LaQuan go to jail for defending his wife, but one thing I know about LaQuan is he will do any and everything for his wife. You know how these motherfucking cops work; you have to stay on them or they will get too relaxed and the file will be stuck in the corner collecting dust. Tonight, I'm going to rep for my cousin. And I'm so sorry I have to say this to you, but fuck the Knicks. Let's go, Heat," I said as I looked at him and started laughing.

"Oh no. Heat fans are not allowed to ride in the Benzo. Let me pull over and let you out."

"Pull over then, baby, because tonight I'm going hard for my girl. Let's go, Heat! And the way the Knicks been playing, I'm quite sure I won't be the only one rooting for them," I said as I looked at Deshawn and winked.

*****

Madison Square Garden was huge. We had courtside seats, too. I was excited. There were a lot of stars in attendance. "Where is Spike Lee? Because I'm about to piss him the hell off once I start yelling, 'let's go, Heat!' This is kind of cool. I would love to go to a women's basketball game, too."

*Damn, it's such a great feeling when you're enticed by both men and women. Now, let me see why Taraine is so star struck by this so-called Mr. D. Wade,* I thought as the game was getting ready to start.

The game was exciting. Both teams were doing their thing, but the Heat was up by 8. D. Wade and Lebron definitely seemed to know each other's next move. They were entertaining on the court and I was enjoying myself far more than I expected. Deshawn was a die-hard Knick fan and I had to be the die-hard Heat fan for Taraine. During halftime we got the chance to chop it up a little. I was starting to feel him more and more. I wanted to see where this was going.

"Are you enjoying yourself?"

"Hell yeah. I'm actually having a great time. It's crazy in here. The crowd is so energizing it's giving me goose bumps. I feel like I'm at a Jay-Z concert and he just brought an unexpected guest on stage and the crowd starts going crazy. I can really get into this. Thank you for inviting me. You opened me up to something new besides the club scene."

"You don't have to thank me, sweetheart; this is what I do. I aim to please!" DeShawn said with a smile.

"I hear you talking. I hope you're still planning on pleasing me after this ass whopping the Knicks are about to receive because it looks like the Heat are on fire tonight. When they come back out I am going to take some pictures, then I'm going to print them and put them in Taraine's room," I said as I began to stare at the thought of Taraine seeing D. Wade's picture on her dresser.

"I always wondered what actually happens to a person while they're in a coma," Deshawn said.

"I always wondered the same thing, Deshawn. Whenever I go to see her, I talk to her as if she can hear what I'm saying. Even though she can't respond to me, I still get this feeling she hears me. I always feel like she's saying, 'Tae, you know you were wrong for that. Tae, that's fucked up, or bitch, you're so nasty.' So even though she's far away mentally, I still love the fact that I can see her and go talk to her when I need to. We are cousins, but we grew up like sisters. We would do everything together. Maybe one day you can come up to the hospital with me. I can guarantee you will feel the love in the room," I said as my eyes began to fill with tears.

"I would love to go with you to the hospital. Just let me know when and I'm there. I'm sorry this unfortunate tragedy happened to her. I'm quite sure she knows how much you love her. I'll give you just one pass tonight, you can rep for the Heat on your cousin's behalf," Deshawn smiled.

"So, does this mean you're joining me, that you are turning your back on the Knicks for tonight?"

"HELL NO! I'm a Knickerbocker for life. Let's make a bet."

"What kind of bet?"

"If the Knicks win, you have to come home with me tonight."

"And if they don't win, what's in it for me?"

"If they don't win you have to come home with me tonight," Deshawn said, laughing.

"What kind of bet is that?" I asked. "You win either way you look at it."

"That's right!"

"That's a bet, but if the Heat wins, I want breakfast in bed, and I want you to serve me with nothing but an apron on."

"I don't own an apron," Dashawn replied.

"Well, you better hope the Knicks win, because if they don't, I want you in an apron. We are in the City; I'm quite sure you will find an apron somewhere."

"Okay, bet," he agreed as he kissed me on my cheek. "It's on."

The second half of the game began and it was just as exciting as the first half. I was screaming so much, I began to lose my voice.

The Heat won just like I thought. D. Wade did his thing and I am officially a fan.

"Yeah, you won this one, but that was just by luck," Deshawn said.

"A win is a win at the end of the day. Now, let's see what I want for breakfast. I want some pancakes, scrambled eggs with cheese, and Kabaska beef sausages," I said as I nudged him gently across his cheek.

"I got you, baby. I always pay my debt. I'm good for it, trust me. I got you. So, did you have fun?"

"Yes, I had more fun than I actually expected. Like I said earlier, I appreciate you thinking of me. You could have taken one of your friends, but you chose me. You get major points for that."

His phone rang. He looked at me and then put it back in his pocket.

We walked around 34th Street looking for tourist shops. Even though I'd been living in NYC all my life, I was feeling like a tourist my damn self. I always drove through 34th, but I never took the time to just walk through the streets at night. It was so beautiful. The weather was beautiful, the sky was clear, and the stars were twinkling. It was unforgettable, and something so different than what I'd usually be doing. I hadn't felt that exhilarated in a very long time. We happen to find an apron that said 'Let's Eat in the City'. We laughed when we saw it. I loved it and he purchased it.

"There's going to be a lot more than eating in the City going on tonight."

"You're so right about that," he replied, laughing.

His phone rang again and he did the same thing – looked at the phone and placed it back in his pocket.

"You can answer your phone. It seems like someone is really trying to reach you."

"Nah, they can wait. I'm spending time with Ms. 'I'm Riding With the Heat'," Deshawn said, laughing.

I started laughing with him. He was so irresistible and I enjoyed being with him.

"Are you a sore loser?" I asked jokingly.

"Yes, I am, but if losing to you is wrong, I don't want to be right."

"You are so corny. You will have to come harder than that if you want to hang with me," I said.

We decided to stop at Cold Stone. They had the best ice cream ever. Their Brownie double scoop with all the works was my favorite. Dashawn said he wasn't really into ice cream, but I fed him some of mine, and after one taste, we were making a U-turn so he could get his own. We took a couple of pictures together and then we made our way back to his car.

"I'm so tired. When we get back to your place, all I want to do is take a hot shower and call it a night," I said.

"I'm cool with that," Deshawn said.

*Yeah right. He knows once I get out that shower all wet and glistening, he is not going to allow me to go to sleep,* I thought.

He turned the radio on and Funkmaster Flex was playing old school R&B. One of my old school songs was playing so I had to turn it up.

*'Let me lay it on the line*
*I got a little freakiness inside*
*And you know that the man*
*Has got to deal with it*
*I don't care what they say*
*I'm not about to pay nobody's way*
*'Cause it's all about the dog in me*
*I want to freak in the morning*
*A freak in the evening just like me*
*I need a roughneck brother*
*That can satisfy me just for me*
*If you are that kind of man*
*'cuz i'm that kind of girl*
*I got a freaky secret,everybody sing*
*'cause we don't give a damn about a thing…'*

I went on and on. "This use to be my shit, Shawn. And I use to be in love with Adina Howard. All I needed was one hour with her," I said as I did my two step in my seat.

Then they started playing Michael Jackson's "Rock With You" which was a classic. Michael's music always does something to the soul. We were jamming.

I start singing…

*I wanna rock with you*
Then he joined in…
*All night*
*Dance you into the*
*Sunlight*
*I wanna rock with you*
*Rock the night away*

Then my favorite song of all time came on. I knew once I heard this song he was definitely going to get it tonight.

"Red Light Special" by TLC.

*'Take a good look at it. Look at it now. Might be the last time you'll have a go round. I'll let you touch it if you like to go down. I'll let you go further if you take the southern route. Don't go too fast, don't go too slow you got to let your body flow. I like em' attentive and I like them in control.'*

I turned towards him and started singing.

*'Baby it's yours. If you want it tonight. I'll give you the red light special all through the night. Baby it's yours. If you want it tonight. Come through my doors take off my clothes and turn on the RED LIGHT.'*

He was blushing and he knew it was about to be on. I was definitely in the mood at this point.

As soon as we walked through the door, the fireworks began. We were going at it hard and heavy. And, once again, his cell phone went off.

*Damn, someone is really trying to talk to him, but whoever it is will not touch bases with him tonight because he is all mine,* I thought.

We walked down his hallway stripping each other's clothes off. By the time we reached the bathroom, we were completely naked and we jumped into the shower. We kissed passionately as the water washed over our bodies.

He washed me and I washed him. He turned me around, bent me over, and gently slid his prize possession inside of me. He wasn't too gentle and he wasn't too rough; it was just right. He had me rethinking this bisexual thing, but I just couldn't help it. I was greedy and I wanted it all. I felt I deserved it all, too.

The shower was great, but we had to be careful about the 'slippery when wet' situation. *One thing I know for sure is this man knows how to please me and I love, love, love it,* I thought.

We got out of the shower and he gave me one of his tee shirts and a pair of boy shorts. I tossed the boy shorts on the chair next to the bed. *Makes no sense to put them on just to turn around and take them off,* I thought.

"Thanks for the tee shirt and boxers, hun, but the cat has to breathe," I said.

He looked at me and started laughing.

"Shantae, you are too much. I enjoy being around you. Are you hungry?"

"No, I'm good, but I could go for some popcorn and a movie."

"Don't have any popcorn. Sorry, baby. How about a drink? I got Peach Ciroc, Svedka, and Moscato Red."

*I'm not really a drinker but I know it will relax me,* I thought.

"I'll have some Moscato, please. Deshawn, don't worry about the movie. Just put some music on and see where it takes us."

I know exactly where it would take us, I thought as I watched him poor me a glass of Moscato.

He sat next to me and we toast to a beautiful night. Then we started tongue-locking. The music was flowing just right and the tee shirt I had on was now off. All of a sudden, the doorbell rang.

"Are you expecting company?"

"No, so let's just ignore them. They will go away."

So we did just that, ignored their ass. I got on top and straddled him. Then the doorbell rang again. They must have heard the music playing and the talking going on between the kissing and rubbing.

"I think you better see who that is or we are never going to enjoy the rest of the night."

So I got up off him, put his tee shirt back on, and walked to the door right behind him. I wanted whoever was at the door to see we were about to get it in and that they were disturbing us.

He opened the door and I heard a voice, but I couldn't see who it was.

"Hey, What's up?" he asked.

When I came from standing behind him, I saw Kandi standing there in a trench coat.

"What the fuck are you doing here?" I asked.

"I could ask you the same damn thing," Kandi said.

"It's obvious what I'm doing here. I was just about to get it on with this chocolate sundae with nuts that's standing before my eyes," I said.

"Oh really, Tae? Are you serious right now?" Kandi asked.

"Hell fucking yeah," I said.

"Oh that's how you doing shit, Shawn?" Kandi asked.

"What do you mean?" he asked with the 'I'm shocked but busted' look on his face.

"You heard exactly what I just asked you, Shawn. I was just here fucking you the other night and now you're in here fucking Tae?" Kandi said furiously.

"I don't owe you no explanation, you're not my girl," Deshawn said.

"Well, what explanation do you have for me?" I asked.

"I really don't have no explanation for you either, Shantae. We already talked and you know I was on some dating shit."

"I understand that, but the both of us had a threesome with you and then you turn around and fuck both of us separately? That's some real slick shit," I said.

Kandi looked pissed off as she slid her way into the apartment and sat on his couch.

"It looks like you guys were really about to get it in," Kandi said.

"Yes we were! We were actually on round two until we were rudely interrupted," Deshawn replied.

"Interrupted? Really, Shawn?" Kandi asked.

"Yes, really!" he responded back quickly.

"So, this is the reason why you haven't answered my phone calls or texts. You have been fucking around with Deshawn, as I suspected, right?" I asked.

"No, Tae, you got it all twisted. I was not fucking him like I told you at the hospital, but you found it so rewarding to embarrass me. You had no trust or faith in me, so why should I give a fuck about your feelings?" Kandi said.

"Kandi, I tried to apologize to you over and over again and you continuously gave me your ass to kiss. I felt like you were lying to me, so I needed to do my own investigation. Which meant connecting with the main culprit Deshawn," I said.

Deshawn looked confused and he didn't know what the fuck was going on.

"Wait a minute. Why are you guys getting into it over who had sex with me? We all had sex with each other, then one-on-one at some point. I am not tied to either one of you. I was just living and having fun. I don't know what happened to end you guy's relationship and I really don't care. I told both of ya'll I wasn't with the drama. That's why I dated instead of committing myself to a platonic relationship," Deshawn said.

I couldn't really say much because even though I had been in a relationship with Kandi for a while, after I started hanging with DeShawn, I grew to like him. He made me comfortable, he pleased me, and he opened me up to a lot of shit.

*I didn't want anybody's feelings to get hurt, but I tried my best with Kandi and she pushed me away, so fuck it. I did me,* I thought to myself as they argued back and forth.

"I should have figured this out because when I was pushing up on you at the restaurant you blew me off. Then, after that little session, I text and called you and still nothing. Then, all a sudden, out of the blue, you hit me up and said you wanted to see me. This shit is crazy," he said and started laughing.

"Is it really crazy, Shawn? Well tell me how crazy you think this is?" Kandi asked, glaring at him. She stood up and opened her trench coat to reveal all of her nakedness.

"Is it really crazy, Shawn?" Kandi asked again.

"You look good, Kandi. Don't get me wrong, but I already have company," he said, closing Kandi's coat.

"You can add another person to your party," Kandi said.

"Nah, baby. This one is private and this right here is uncalled for. Were you drinking or something? How are you just going to invite yourself to someone's house? Why did you think that was okay?" he asked.

"I called you like four timed and I left you a message telling you I was on my way and that I had a surprise for you," Kandi said.

"I understand that, but you didn't get a response from me. I was already engaging in the plans I had for the night. I was already with the person I wanted to be with."

"So, you're the one who kept blowing up his phone? You were really trying to get him, huh, Kandi?" I said.

"Check this out, Kandi. Another threesome would be great right about now. I would love to indulge in that once more, but to be honest with you, for some reason, I'm not interested in doing that with you guys anymore. You're sexy as hell, but I'm not feeling you like that. The sex was good, but you're not the chick I want to be with."

"You didn't say that when you was fucking me," Kandi said.

"You're right. I didn't say that. Just because we fucked don't mean I have to be all into you. Don't let your beauty make you feel you can't be rejected because, as of right now, I'm letting you know I don't want you. Don't forget you were the one calling me and not the other way around," Deshawn said.

"You are so right about that, but prior to me calling you, you were the one chasing me," Kandi said.

"Yes, I was, baby girl, and you ignored me every single time. One day you decided to call me, you wanted to fuck, and I'm a man, so I gave you what you wanted. Don't take it personal. I just found someone I'm more attracted to and it goes way beyond her looks."

"But that's my girl," Kandi said.

"Oh, now I'm yours. I couldn't reach you for how long? I apologized for how I carried on, but it's clear to me you had other intentions. Deshawn is right, we did connect," I said as I looked at him.

"I'm sorry if you got caught in the middle of the bullshit, Deshawn. Was I using you? Honestly, yes, I was in the beginning, but after our first time alone, I realized there was something about you. Even though I shouldn't be, I am a little hurt by all of this. At the end of the day, you're a man – a single man – and you were just doing you. As for you and I, Kandi, we are done. I was going to bring your shit to your house anyway, so let me get the fuck out of here and do what I intended on doing anyway. Which was to leave your stuck-up Ms. Sweet and Quiet ass alone," I said.

As I started walking to his bedroom to get dressed, he pulled me back.

"Please don't leave, Shantae. I want you. You're the one I want," Deshawn said.

"Oh, you want her, motherfucker?" Kandi asked.

"Yes, I do. Shantae and I click. I love her style, she beautiful, charismatic, and open-minded. On top of that, we get along very well," Deshawn said, grabbing Shatae's hand.

"I'm sorry once again, but I'm really feeling you. You know deep inside there's something between us. It seems like we all played a game with one another. I don't want to be with Kandi. I don't really know what's happening between the both of you, but I want you, not her," he said.

For the first time in a long time, I found myself getting emotional. I haven't felt all crazy in love in a while. I still loved women. I'm not so sure about Kandi, but there was just something stronger brewing between Deshawn and me. What started out as me doing some detective work turned into something more personal. I looked at him and listened to what he had to say, and for some reason, I believed him. I believed he was feeling me just as much as I was feeling him.

He walked towards the door, opened it, and asked Kandi to leave. She turned to look at me, then she turned around and left.

"Fuck both of ya'll. Ya'll are both right for each other," Kandi said as she walked out of the apartment.

Deshawn closed the door behind her. He walked over to me, grabbed me by my hand, and walked me over to the couch. He wrapped his arm around me and we sat there silently.

Everything that just occurred had really begun to sink in.

He tilted my face in his direction.

"Shantae, what I expressed to Kandi was real, and if you're willing to give us a try, I'm ready for that. I can do the monogamy thing. Do you think you can?"

"There's so much going through my mind right now, Deshawn, but I'm open to it and I'm willing to give us a try. And yes, I can do the monogamy thing if I'm really feeling that connection."

"So, let's make this official."

"Okay, it's definitely official, baby. I just hope you're worth it," I said as I looked at him with a straight face.

"Oh, I'm worth it, believe me. I'm worth it," he said with a smile on his face.

He grabbed my hand and pulled me towards him. I rested my head on his chest and smiled at the feeling of giving this relationship a try, but I was still in shock.

What the fuck just happened? I wasn't really sure. I don't know what tomorrow may bring, but I know I am able and willing to give it a go. I could hear Taraine's voice in my head saying, 'Here you go again, bitch, with these games. You don't know who you want, but then again, you think you're God's gift to the human species.'

You're damn right, but for right now, I have diverted to the male species. Damn, I need to go to the hospital to tell Taraine about this shit here. I'm about to blow minds with this one, I thought as I closed my eyes and relished in the moment. I was falling in love with a man...or was I?

# Under No Circumstances

## Kelly

"Hello, 911? Yes I need for you to send the cops to my home. I am being stalked by my children's father," I said as I peeped through my window.

"Can you see him?" the operator asked.

"Yes, I can see him standing behind a tree that's directly in front of my house. Please send the cops to have him removed."

"Give me your name and address," the operator said.

"250 Hart Street and my name is Kelly Warner. Please hurry because it looks as if he's walking towards my door."

The operator called it out over the radio.

"Don't go near the door, ma'am; the police are on their way. Please stay on the line until they arrive. Do you still see him?" the operator asked.

"Actually, no. I don't see him anymore."

I decided to go into the kitchen and get a knife and my hammer.

*If this bastard tries to come at me in any way, he's going to wish he never had. I will fight to the death of it,* I thought as I went back to my window to take another look.

"Where are the police?"

Although I didn't see Keith anywhere in sight, I knew he was still lurking around in the area.

"You don't have to look out the window no more. I'm right here," Keith said.

"Are you okay, ma'am?" I heard the operator ask, but I was frightened by the sight of Keith standing right in front of me.

"Shouldn't you be home with the kids? Why are you out here watching my every move? I want you to leave now."

"Please Kel, let me talk to you. Just hear me out. I want you back. I want us to be a family again."

"No, I will never get back with you. You're crazy, you're manipulative, and now you're a stalker. All I want you to do is leave my home. That's all I want from you, Keith."

"I will leave, but I'm taking you with me."

"I'm not going any fucking where with you," I said as I gripped the knife tightly in my hand.

"The kids need you. I need you. So get some of your clothes and let's go," he said aggressively.

"You made me seem like I was an unfit mother in court. You told the judge I neglected my children and you told her I cheated on you. You made up all these lies to make yourself look better. You got what you wanted. Now get the fuck out. The police are on their way, so I would advise you to leave before they get here and lock your ass up for trespassing!" I yelled.

"I am leaving Kel, but I'm not leaving without you," he said as he came walking towards me.

He then reached to grab me by the arm and all I saw was red.

"Get the fuck off me, bastard. You low-down piece of shit."

I tried to pull back and when he bent down to pick me up. I lost it and started jabbing him in the back with the knife. The more I jabbed, the harder he fought to lift me up over his shoulders. It seemed as if he wasn't feeling a thing.

"I hate your motherfucking guts!" I screamed as I continued stabbing him.

Suddenly things went from red to black.

*I love my kids and I would die for them,* I repeated over and over again.

"Hello? Ms. Warner, can you hear me? Ms. Warner…" I heard a voice say continuously

*****

When I opened my eyes, I realized I was in a hospital bed and I was strapped to the bed.

"Hello, Ms. Warner. I'm here to ask you some questions."

"Questions about what?"

"About the incident that occurred in your apartment," he said.

"You tell me what happened because I don't know what you're talking about. Why am I strapped to this fucking bed? Take these straps off of my arms and my legs right now. I demand to know what all of this is about. What the hell is going on? Why do you want to question me?"

"Ma'am, there was an incident in your home between you and a man by the name of Keith. I just need you to tell me what happened so it can be put on record," the officer said.

"Who the fuck is Keith? I don't know no-one by the name of Keith."

"Ma'am, you called 911 and when the police arrived they found you continuously stabbing a man and screaming how you would die for your kids," the officer said.

"I'm sorry, officer. I will tell you again. I don't know anybody by the name of Keith, and furthermore, I don't have any kids. Now can you please remove these straps? What is this shit all about? Why am I strapped to this fucking bed? What the fuck is wrong with ya'll? Why the fuck am I here? I want to go home."

"Thank you for your time, ma'am," he said as he got up from the chair and walked towards the doctor.

"What the fuck do you mean 'thank you for your time'? If you don't take these damn straps off of me, Mr., Mr. please. Why are you doing this to me?"

The more he ignored me, the louder I yelled. The doctor walked back towards my bed.

"Doctor, can you be ever so kind as to take the straps off of my arms and legs?"

"Yes, I will do just that, but I need for you to cooperate with officer Swartz," he said as he turned back to the officer to make sure he said his name correctly.

"Oh, so your down with him too, huh, Doc? All I need is for you or him –I don't give a damn which one of ya'll do it –but somebody needs to let me free. I guess you guys don't know I'm a little seven-thirty. I never fuck with anybody but if you come at me wrong, I will lose my damn mind."

The doctor turned towards the officer and said a couple of words. None of which I could understand as I tried my best to read his lips.

"Oh, I see both of you are trying to take me down. This is my world. You will never take me down in this lifetime."

I continued yelling and breathing hard. The next thing I knew, the doctor was walking towards me with a syringe in his hands.

"Oh, so now you're trying to shut me up, Doc? You can't beat me, Doc. You're nothing but a coward. You and that fake cop," I said, looking directly into the officer's eyes.

I fought hard trying to take the straps off and had no luck. I looked up at the doctor as the tears begin to fill my eyes.

"Why would you do this to me, Doc? I'm a good girl," I said as I felt the liquid from the syringe work its way through my veins. I felt as if I was falling into a deep dream before everything went black.

# Real Love

## Taraine

*You know, God, I love you with every single part of my being. I consider myself to be your number one fan. I just need to know what you are trying to show me. I'm just laying here trying to figure it all out. I'm a fighter, a survivor and I am a woman of tolerance. I mean, really, what is it God? Because I'm lost and I just don't understand what's going on here. I know this is all in your plan, but couldn't we have discussed this amongst each other? Well, I will tell you this, God. I am tired of living in my own mind. I know you have chosen me for a reason which may never be revealed, but is there any way you can give me a little hint? Don't get me wrong, God because I trust you with all my heart, every inch of my body. You are the owner of my entire being and I'm grateful that you chose me. I'm just ready to get out of this shell. But if you want me here for twenty more years, I understand. Besides, do I really have a choice? But hey, if you can find it in your heart to release me back into the world in the physical form, I would really appreciate it. You know how we do. Of course you do, you're the big G.O.D. Did I forget to mention my family and friends need me, and I need them as well? I just wanted to share that with you. I don't want to take up any more of your time. I'll just be here waiting until you decide it's time. Your number one fan…Taraine*

"Hey, beautiful!"

*Wow! It seems like forever since I heard that,* I thought as I heard LaQuan say those magical words to me. Those magical words that would send chills up and down my spine.

"I see Kelly came and gave you another makeover. You are so beautiful, even in your sleep. I miss you so much, and so do the girls. Sometimes Nicera wakes up out of her sleep screaming and calling for her mommy. I try to console her the best way I can, but there's nothing like a mother's love or touch. I wish I could just bring you home and let God take it from there, baby. The medical bills and the private investigator are beginning to dig deep into my pockets, but whatever it takes, I'm willing to do. You are my everything, Taraine, and if I could trade places with you, I would. The investigator says he's closing in on the accomplice. I sure hope so, with all the money he's charging. But like I said, when it comes to my family, I would rather die broke than to walk around not knowing who did this to you and why," LaQuan said.

*You claim you want to find out who did this to me, LaQuan, but you really don't want to know. And that investigator is not doing his job because you're sleeping with that bitch. Why, LaQuan? Why would you betray me like this? I thought we had an unbreakable bond. You couldn't even wait until I was dead and buried. Oh no, LaQuan, not you. You decided to do this shit while I'm lying here trying to fight my way back to you and my girls. I could have let go a long time ago, but I thought it was our love for one another that was keeping me here. That bitch is trying to take my life and you're too blind to see that. Can you stop lusting over that bitch long enough to recognize she doesn't love you?*

"I hope you hear me, Moc. As a matter of fact, I know you hear me. That's why I'm here talking to you," LaQuan said as he grabbed Taraine's hand.

*When is the last time you've been here, LaQuan? I haven't heard the sound of your voice in a long time. But I guess you're so involved in your newly found relationship that you lost sight of what we were to one another, what we shared. I know you were lonely, Daddy, but do you think I'm not lonely lying here trapped inside my own mind, my own world? Don't you think I miss the touch of your soft lips on mines, our hands intertwining making us one? The love we use to make day in and day out? Where is that LaQuan at? I don't know, but he's not here with me.*

I began to cry on the inside as I came to the realization I was losing my man. I was losing my man, my daddy, my BooBear, my best friend, and most of all, I was losing my husband to this murderer.

"Your hands are so soft," LaQuan said as he kissed them. "Taraine, I need you to come back to me, baby. I don't want to live without you another day. You are my precious gift, and there is no one in this world that could ever replace you. I'm so sorry I wasn't there for you. I made a promise to always protect you and I failed you, Moc. I failed big time. I don't think I could ever forgive myself," LaQuan said as he began to cry.

I could feel his soft lips as he began kissing me on my cheek and lips. I listened to him as he began to cry uncontrollably.

"I know there's a God because he has been there for us through thick and thin. I'm just asking for him to release his angels into our lives one more time. I need my wife! I need her here with me. I want us to grow old together. There is still so much living for us to do, so much we still want to accomplish. Raise our beautiful daughter's together, maybe even try for a little boy. I want to live the life we were supposed to live. The life we were meant to live. So, I'm begging you, please let her come back to me, back to us," Laquan said as he prayed over my body.

*Do you hear my baby, God? He needs me, he really need me. Maybe I was wrong. Maybe that bitch didn't have him completely and I still have a chance to claim my throne. This is real love, and it's always been that way from the very beginning. Please reunite us, Father. I beg you, please.*

LaQuan sat back down in his chair and continued to pray.

"I know you haven't heard me recite this to you in a while. I thought maybe you had gotten a little tired of hearing this, but I need for you to hear and feel my love for you, Taraine. I need for the love of my life to find her way back to me.

*Pretty women wonder where my secret lies*
*I'm not fit or built to suit a fashion model's size*
*But when I start to tell them*
*They think I'm telling lies*
*I say*
*It's in the reach of my arms*
*The span of my hips*
*The stride of my step*

*The curl of my lips*
*I'm a woman*
*Phenomenally*
*Phenomenal Woman*
*That's me*

"That's her, God. She's my phenomenal woman and I need her here. I will be here to recite this to you every day, Moc because I know you hear me, and I know this poem is all about you," LaQuan said.

*I walk into a room*
*Just as cool as you please*
*And to a man*
*The fellow stand or*
*Fall down on their knees*
*Then they swarm around me*
*A hive of honey bees*
*I say*
*It's the fire in my eyes*
*And the flash of my teeth*
*The swing of my waist*
*And the joy in my feet*
*I'm a Woman*
*Phenomenally*
*Phenomenal Woman*
*That's me*

"Do you hear me, baby? That is you, you are phenomenal – you're remarkable and I love you. These tears I shed for you because I know you hear me and I know you feel me."

*Men themselves have wondered*
*What they see in me*
*They try so much*
*But they can't touch*
*My inner mystery*
*When I try to show them*
*They say they still can't see*

*I say*
*It's the arch of my back*
*The sun of my smile*
*The ride of my breast*
*The grace of my style*
*I'm a Woman*
*Phenomenally*
*Phenomenal Woman*
*That's me*

"You hear that, baby? I know what was in you. I recognized all your great qualities. I learned your inner mystery, it radiates all over you. You are and always will be my guiding light," LaQuan said as he began kissing my forehead and squeezing my hand tightly.

*Now you understand*
*Just why my head is not bowed*
*I don't shout or jump about*
*Or have to talk real loud*
*When you see me passing*
*It ought to make you proud*

*I hear you, baby, and I definitely feel you. I feel you touching me, baby. Yes, I can feel your heart beat in sync with mines. Is this a dream or is this real, God? Because I can feel him! I feel him squeezing my hands tightly.*

My heart began to race faster as I slowly opened my eyes. All I could see was the bright light, which made me shut them quickly. I tried again to see if what I thought was happening was really happening. I could see the silhouette of LaQuan's tight muscular body. I shut my eyes once more. The dark seemed so much more comfortable, but I've been in the dark for far too long, so I knew I had to give it my all. This time when I opened my eyes, I was looking directly at LaQuan as I watched the tears fall slowly down his cheek.

He must have lost his train of thought as he began to repeat the poem.

*Now you understand*
*Just why my heads not bowed*
*I don't shout or jump about*

*Or have to talk real loud*
*When you see me passing*
*It ought to make you proud*

I tried my best to divide my lips and I also tried to squeeze his hands.

*I hear you baby, I'm here,* I thought as I was finally able to part my lips to finish reciting the poem with him.

I say:

*It's the click of my heels*

I guess he couldn't hear me because he kept reciting the poem without reacting to my voice.

*The bend of my hair*
*The palm of my hand*
*The need of my care*
*Cause I'm a Woman*
*Phenomenally*
*Phenomenal Woman*
*That's me*

We said in unison.

"That's me, baby!" I said.

LaQuan opened his eyes. He wiped his tears away and looked at me again.

"Baby, are you here? Is this really happening or am I just imagining this?" I said.

I tried to continue talking but my throat felt very dry. I coughed a little and tried to speak once more.

"Is that really you, LaQuan?" I asked.

He jumped up and started kissing me all over.

"Baby, you came back to me!" he said as he touched my face gently and began kissing my lips. "I love you so much, Moc," LaQuan said as he reached over to press the emergency button to alert the doctors.

I looked around my room. It was filled with cards, teddy bears, and white roses.

"Welcome back, baby! I've missed you so much," he said as the nurses rushed into the room to see what the emergency was.

"What's the problem?" one of the nurses asked.

"There's no problem, nurse. I would actually call this a miracle!" LaQuan said as he stepped aside and allowed the nurse to see the miracle he was witnessing right before his eyes.

The nurse then paged the doctors. As the doctors walked through the door, they all smiled and were amazed by the sight of their patient with her eyes wide open. They automatically began to talk to me just to make sure it wasn't my reflexes.

"Hello, Mrs. Cummings. Can you hear me?" the doctor asked.

I slowly nodded my head yes.

"Do you understand what I'm saying to you?" the doctor asked.

Again, I nodded my head.

"Can you try to talk to me?" the doctor asked.

I cleared my throat before speaking. "Yes, doctor. I can hear you, see you, and feel you. And I must say, besides my husband, I think you're the greatest being I have laid eyes on this far," I said, giving them a weak smile. "My throat is very dry…it feels a little tight."

"Okay, we'll get you some water," He looked towards his nurse and she rushed out the door to get some fresh water.

The doctor continued checking me from my head to my toes. He ordered some tests to be done and for my blood to be drawn.

"I don't want to put too much strain on you all at once. You have been in this hospital, in this very same position for a very long time," he said as he continued checking me thoroughly.

"Can you wiggle your toes for me?"

I wiggled my toes just as he asked.

"Are you able to lift your legs?"

I was also able to lift my legs up and down slowly.

"I will start you on a liquid diet and then you can gradually work your way to solid foods," the doctor said.

He looked at LaQuan and said, "You're right. This is a miracle. I'm happy to see how you have fought to come out of this coma. The love and support of your family and friends has really done a great deal for you. It touches me when the outcomes turns out like this. I will be back to check on you in just a little bit. I need to make sure all the other doctors make their rounds to check on you," the doctor said as he headed out of the room.

LaQuan sat in the chair next to my bed and began making calls.

"Deb, I need you to bring the girls up to the hospital as soon as possible!" his voice was brimming with excitement. LaQuan could hardly contain himself. "Yes, everything is okay! Please bring the girls here to see their mother. We'll talk about what's going on when you get here. I love you, too, Deb," LaQuan looked at me and smiled. Then he leaned over and kissed my forehead. "I love you, Moc," LaQuan said, caressing my cheek. He couldn't stop touching me. It was like he was trying to reassure himself that I was really back.

I couldn't stop smiling. "I love you too, daddy. I can't wait to see my girls. How long have I been in the hospital? I asked.

"Too long, baby!" LaQuan said.

"How long is too long, boo bear?" I asked.

"Almost a year, baby. But it felt like a lifetime. Everybody has been here praying for you and just waiting for the day you would open those beautiful eyes of yours. And look – you finally did it! It has been rough, baby, but I must say the people in your life are definitely trustworthy and supportive. They have been there for me, the girls, and Deb. Your mom is also a trooper. If it wasn't for her, I might have been lying in bed right next to you," LaQuan said as he shook his head at the thought. "I'm not trying to push you, baby, but we will have to talk about what happened to you. So, do you remember anything? Can you describe the motherfucker who did this to you?" LaQuan asked angrily.

"Yes, I can, baby."

"Let me call the investigator now that you're awake. It's time for this motherfucker to go down," LaQuan said. He began pacing back and forth while looking for the investigator's number.

"Mr. Weis, ah, this is LaQuan Cummings. When you receive this message please return my call. My wife came out of the coma and she's able to talk. I'm quite sure she can provide you with more information," LaQuan said on the detective's voicemail.

As I listened to LaQuan leave his message on the phone, I began to get flashbacks of what happened to me. The thought of it made my heart race and my head hurt. The more I remembered, the harder the anxiety came on.

"What's wrong, baby?" LaQuan asked. "Please, Moc. Calm down, please, baby. I can't lose you again," Laquan said as he wiped the sweat from my forehead.

He reached for the call bell to alert the nursing staff.

Once the nurse entered the room and realized what was happening, she called for the doctor to be paged.

"Mrs. Cummings, I need you to relax. If not, I will have to give you a sedative," the nurse said as she tried to get me to relax.

I looked at her as the tears began to flow. As much as I wanted to calm down I couldn't. My emotions were running high and the more I thought about the incident, the more my heart ached.

"I think I may have pushed her too much. Maybe I shouldn't have questioned her about what had happened," LaQuan said, the fear apparent in his voice.

"Yes, I understand," the nurse said. "But the most important thing is that she take it easy right now."

The doctor spoke to the nurse as he began doing a thorough examination. He checked my vitals and discovered my pressure had elevated extremely high. He gave orders to the nurse to give me a dosage of Atenenol 100 mg.

"You have to remember she's still in a fragile state of mind. Just give her a little time, that's all I ask of you. I'm still waiting for the test results to come back, but everything looks fine so far. But we have to be sure. Just take it easy, okay, Mr. Cummings?" the doctor ordered.

"Yeah, I hear you, doc," LaQuan said as he sat beside me and held my hand. "I'm sorry, Moc. I'm not trying to stress you out, trust me."

"I know you're not, boo bear. It's okay," I said as I grabbed his hand and held it tight.

Deb came walking in the door with Nicera and Raine'. When she noticed I was wide awake, she placed her hands over her mouth in shock. My babies ran toward my bed yelling 'mommy'. The closer Debra got, the more overwhelmed she became with joy.

"Are my eyes deceiving me? Am I seeing right?" Deb asked as the tears rushed down her face.

"Yes, Deb. I'm back," I said with a weak smile.

My mother stood beside my bed and touched my cheek gently as she wiped away my tears. She bent down to wrap her arms around me and then she looked back at LaQuan.

"God heard my prayers," she said.

"Yes, he did, Deb. And he heard mine, too," he said.

"Look at my babies!" I smiled. "Come give mommy a kiss," I said as I watch Nicera grab Raine's hand and walked towards my bed. "I missed my babies. You guys are so beautiful and ya'll got so big. My two little princesses, I can't believe this. I missed almost a year, of my girl's lives," I said as I held them tight and they held me right back.

It felt so good to feel their little arms wrapped around me and the kisses from their tiny lips on my cheeks as they giggled with happiness in their heart.

"Where are my girls at, LaQuan? Did you call them?" I asked.

"No, I didn't call them yet, but I will a little later. I don't think you should overdo it. Remember what the doctor said. We shouldn't try to do too much too fast. You know once they all come up here it will be a session and a party all rolled into one. I'm just glad to have you back here with us mentally and physically. Everything will happen in due time, okay, baby?" LaQuan asked as he kissed me gently on my lips.

We celebrated amongst ourselves just talking and doing a lot of kissing and hugging. The doctors were in and out checking on me, drawing blood, and taking my vitals every five minutes. It didn't bother me at all. I was just so happy to be in the presence of my family; to see their beautiful smiles was more than I could ever ask for. When visiting hours were over, my mom took the girls home. LaQuan decided to stay with me overnight. After they left, he got in the bed with me and he held me tight.

"I'm not leaving you tonight, baby. I'm going to lay here with you until you fall asleep and then I will get in the chair and watch you sleep. I'm not taking any chances, Moc. This experience showed me what love is truly about from another aspect. I see you so differently, baby. You are definitely my hero. I missed you so much, but my inner being never allowed me to give up. I always knew in due time you would come back to us. I am just curious about one thing, Moc. What was it like to be in a coma?" he asked.

"To be honest, daddy, I didn't know what was going on. It just felt like a never-ending dream at times. Then, there were times when I felt like I was going from one dream to the next. The weird thing about it was I always could hear you guys, or at least I thought I could hear you. I do remember trying to talk to all of you, but no one would respond back. Now, I'm confused, baby. I do know, when you started reciting Phenomenal Woman I started feeling chills throughout my body. It touched my heart as I listened to you and I just felt the need to say it with you. God gave me the strength to do just that. Like you said, LaQuan. You believed in me, and you believed in us. You are my soul mate, baby, and it's clear to see it was time for us to be reunited. I'm just so happy and can't see myself without you, not in this lifetime," I said.

"Even if it took forever, I knew that I would never leave you, Taraine. You are my everything, my always and forever, and nothing will come between us – not even a coma. Now, I need you to get some rest. I'm not going anywhere, ever," LaQuan said as he kissed me gently on my forehead.

"I know, baby; infinity love," I said as I closed my eyes. I felt like I was wrapped in the arms of my Angel. He was heaven sent and no one could ever divide us, no matter how hard they tried.

*****

I was awakened by the doctors making their rounds. I didn't care. I was grateful to be alert and wide awake.

I looked over at the chair and LaQuan was gone.

*Where's my, baby?* I thought as the doctors and interns made their way to my bed checking and observing the patient who miraculously woke up from a coma.

My doctor came over to me and did another examination.

"Mrs. Cummings, your test came back fine. I'm going to send you to rehab for the next couple of days and if things go well, you will be going home to your family, but remain an outpatient at the rehab clinic. How does that sound, Mrs. Cummings?" he asked.

"That sounds like music to my ears, doc. I am looking forward to going home. There's so much catching up I have to do."

LaQuan came walking into the room with two dozen of white roses in his hands. He knew I had a love for white roses. They were just so beautiful to look at. My room already looked like a flower shop and it smelled good as well.

"Good Morning, Moc!" LaQuan said as he walked up to me and kissed me on my forehead. "I was trying to get back before you woke up, but I see the doc beat me, huh."

"That's okay, baby. Thank you for the roses; they look beautiful."

LaQuan pulled out one rose and handed it to me. I took a long sniff and closed my eyes as I took in the sensual aroma. I felt as if I was walking through someone's garden.

"I love the scent of a rose, daddy; it just makes me feel so alive."

"I'm just happy to be able to look into your beautiful brown eyes and know that you are looking right back at me."

"So, doc, how's my baby coming along?" LaQuan asked.

"Just as I told your wife, her test came back fine. I scheduled her for rehab for a couple of days and we'll see what happens from there. If she gets through rehab with no problems, she's all yours and she can continue rehab as an outpatient," the doctor said.

"Do you think my wife will be able to talk to the detective about the incident, or is it still too soon?"

"She should be good, but the detective shouldn't come on too strong at one time. If it gets to be a little overbearing Mrs. Cummings has every right to say she feels uneasy," the doctor said.

"Okay, doc."

"I'll see you soon, Mrs. Cummings. Take it easy now," the doctor said as he walked out the room.

"Baby, you know I had to get you some breakfast even though they got you on liquids. I won't feed you too much, just a little taste. You know I have to feed my baby," LaQuan said as he looked at me and smiled.

"Thank you, BooBear, but I really don't have an appetite. How about I drink some of the orange juice and you sit right here and let me feed you?" I said with a wink.

"So, are you ready to talk about what happened that day, Moc? I will understand if it's still too soon, but to be honest, that motherfucker has been on the run long enough. Now that you're alert, it's time to put that bastard where he belongs," LaQuan said as he pulled his chair beside my bed and sat down waiting for me to feed him.

"Yes, I'm ready to talk to the detective, daddy. But I just need to let you know it wasn't a "he" it was a "she" that did this to me. Lance's fiancé is the one who shot me," I said as the tears began to form from the anger I was feeling.

"What?" LaQuan said as he jumped up out of the chair.

"Yes, baby. It was Lance's fiancé, Sidora. She came to the house on a mission, which was to rob us and take us down by any means necessary. She said she was your cousin. I tried to call you but it went to your voicemail. We were talking and sipping on some wine for a while and then the bitch just flipped on me saying she was going to make you pay for setting Lance up. Lance told her it was your fault he was locked up and you were the reason why he was locked up. She kept asking for the money and jewelry, but most of all, she wanted to hurt you. She was there for revenge. She wanted you to feel pain just like she did, and eye for an eye. I took her to the bedroom to throw her off a little and she started bugging out. I believe she hit me and I blank out. She was searching through the house and that's when I noticed the ice pick we had used the night before. I told her the safe was in the girl's room. I acted as if I was going in the girl's closet and I turned around and stabbed her with the ice pick in her chest. The next thing I knew, shit was black. She shot me, baby," I said as I put my face in my hand and started crying hysterically. "That bitch shot me, LaQuan. And this is all because of your bitch ass cousin Lance. Did you ever meet her while they were together?"

"No, baby. I never met her before. I mean, he talked about her a lot, but that's as far as it went. Do you think you would be able to pick her out in a line up or mug shot if you had to?"

"Hell yeah, I can. Besides, she has a huge mole on her face you can't miss. I will never forget her face, LaQuan....ever," I said angrily.

"I'm so sorry, baby; so sorry this happened to you. I have to call Detective Weiss because all this time he has been searching for a man," LaQuan said. "Damn! This motherfucker still trying to come at me and my family from all directions, but that shit must stop here," LaQuan said as he paced back and forth.

"He tried to hurt us, baby, but look. I'm still here, I'm a survivor," I said, but he was too hot and I don't believe he heard a word I said.

"Baby, do you hear me? LaQuan? LaQuan..." I repeated. "Look at me, baby. I'm still here. They didn't win this battle," I said.

"Yes, I hear you, Moc, but this should have never happened. And to make matters worse, that bitch is probably walking around thinking she took you out. She thinks she got away with murder, but trust me, it's our time, Moc, and it ain't over until it's over," LaQuan said angrily.

"Hey, baby, let's not lose focus. What we need to do is fall back for a moment, take a little bit of time, and let's just think logically about this. At the end of the day, I survived being shot, and I came out of that damn coma, so I am victorious. Yes, almost one year of my life has been put on hold. Let's just say I was on sabbatical, okay? I want revenge but we have already lost so much and we overcame a lot of obstacles. All I'm asking is that you let the detective handle this situation, please? Let's just do it the right way. I'm ready to leave NYC and start a new life, new beginning, just like we had planned before all this occurred. How does that sound?" I asked.

I wanted to let him be the man in charge, but I knew I had to take control of how things were going. I would never give Lance or Sidora the satisfaction of stealing our joy – enough was enough.

"That sounds good, Moc. I hear you. Trust me, daddy always hears you. I love you and my babies enough to let the police handle the situation, but they better act fast," LaQuan said.

"Baby I need you to come talk to me, come sit right here so I can look into your eyes."

LaQuan walked towards me, sat next to me, and smiled.

"I'm serious, LaQuan. I need you to look me in my eyes and promise me you are going to let the detectives, police, whoever handle this for us."

"I promise, Moc. I will let the police do their job."

"Thank you very much. That's why I love me some you, daddy. We have a lot of celebrating to do. Leave that bad energy on the other side and come love your Mocha Chocolate. I've been missing the hell out of my baby," I said as I patted my shoulder inviting him to lay next to me and cuddle.

"When I went to get your roses I decided to call your girls and let them know my baby is back, so I guess they will be here today having one of your girl's sessions," he said as he looked at me and smirked.

I started laughing.

"What's wrong with my girl-sessions?"

"Nothing at all, Moc. I just don't want no parts of it. But none of that matters right now. What matters most is you being here, loving me, and me loving you back. We are going to live life to the fullest; trust me, baby. Me, you, and the girls are going to be just fine. They missed their mommy so much. I did the best I could, but there's nothing like a mother's love," LaQuan said.

"I'm quite sure you did a fantastic job," I said.

The nurse from the rehab department came to pick me up for my first therapy class. They wanted to see how well my reflexes work and if I was able to walk on my own. Lying in that hospital bed for all those months may have done some damage, but I was going to pray for the best and pray I could walk out of that hospital on my own without the help of a wheelchair or cane. To be honest, I was just happy to have my life back, so even if I had to use a wheelchair or a cane that would be okay. But I would work my ass off to get where I need to be.

*****

When I first got up to walk, my legs seemed very weak and wobbly as was expected. I grabbed onto the bars and slowly dragged my legs. It felt like I had 50-pound weights on each ankle and the weights were winning the battle. I had to focus as I told myself over and over. This battle was mine and I wasn't going to be defeated. I survived many obstacles in life and therapy was next. The nurse told me therapy was only for an hour. I asked him could we go and extra hour... perseverance was the key. Determination was the factor and I wasn't giving up. I was a force of nature and that bitch needed to know she wasn't stopping nothing.

"You were outstanding, but I don't want you to overdo it," the male nurse said.

"I hear you, sweetheart, but I'm on a mission. I've lost too much time without my family. The world has missed my presence, so I have to shake it off and get back to business. Time stops for no one, you feel me? You see this wig I got on? It's so not my style, this has my girl Kelly written all over it. I have to get my sexy back. It's time for me to get back into the world and live, live, live. You feel me, hun?" I asked as I put my hand in the air to give him a high five.

"Oh yes, I feel you," he said as he admired me from the sideline.

"Awh, you're so sweet, and I'm glad you see it my way. So, me and you tomorrow I hope because I'm feeling you. Me and you see eye-to-eye," I said as he wheeled me back to my room.

As soon as I rolled into my room, all I heard was "welcome back, bitch!" Of course it was Fatima, then I looked over and saw Shantae crying while showing her pearly whites. They both came and hugged the hell out of me.

"LaQuan told us you went to therapy. How did therapy go?" Fatima asked.

"It went well. You know me. I'm going to push until I can't push no more," I said.

"Okay, babe. I guess I'll give you some time with the ladies. I will bring Nicera and Raine' with me when I return, okay? Love you, Moc. Please make sure ya'll watch over my baby while I'm gone," he said.

"Oh, LaQuan, we will take care of your Mocha Chocolate," Fatima said laughing.

"Be good, and don't overdo it," he said, placing his soft lips on mines and kissed me as if he really didn't want to leave me.

*****

"We missed you so much, Tee, and we have so much to tell you, especially me," Fatima said as she sat in the chair next to me.

"Oh really? Well, before you start running your mouth, I just wanted to say sorry for your loss. I'm even sorrier that I was unable to support you when you needed it most," I said as the tears fill my eyes. I felt as if I was the one who had the miscarriage.

Fatima and Shantae both looked at each other in shock.

"What's wrong?" I asked. "I could hear ya'll bitches every time ya'll came up here to talk to me. Ya'll just couldn't hear me talking back, which was probably a good thing at times," I said.

"The loss was such a draining experience for me; it affected me far more than I expected it to. I'm still trying to heal. Khalief and I had a little memorial for her. The hurt is at a minimum, but trust me, it's something I will never forget. We decided to name her Angel and I know she's a little Angel living in them golden gates with grandma Flo-Jo and my mother. I know they are spoiling her," Fatima said as her emotions began to get the best of her and she started to cry.

"It's okay to cry, Tima. And like I said, I'm sorry I was unable to be around when you needed me the most."

"I'm just glad to have you back. This year has definitely been rough on all of us with you gone," Fatima said as she rubbed my hands gently.

"How are you and Kandi doing? Did you guys make up? She came here crying about something you had done to her. I always told you, Tae. Inviting other people into your bedroom is nothing but trouble. You know how you are, Miss God's Gift. So what's going on? Did ya'll fix that little situation or what?" I asked.

"Well, Kandi and I are a done deal, and the guy we had the threesome with, DeShawn, we're together now."

"Huh?!" I said with the 'what the hell is going on' look on my face.

"We're taking it slow, just trying to get to know each other a little better. All in all, he's a very nice man. I'm getting to know him and he's really a breath of fresh air, Tee," Shantae said.

"Oh, so you back to doing men, huh?"

"I guess so for now, but we'll see what happens. You know how I get down, but I can't wait for you to meet him," Shantae said smiling.

"Yeah, I have to bring Khalief here to see you. What were the odds of me ending up with him?" Fatima asked while shaking her head.

"Life is so strange and unpredictable. All I know is I'm back bitches and we're going to live it up like there's no tomorrow because let's just be honest, you never know. We have no control over when our lives will end. So why not enjoy and live every day as if it was your last," I said. "What's up with Kelly and Slim?" I asked.

"Kelly, unfortunately, is in an asylum. Keith continued harassing her and she completely lost it. She stabbed him like 35 times, but the motherfucker survived. Now that's when you know a motherfucker is crazy. They always say it's hard to kill a crazy person and he made me a true believer. I went to go check on her and it's as if she's not there mentally. I'm not even sure if she recognized me at all. The doctors said she has no recollection of what happened in her house and she talks as if she doesn't have any children. It was so sad to see her like that. That motherfucker pushed her way too far and now the kids are without their mother and possibly their father. He's still living, but he has a lot of complication from the stabbing," Fatima said.

"Slim is doing her thing in Philly. She and Ron are doing much better. She found some psychotic bitch named Dee to roll with out there. The first time I met her, I knew something wasn't right with her. You know Monica can be so naïve at times, so I fell back and eventually that bitch showed her true colors. When you get the chance to talk to her, I guess she can tell you what's going on in her life, but for right now, it's all about you. We've missed you so much, Tee. We prayed and prayed. God must have got tired of us begging, pleading, and crying, so he decided to send you back to shut us up," Fatima said.

"Yes, now it's time for us to hit up some clubs," Shantae said as she looked at me and started laughing.

Fatima and I both looked at each other and started laughing.

"Still the same ole Tae I see."

"Give me just a little more time, Tae, and I'll be ready to hit up all the clubs with you. We are still leaving NYC, but you guys can come visit me and I'll come visit ya'll. I think it's time for us to start venturing out; it's time for us to see other parts of the world. First, I need them to catch her ass, the bitch that did this to me. This is not over," I said angrily.

"What do you mean HER?" Fatima asked.

"Lance's fiancé is the one who shot me."

"Get the fuck out of here. Where the fuck did she come from?" Shantae asked.

"I don't know, but that bitch came for revenge. Lance filled her head up with all sorts of lies. It's all good. That bitch thought she took me out, that she left me for dead. Well, she got it all wrong. I'm quite sure she's in Philly laid back thinking she got away with murder. God told me he "GOT ME" and he sent me back to my family and friends. God said, 'It ain't over until he decided he was ready for me', not some crazy deranged women stuck on destroying my family," I said.

"But you know what? We are not going to focus on that right now. Like I told LaQuan, leave it to the authorities. When I'm released from this hospital I'm doing it up real big. Right, bitches?" I yelled with both hands in the air.

"Yes!" they both shouted in unison.

"Living Life to the fullest, that's what it's all about, ladies – living life to the fullest," I said with a huge smile on my face.

A couple of hours later, LaQuan returned with the girls, and also with my mom and detective Weiss. He questioned me for a while. When I told him it was a female he didn't look surprised at all. I guess these days you can't put a thing past anyone. Once he left, we were able to enjoy the rest of our visit together. I was just glad to get it over with. I lay and listened to the sound of Nicera as she began singing her ABC's. She sounded so adorable. Raine' started singing along with her, she didn't have the letters down pack, but that's okay. Mommy was back, and I knew with time, things would be back to normal. I loved watching LaQuan interact with the girls. I knew he was a loving man, but it felt good to see it all over again as I watched Raine' squeeze his cheeks together as she sang along with her sister.

"Are you ready to get out of here?" Deb asked.

"You know it, Deb. All I need is some of your lasagna and some mac and cheese and I'm good," I said, rubbing my belly.

"These girls have really missed you and so has your husband. He has done exceptionally well with them I must say. At one point, he just looked so broken hearted but he always said he was never going to give up on you. He always believed you would find your way back," Deb said.

I just looked at her and smiled. I was very grateful to have him in my life and I know God put us in one another's life for a reason, I thought as I continued watching him play with the girls.

# Closure

# Taraine

I wasn't able to go home in a couple of days like I thought. I had to remain in the hospital for another two weeks, just to make sure everything was at its best before they decided to release me. LaQuan came to pick me up. I was filled with so much joy and my emotions were running wild. I was a little overwhelmed by it all, but I was still happy that I was given the chance to be with my family.

LaQuan said we were going to stay at the Marriot until we were able to move to Georgia, which was where our house was located. He said he never slept in our house after the incident took place. It was just too painful for him to go back there.

"I need to go back there, LaQuan."

"Why would you want to do that?"

"It's just something I need to do."

"Okay, Moc, if you say so."

When we got to the house I felt all right up until I took my first step inside the living room. That's when everything hit me hard and anxiety began to take over. I took a deep breath and continue walking through the house. I was determined not to let Sidora take over my life. I wasn't going to allow her to control my thoughts and feelings.

This is where it all began and this is where it will all end, at least until they catch her ass.

"Your mom said she will move with us to Georgia. She wants to help you while I'm at work. I have a good feeling about this, Moc. Everything will be all right, trust me. We will start exactly where it left off before this shit happened. We'll be all right," LaQuan repeated again.

"I know it will, BooBear. I just needed to come here one last time for closure," I said as I walked towards the girl's room which is actually where she shot me. I stood at the door for a moment but felt nothing. As I walked inside, all the events that occurred that day took over completely and all I could think about was my will to live for my family. That's why I'm still here. I thought as I started to cry.

LaQuan came behind me and held me tight.

"Let it all out, Moc. This is the end, baby. It's time to close one chapter and move on to the next chapter. You will never be able to erase what took place here, but I will do whatever it takes to take away the pain. Do you trust me, Taraine?" LaQuan asked as he looked into my eyes.

"Yes, I trust you."

"What have I always told you, Moc?"

"To live life to the fullest!"

"Exactly, and that's what we're going to do. There may be some bumps and bruises along the way, but as long as we got each other that's all that matters. They couldn't stop us then and they definitely can't stop us now because we won't let them," he said as he grabbed my hand and walked me out of the room.

*****

When we arrived at the Marriot, LaQuan had the room filled with my white roses. He also had a dozen of blue roses, which I'd never seen before. They were beautiful and unique. It was a huge suite, more than enough room for me, LaQuan, and the girls.

I'm going to go pick up the girls now. I just wanted to spend some time alone with you first. Is that alright with you beautiful?"

"Yes, it is," I said with a smile.

"Get comfortable. I'm going to make you a nice hot bubble bath."

The bathroom was nice and big with a huge whirlpool tub.

The water was nice and warm and filled with plenty of bubbles. It seemed like forever since I'd taken a hot bubble bath. Oh wait, it has been more than a minute, actually almost a year. LaQuan had candles all around the whirlpool. He helped me in the tub, made sure I was comfortable, and then he stepped out the bathroom. He returned with a bottle of wine and two wine glasses in his hand. He undressed and then he joined me in the tub. He was still as sexy as the first day I'd laid eyes on him. He had a bowl of strawberries and some whip cream. He dropped a strawberry in both of our wine glasses and then made a toast.

"You are as beautiful today as you were the first time I saw you. God sent me my Angel and someone tried to take you away from us, but, baby we're unbreakable. I thought they knew that, baby. What God has put together no man or woman can put asunder. You are my everything, Moc. My beginning and my end, and I plan to spend the rest of my life with you," he said as tears rolled down his cheek.

"I want to say thank you for being you. You are a remarkable man and I'm so glad you came into my life. You have accepted Nicera as your own daughter and I love you for that, BooBear. I couldn't have asked for anyone better. Thank you for sticking by me all this time. Thank you for believing I would come back to you. Thank you for being my rock, my beginning and my end. I love you forever and always," I said as I began to cry.

The music played low as we relaxed and enjoyed each other's company. LaQuan massaged my body with tender loving care. All I could do was lay back and enjoy the moment. I felt a little insecure about how I looked, but LaQuan looked past that. All he saw was my beauty radiating from the inside out. My hair, skin, or weight wasn't at its best from lying in that hospital bed for so long, but because of him, I felt like the most beautiful women in the world. I still had on the wig Kelly gave me. He gently pulled the wig off. He could tell I was a little embarrassed.

"It's okay, Moc. I just want you to relax and be free and know that I love you no matter how things appear. I'm here and I love every-thing about you. We will heal together. I always told you I had your back and it was all about us. Just know that I still love you and we are going to heal together," he said as he spoke to me with his eyes and heart.

"I know, BooBear, it's just me. I feel awkward and slightly embarrassed about the way I look."

"You have the look of a survivor. I know how beautiful you are and so does everybody else. All you need to do is be strong mentally and everything else will follow, but for right now, relax and be at peace," he said as he stood up to climb behind me in the whirlpool. I leaned back and enjoyed being in the arms of the man I loved. It felt good just to be loved unconditionally.

We got out of the tub and made our way to the bed. He grabbed the massage oil off the dresser and gave me the best massage ever from my head to my toes. My body began to quiver. I was excited but yet afraid. I wondered if I still had it – was I still able to make love to him like before. He came up to me and kissed me gently.

"Don't worry, Moc. Daddy won't hurt you," he whispered in my ear and began kissing me again.

"Okay," I said as I kissed him back.

"Relax and let me take care of you! Let me show you how much I love you and how much I missed you."

He kissed me and I did just as he said. I relaxed my mind, body, and soul and I enjoyed the moment. His strong hands on my body felt so good. The heat of passion that was coming on heavy and strong had me falling in love all over again. I loved the way he looked into my eyes as if they were the most beautiful work of God. I trembled as if it was my very first time. He nibbled on my ear gently as I stroked his strong sculpted back.

"Relax, Moc. I promise not to hurt you," he whispered in my ear. I love you, Moc. You know you are my world and I will do whatever it takes to protect you, provide for you, and comfort you," he said, exploring my body with his hands and his tongue. When he kissed me it was such a turn on. He kissed so seductively, but the passion was electrifying. I love the way he made love to my body. All I could do was close my eyes, listen to our heartbeats, and know this was an undeniable love. He was and is my everything. LaQuan was my Phenomenal Man.

I wasn't quite myself yet, but I felt alive. I was alive and well. All I could do was smile, smile at the pleasure of having such a wonderful husband. I was so in love with him and I finally realized why I was one of the chosen ones. *This was my destiny; to feel love, to respect it, and to know I deserved to be with a man who loves me in this manner,* I thought as I dozed off to sleep.

# Disconnected

## Monica

"Hey, Ron. Are you finished packing? I want to leave here around 6 p.m.," I yelled to my husband as I heard my doorbell ring.

"Who the hell is that? I don't have time to be entertaining people. I need to get to NYC," I mumbled as I walked to the door.

I looked through the glass door and realized it was Dee's crazy ass. *Oh, damn! I can't act like I'm not home. She already saw me walking towards the door as she peeked in through my side window,* I thought.

"Hey, Dee! What do I owe this visit?" I asked as I opened the door. "I haven't seen you in a couple of weeks."

"I know, girl. I've been trying to get myself together that's all. What's up with you?" Dee asked as she let herself in my house.

"My husband, and the kids and I are on our way to the NYC. My best friend came out of the coma and her husband and Fatima are throwing her a surprise party. Look at the invite, it's beautiful. I'm so happy for my girl; she came out of that damn coma. She has always been a survivor and she proved that the day she woke up," Monica said as I handed her the invite.

"Oh wow, she's beautiful," Dee said as she stared at the picture on the invite.

"How did she end up in a coma again?" Dee asked suspiciously.

"She was shot twice. Once in the chest and once in the head. All this time we all were thinking it was a fucking man who did this to her, when all the while it was a psychotic bitch. A sick ass woman who was out for revenge due to lies her crazy ass man put in her head. She shot Taraine and thought she left my girl for dead, but little did she know my girl is a fighter and she fought her way back to her family and friends," Monica said with a smile on her face.

"Wow, I'm happy to hear that. I wish I could have visited her when you went to see her in the hospital. She sounds like a truly amazing and strong woman."

"Yes, she is. That's my girl, Dee. I am so happy. She and LaQuan have this undeniable love for one another. He held on strong because he knew his love for her would bring her back and I feel she survived this because of the love she has for him and their children. Real love is not easy to come by, but once you get it you better value it."

"Damn, I wish I would have known. I would have took the ride with you to NYC," Dee said as she continued to stare at the invite.

I know, right, but you will get the opportunity to meet her when she comes to visit me. This party is RSVP only; I would have needed to know a lot sooner."

*There's no way in hell I was inviting you to my girls party with your crazy ass,* I thought as I watched her stare at the invite.

"I would love to meet her in the near future," Dee said as she handed the invite back to me.

"How are things going with you and your man?"

"We're just fine. We will be together eventually," Dee said.

"Okay, so you guys made up and decided to reconnect?" I asked just out of curiosity.

"Something like that. These days you can never be too sure about anything. I still have some things I need to do and I just recently found out I need to finish some personal matters I started before I can get back on track. Once I take care of this distraction, then I can focus on my personal life much better," Dee said.

"Okay, Dee. Well I wish you luck, girl. If you need someone to talk to you know you can call me."

"Thanks, Monica. I really appreciate that. Well, I'm going to let you finish packing. Have a safe trip and I'll see you when you get back," Dee said.

"Okay, Dee. I'll call you when I get back," I said as I closed and locked the door.

*Please, bitch. I will not be calling you when I get back; you have too many issues. We are officially disconnected,* I thought as I proceeded back to my packing.

"Okay, boys, are you guys ready? It's road trip time," I yelled with excitement.

# The Party

## Fatima

"Wow, Q., I'm impressed; the party planner did a great job. The food looks delicious as well. Taraine is going to be so surprised. I know she don't see this coming. You think she knows what's going on?" I asked.

"No. I don't think she has a clue. That's the good thing about it," LaQuan said.

"Awh, give me a hug. I love you so much, Q."

"I love you too, Fatima. You know we've always been cool from the very beginning and you're right, the party planner did do her thing. I'm impressed as well, but your cousin deserves this," LaQuan said.

The décor was Platinum and White, the table and chairs were set up real nice leaving more than enough room for people to get their dance on right in the center of the ballroom. There was a banner that said 'Welcome Back, Taraine!!!' There was also a second banner that said 'To New Beginnings!!!' There was a souvenir table which consisted of a wine glass filled with Hershey kisses and a silver ribbon tied around the center of the glass. The ribbon said 'God Bless the Child'. There were two cakes; one with Taraine's picture on it and the other one had a picture of Taraine and her family. The DJ was setting up his system making sure everything was on point. *Everything looks beautiful. Taraine will definitely feel the love from all her family and friends. I'm so excited!* Fatima thought as she looked around and smiled.

"Okay, Q. I am going home to get ready. Please get your wife here by 8 p.m., do you think you can do that for me," I said laughing.

"Yes, I can do that for you, Fatima, I hope," LaQuan said with a smirk.

"I told her I wanted to take her out to dinner and that she should put on her very best. She said her and Tae were going out shopping, but yeah, we will be on time. I promise you we will be on time. Trust me."

*****

Khalief and I arrived at 6 p.m. It had been a while since he and I had been out amongst people. We were doing a lot of healing and preparing for our future. I know there have been plenty of days when he wanted to give up on me, but he understood what I was going through mentally. It wasn't easy for either of us, but we were getting through the bumps and bruises and working on getting pregnant again.

People started arriving around 6:30 p.m. They were dressed to impress as mentioned on the invite. Some of Taraine's coworkers and acquaintances from her school came out. Even some of her students she counseled came with their parents. People were ready to eat, drink, and have a good time celebrating with Taraine.

Deb arrived with Raine' and Nicera. Deb looked divine and the girls looked like little princesses. There were chaperons escorting people to their assigned tables. You could tell the guests were impressed as they mingled, talked, and enjoyed the music the DJ was playing. Some were on the dance floor doing their two-step as the DJ played old school music, like the classic "Before I Let Go" by Frankie Beverly and Maze.

Shantae had arrived with her son Messiah and her boyfriend Deshawn.

Monica had arrived with her husband Ron and her two boys Quincy and Michael.

"Hey, Chica! What's going on? You look good, girl. You're glowing too. What's up with that?" Monica said as she walked over to where Shantae was standing and gave her a kiss and hug.

"You know me. I'm always going to be happy by any means necessary. Now, since I got that out the way, I would like to introduce you to my boo-thang, Deshawn," Shantae said.

"Your what?" Monica asked with a look of surprise on her face.

"You heard right, my boo-thang, my man," Shantae said with a smile on her face.

"I hear that. Well, anyway, Mr. Boo-Thang, how are you doing? I'm Monica."

"Nice to meet you!" DeShawn said.

"Same here. I can't wait to see my girl, Tee. You know she's going to be so surprised and happy," Monica said.

"Yeah, wait until you see her. We went shopping. But she thinks LaQuan is taking her out on a special date. It was killing me not to tell her. You know I can't keep any secrets, but I managed to keep my mouth shut. She deserves all of this and so much more. When I think about seeing her lying there looking lifeless makes me more grateful for life all together. I'm glad that she's in a healthy state of mind and that she's ready to move on with life. Well, you and Ron are looking real happy. He must be laying the pipe down," Shantae said.

"Yes, he is, Tae. The tables have finally turned. I think our communication has gotten much better. He's much more comfortable and very at ease in the bedroom when it comes to the delicatessen," Monica said with a wink.

"This sounds more like a woman-to-woman conversation, so I think I'm going to get me something to drink. Do you want anything, baby?" Deshawn asked.

"If they're serving liquor bring me a Coconut Ciroc, baby," Shantae said.

"Could I get you something, Monica?" he asked.

"No, I'm good, hun. Thank you for asking," Monica said.

"Girl, what happened with Kandi?"

"That's a long story, girl. She may come tonight, I'm not sure, but DeShawn is the one who engaged in the threesome with us. I will call you and bring you up to date on everything that took place between all three of us. As of right now, we are here to enjoy life and party with absolutely no drama," Shantae said.

"You got that right. And they're playing my song, so let me go get my husband so I can grind all on his chocolate ass," Monica said.

"Okay, just remember this is a family-friendly occasion, so be-have. None of that winding and grinding shit with you and your husband tonight," Shantae said.

"I know, chica. We will be on our best behavior tonight," Monica said as she winked and walked up to her husband and pulled him to the dance floor.

# *Love of My Life*

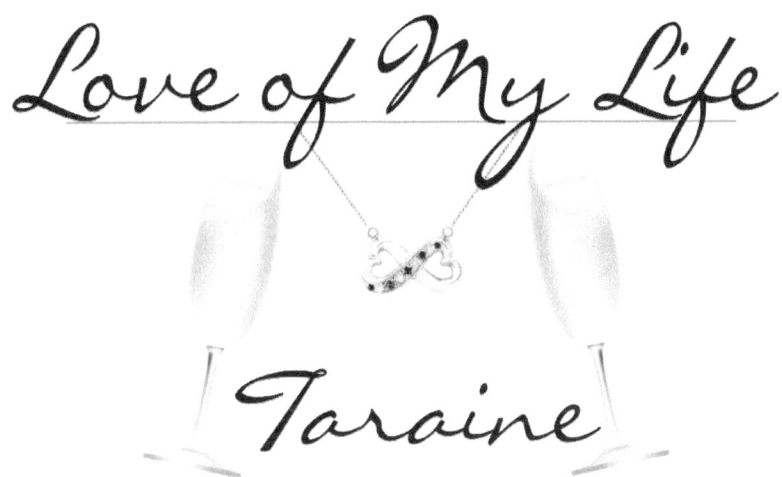

## *Taraine*

"So where are we going tonight, LaQuan?" I asked joyfully.

"Why are you so nosey?" he asked.

"You know I hate surprises."

"Well, you're not getting a word out of me tonight?"

"Well, maybe if I kiss you right here, and over here, it's no telling what I can get out of you."

"Not tonight, Moc. I'm not letting you have your way tonight."

"Oh really?" I said as I kissed his neck again and slowly made my way to his lips. He could never take it when I made love to his lips.

"Please, baby," I said as I sucked his bottom lip gently.

"No," he replied sternly.

I laughed on the inside, then I took over. I didn't really care to know where we were going. I was looking forward to my surprise, but first, I wanted to enjoy what was standing before me. I thought as I began seducing him. I know he loved when I did the 'take-over'. I know he loved when I did the 'take-over'. I was gentle to me my first night home; he made love to me mentally, but after that, all we did was make love— each and every night, and I wasn't planning on skipping tonight. I thought as I pushed him on the bed.

"Moc, what are you doing? We have dinner reservations for eight o'clock."

"Okay, baby, but I have reservations of my own. As a matter of fact, we're fifteen minutes late," I said, climbing on top of him. I put my finger to his mouth as he opened it to talk.

"Shhh, don't talk; just lay back, relax, and enjoy the moment, baby," I said as I began to go to work on him.

"I want to say thank you for being God's gift to me. I love you and I will show you how much every chance I get," I said, kissing him on his well-sculpted chest. I explored his entire body with my tongue the exact way he explored mine. The look on his face told me he enjoyed every moment. I climbed on top of him and made love to him passionately. I desired him and I took my time so he could experience every feeling imaginable. I wanted to take him there and that's exactly what I did. We were one and when we reached our peak, it was electrifying. I lay on top of him and listened as his heart raced.

*Oh, yeah! The bitch is back in full form,* I thought as I smiled at life, it was definitely good. If loving him is wrong I don't want to be right.

"Daddy loves you, Moc," he whispered in my ear.

"Moc loves her Daddy more," I whispered back in his ear.

*****

After LaQuan and I showered together, we got dressed. Of course, we were running way behind schedule, but it was all worth it. We looked at each other and smiled because we knew we were doing it; we were looking good. He was my King and I was his Queen and we were dressed to kill.

I was so excited about our dinner date. I couldn't recall the last time I felt this good about going out in a long time. On our way there, LaQuan called the restaurant to tell them we were running a little late and we should arrive in the next 15 to 20 minutes. That's what I love about my baby. He had street smarts but he knew how to be sophisticated as well.

We arrived at this beautiful restaurant; from the outside, it looked like a huge hall. The lights were beautiful. It kind of put you in a romantic mood. I was feeling this before we had the opportunity to enter the place. 'You go baby', I thought to myself as I held his hands and walked right beside him. When we walked inside, it was even more beautiful than the outside.

"What is going on, baby?" I asked.

Suddenly, everyone yelled "SURPRISE!!!"

I was so surprised and touched, all I could do was turn around and hug LaQuan. He grabbed my hand and walked me inside. The more people I recognized, the more my heart was filled with joy. Raine' and Nicera ran up to me and I held them tightly.

"Oh my God!" I said as I walked into this room full of love. I could feel it all over me. I had chills dancing throughout my entire body as I took a moment to look at each and every face. My heart skipped a beat when I recognized some of my children I counseled.

*All this for me!* I thought.

"How did you guys pull this off? I'm so overwhelmed, guys; ya'll just don't know how this makes me feel. This is so beautiful and I'm so grateful," I said as I took in all the applause.

I began feeling like a star as everyone began walking up to me to hug, kiss, and tell me how much they loved me. Many told me how beautiful I looked, and to be honest, I felt beautiful and I felt loved.

"Tee, stop crying. You're going to mess up your makeup," Fatima said as she dabbed my face gently, making sure my mascara didn't dribble down my cheeks. "Girl, you are looking fab tonight."

"Thank you, Tima. I feel fab tonight," I said.

"Hey, girl!" Monica screamed as he held me tight.

"Slim Boogie, I'm so glad to see you."

My students from the Behavioral Out Reach Program came to give me a hug. They had cards and flowers for me. This was definitely a surprise of a lifetime.

LaQuan walked me to our table. It was filled with photos of us, my girls, Deb and I, my family, and friends. It was breathtaking and I had to take a moment to take it all in. Deb came to me and just held me tight. I held her right back. I don't remember a time when we held on to one another like this. I knew she loved me with all of her heart, but at that very moment, I felt something deeper than I ever felt before. She probably felt the same thing, which was stronger than that four letter word LOVE. Whatever it was, I was glad to feel it.

After everyone ate, Fatima took to the mic.

"If anyone would like to say a few words to Taraine, here's your opportunity," Fatima said.

One-by-one, people started coming up and saying something special about me. When Deb took the mic my heart raced.

"I just want to say I am so grateful to have a daughter like you. I know to you it may seem as if I was rough on you as a child, but it was tough love. I wanted the best for you. You have grown to be the best daughter a mother could ask for and I'm so thankful to God for bringing you back to me, to us. Thanks you," she said. She looked up and the tears began to fall gracefully down her cheeks.

"I love you to, mommy," I mumbled and then I blew her a kiss.

"Good evening. My name is Shantae. I'm Taraine's favorite cousin," Shantae said and began to laugh at the look on Fatima's face. "I'm not going to talk too long, although I can when it comes to this particular woman."

"This beautiful woman we are all here for is one of a kind. She says what's on her mind and she also tells you what you need to hear, but it's always projected with love. Taraine, when you were in that coma, or as I like to say, 'the extended vacation', and I needed to talk about my issues, I knew exactly where to go. I would sit next to your bed and tell you what was going on in my life and it always seemed like you had a way of giving feedback. It just seemed like whatever you would have said to me—if you were capable of talking—would enter my mind. I know, it was weird, but it happened every time I paid you a visit," Shantae said as she dabbed at the tears rolling down her face. "Like I said, I could go on forever, but I'm getting a little too emotional and I'm not about to show my soft side. I'm not one for all the crying, so with that being said, I just want to say I love you and thank you for teaching me to live every day as if it was my last," Shantae said as she passed the mic and ran straight to the ladies room.

"Would anyone else like to say a few words to Taraine?" Fatima asked.

Nicera raised her hand trying to get Fatima's attention.

"Okay, come up to the mic, baby girl," Fatima said.

Nicera ran up to the mic as Raine' followed behind her.

"I want to say I love my mommy," Nicera said as Raine' jumped in and said, "I love my mommy, too. And, mommy, can I have some cake?" Raine' shouted into the mic.

Everyone started laughing and clapping showing them a little love.

They walked back over to our table and all I could do was grab my babies and hug them tight; they were my reason for living.

# It's Over

## Shantae

"Hey, you look familiar," I said as I walked into the ladies room to fix my makeup I destroyed from crying. "Oh, you're Monica's friend Dee, right?"

"Yes, and you're Shantae, if I'm not mistaken," Dee said.

"Yeah, but you can call me Tae. So, you drove down with Monica and the boys?"

"No. I left a little after them. I'm staying with my relatives in the Bronx," Dee said. "Okay, well I'm about to go out here and get my dance on," Dee said as she exited the bathroom.

"Okay, Dee."

I looked in the mirror to make sure everything was looking good, and just as I was about to exit the bathroom, Kandi entered.

"Oh, you thought it was over, bitch?" Kandi said as she stood right in front of me blocking the door.

"What do you mean *over*, Kandi? It is over. You and I are done. I moved on and I'm hoping you did the same thing," I said.

"I guess you thought shit was going to be that easy, huh, bitch? From the very beginning, I told you if you fuck me over there were going to be consequences to pay. I guess you thought I was joking," Kandi said.

"I don't know if you were joking or not, only you would know that, but I tell you this, Kandi. I'm not going to stand here and let you talk to me in this manner. I'm not going to be in the restroom arguing or fighting with you. I am here to celebrate my cousin's life and I'm not with the drama."

"Oh no, Tae. I'm not for the drama either, nor am I here to fight with you, but I'm definitely here to put this bullet in you," Kandi said as she pulled out a small pistol. If I can't have you to myself, nobody will."

As soon as I realized she was about to pull the trigger, I tried to rush her and knock the gun out of her hand. It all happened so quickly and before I knew it, she had shot me in my chest. I could feel a burning sensation in my chest. I fell to the floor as she stood over me.

"He could never love you the way I could," Kandi said as she kneeled down and gently kissed me on my lips. "I will love you until the day I die," Kandi said, standing up to fix her form fitting dress before exiting the bathroom.

I tried to scream for help, but the music had drowned out my cries. I closed my eyes and prayed for someone to find me as my eyes began to get heavier and my heart began to beat less. I struggled to breathe.

*Please somebody – come find me before it's too late,* I thought as the lights began to dim.

# It Ain't Over Until It's Over

## Taraine

Detective Weiss walked into the hall room with a couple other detectives beside him. LaQuan automatically spotted them when they walked in and approached them to find out what was going on. They had to have some detrimental information making them appear here at the party.

"Hey, Weiss. Are you here on official business, or are you here to partake in the events?" LaQuan asked.

"Oh, Mr. Cummings, I wouldn't miss this for the world, but I'm here on business. I'm here to tell you we're about to make a move on Sidora. I sent some of my affiliates in Philly to check some things out for me. Sidora goes by the name 'Dee' in Philly. The description Taraine gave was a dead ringer. The mole on her face was definitely a dead giveaway. I have a feeling she may be in the surrounding area. That's why I'm here with my partners," Detective Weiss said.

"Well, I'm glad you guys are here. It makes me feel better knowing you're on your job, Weiss," LaQuan said, extending his hand to shake the detective's hand. "I'm going to let you do what you do and I'm going to step back over there with my beautiful wife. I have to protect her. I already failed her once. I can't slip up again," LaQuan said, turning and walking away. He proceeded to the DJ booth and grabbed the mic.

"First of all, I want to thank everybody for coming out tonight and celebrating the life of my beautiful wife. I would like to say I love you so much, baby. You have brought me so much joy from the very first day we met. I know we have a love that will last a lifetime and I'm just grateful to have this second chance with you. If this world were mine, you would feel no pain; just love and happiness. I'm grateful for my two beautiful daughters and my beautiful family. You guys complete me. I can't praise you enough, Taraine. You are a remarkable woman, you're my everything, my 'Phenomenal Woman' and there could never be another you. I love you, Moc," LaQuan said.

"I love you too, baby," I said as she walked over to LaQuan and kissed him with so much passion.

I turned around and picked up the microphone.

"This is supposed to be a celebration and I know you guys are tired of crying and messing up your beautiful faces and fabulous dresses. I just want to thank you for all coming out and celebrating life. I'm so blessed and thankful to God, my family, and friends for giving me the strength to fight. I love each and every one of you, and on that note, I don't know what ya'll came to do, but I'm here to party. So if ya'll will excuse me, I'm going to kick off these stilettos and get my dance on with the love of my life. Let's party like there's no tomorrow; we only have one life to live. Well, in my case, two, but anyway – let's party," I said as I took off my shoes, grabbed LaQuan's hand, and made my way to the dance floor.

The girls came on the floor and we all danced together. I was having the time of my life as I looked around at everyone as they made their way to the dance floor as well.

Then the DJ slowed it down and began playing one of my favorite songs. "If This World Were Mine" by Luther Vandross and Cheryl Lynn.

LaQuan held me tight as he begins singing in my ear.

*If this world was mine*
*I would place at your feet*
*All that I own*
*You've been so good to me*

*If this world was mine*

Then I begin singing to him.

*If this world was mine*
*I'd make you a King*
*With wealth untold*
*You could have anything*
*If this world was mine*

It felt as if we were the only one in the entire hall as we looked into each other's eyes, danced, and once again, made love mentally.

"Could I have this dance, please?" I heard a familiar voice ask. As I turned around to put the voice with the face, I found myself staring into the face of the psychopath that shot me and left me for dead.

"It ain't over until it's over, bitch," Sidora yelled and she pulled out her pistol and pointed it directly at my temple.

All I saw was chaos. With all the chaos, I heard a loud noise. And then, there was darkness.

*****

I managed to open my eyes as I lay on the floor gasping for air. I tried to hold on to every moment as I turned my head and watched as people ran for their lives. The screams and cries saddened me as I watched them handcuff the psychotic bitch with the mole on her face. I thought about how I survived it once and could do it again as my children's faces began to flash before my eyes. I heard the sound of LaQuan voice as he begged me not to leave him. It was becoming more difficult for me to breathe as I felt compression on my chest.

"Come back...come back..." was all I heard as if from a distance as air was being pumped into my mouth.

I gasped as my body jerked once, twice, and then a third time. I opened my eyes to the sound of a loud beeping noise. My eyes quickly closed back into darkness to block out the bright light. I tried to open them once again, and this time, when I got them open, everything seemed a little clearer. I looked to my left and then to my right and was very confused.

*What happened? Where am I?* I thought.

I reached up and felt the bandages on my head. I looked around once more and recognized I was in a hospital room which was filled with dozens of white roses. I closed my eyes again, but this time when I opened it, I heard the voice of an Angel.

"Hey, Moc. I knew you would find your way back to us, baby. You never cease to amaze me," he said, kissing me on my cheeks.

I looked at this handsome man and wondered who he was and why was he calling me 'Moc'…

Stripped by Passion

# About the Author

Inspiring, prolific and courageous; Mahagony Redd defines the dynamic voices behind the women of Stripped by Love. Mahagony Redd was born and raised in Brooklyn, New York. She attended the College of New Rochelle where she received her B.A., in Psychology. Mahagony Redd uses her personal and professional experiences to unleash her premiere novel Stripped by Love. She is also a former officer of the NYSDOC and a former employee for NYPD. She resides in Brooklyn, New York with her two children Maliya and Derrick Grinnage.

www.ingramcontent.com/pod-product-compliance
Lightning Source LLC
Chambersburg PA
CBHW021242260626
47155CB00004BA/1274